Ancient
Ghost
Stories

This edition is first published in 2023 by Flame Tree 451

FLAME TREE 451
6 Melbray Mews,
Fulham, London SW3 3NS
United Kingdom
www.flametree451.com

Flame Tree 451 is an imprint of Flame Tree Publishing Ltd
www.flametreepublishing.com

A CIP record for this book is available from the British Library

Print ISBN: 978-1-80417-595-8
ebook ISBN: 978-1-80417-599-6

23 25 27 28 26 24
1 3 5 7 8 6 4 2

The stories in 'Sumerian Stories of the Netherworld' are reprinted
from *The Electronic Text Corpus of Sumerian Literature*
(http://www-etcsl.orient.ox.ac.uk/), Oxford 1998–. Copyright © J.A.
Black, G. Cunningham, E. Robson, and G. Zólyomi 1998, 1999, 2000;
J.A. Black, G. Cunningham, E. Flückiger-hawker, E. Robson, J. Taylor,
and G. Zólyomi 2001. The authors have asserted their moral rights.

Cover image was created by Flame Tree Studio, based on elements
courtesy Shutterstock.com/Viacheslav Lopatin/Joel Askey.

Printed and bound in China

Ancient
Ghost
Stories

With an introduction by
Camilla Grudova

Contents

A Taste for the Fantastic

From mystery to crime, the supernatural and fantasy to science fiction, the terrific range of paperbacks and ebooks from Flame Tree 451 offers a healthy diet of werewolves and mechanicals, vampires and villains, mad scientists, secret worlds, lost civilizations, escapist fantasies and dystopian visions. Discover a storehouse of tales gathered specifically for the reader of the fantastic.

Great works by H.G. Wells and Bram Stoker stand shoulder to shoulder with gripping reads by titans of the gothic novel (Charles Brockden Brown, Nathaniel Hawthorne), and individual novels by literary giants (Jane Austen, Charles Dickens, Emily Brontë) mingle with the intensity of H.P. Lovecraft and the psychological magic of Edgar Allan Poe.

Of course there are classic Conan Doyle adventures, Wilkie Collins mysteries and the pioneering fantasies of Mary Shelley, but there are so many other tales to tell: *The White Worm, Black Magic, The Murder Monster, The Awakening, Darkwater* and more.

Check our website for regular updates and new additions to our curated range of speculative fiction at *flametreepublishing.com*

Introduction

Some months ago, I was walking with friends in rural Perthshire, mountains looming in the distance, on a road said to be Roman. I don't remember how the subject of ghosts came up, but one of my friends, who was a chef, told us about a colleague of his who had worked at an old manor house turned hotel. A little girl came into the kitchen while he was preparing breakfast and asked if she could help with anything. He said no thank you, and later remarked to the guests how polite and sweet she was. None of the guests had a daughter and he was told by other staff members that the little girl was a ghost who often appeared. This memory came into my head when writing this introduction, as it seemed to have more in common with ancient ghost stories than the spooky ones that get told in modern times. In many of these ancient stories, ghosts are not terrifying, but ever present, an everyday fact of life. Ghosts appear here not just as the disembodied once living, but reanimated corpses, spirits, demons and invisible beings. The stories have been passed down by scribes, on clay tablets and pot shards, sitting silently in museums.

In the ancient world, the ghosts of Trojan soldiers are common enough to be weather forecasters (if the ghostly soldiers are dusty, it means drought, if sweaty, rain) and the Underworld is accessible through doors and holes – the first three tales in the collection, from ancient Sumer, bring us down into the Underworld, a theme later repeated in an excerpt from Homer's *Odyssey*. Most interestingly, the dead appearing in dreams or 'visions' of any sort are counted as just as real an encounter with ghosts as during lucid, waking hours. By this standard, most contemporary readers have seen ghosts: dead grandparents and friends appearing in our dreams, grief dancing them around in our unconscious.

In one example from ancient Rome ('Quintilian's Tenth Declamation', *see* page 91), a bereaved mother's son comes and cuddles her in her dreams. Her husband isn't pleased his son has left the Underworld – you can either read him as cruel or as mindful of his wife's mental peace – and hires a sorcerer to put spells on the boy's tomb to lock him in. The son, trapped, bashes his soul against his grave, unable to visit his mother or anyone.

It is not just the ghosts of humans who appear in dreams: in another Roman story by Virgil, 'The Culex' (*see* page 96), a shepherd kills a gnat who then appears in his dream. The gnat, who saved the shepherd from a snake he didn't see, berates the shepherd and describes the horrors of the Underworld. The shepherd, when he wakes, builds a monument to the gnat, with offerings to appease his spirit.

The dead who don't have proper burials or offerings come to complain, or are called upon for advice. A husband (Periander, *see* page 99) has to 'give' his dead wife nice new clothes by burning them on a pyre before she will give him some useful counsel. Ghosts annoyingly get in the way of digging canals in Nero's Rome, and must be ignored. They will eat and drink with people, or they must be fed with offerings. They will save their lives and cut their hair. They cause joy along with fear.

In Peru, spirits are often embodied in fetish objects. Lakes and mountains were places where ancestors crossed over to the next world. In Japan, ghosts appear as balls of fire with faces (they can be benign or vengeful), while in Greece and India, it is required to burn bodies in order for the spirits to find peace and pass on. In China, ghosts are everywhere and ever present and ever influencing though they cannot be seen or heard. In ancient Greece, ghost sightings trigger the same excitement as our era's celebrity sightings: there goes dead Achilles! Did you see him? Hector too! And the Emperor Nero!

Nowhere does the line between the dead and the living become more transparent than in ancient Egypt. In 'Setne and the Mummies', a boy walks into a tomb to steal a magical book from the dead, *The Book of Thoth*. A family are waiting there, dead but living, and warn him not to take it as it killed all three of them. Setne does by force, but when he suffers nightmares, and under the advice of his father, returns the book. *Ancient Ghost Stories* also includes a description of Egyptian burial practices, the idea of the afterlife bound up in materiality: the dead are preserved and given food for the afterlife to continue as they were in their tombs.

The stories can also be humorous; in 'An Account of Reanimation', the Roman writer Apuleius, the comedic writer of *The Golden Ass*, has a corpse breathing again, brought back to life, simply to ask the magician why they have done so.

Others are romantic. In 'The Brahman and His Bride', a young man whose bride dies after stepping on a snake gives half his life to bring her back from the celestial regions, and they live happily for a shorter period than the average life, but preferable to a longer life alone.

As someone who writes weird or peculiar stories, instead of horror, I felt a particular affinity with these sad, touching, funny and mostly unfrightening stories (the one exception to unfrightening being 'The Drowning of Thorkell' from the *The Laxdaela Saga*, in which 'blue and evil bones' are found under the floorboards of a house, the cause of an apparition crawling over people in their sleep and dropping a hot mysterious liquid on them). These ancient stories will appeal to readers of Gogol or Kafka. They are intimately human, and make us question our own distant relationship with death and the dead. Going back to my walk in Perthshire: the difference between that ghost story and these was indeed the distance: I did not know if my friend telling the story believed it, it was a classic 'friend of a friend' tale, in a world where belief in the afterlife is uncommon. These ancient stories bridge the gap between the living and the dead for the modern reader.

Camilla Grudova

Ancient
Ghost
Stories

Sumerian Stories of the Netherworld

Ancient Sumerian Scribe

The following three stories have been translated from ancient clay tablets, revealing a circular and almost musical style of expression which the anonymous scribe or scribes used in recording these ancient Sumerian tales of the afterlife and the spirit realm.

Inana's Descent to the Netherworld

From the great heaven she set her mind on the great below. From the great heaven the goddess set her mind on the great below. From the great heaven Inana set her mind on the great below. My mistress abandoned heaven, abandoned earth, and descended to the Underworld. Inana abandoned heaven, abandoned earth, and descended to the Underworld.

She abandoned the office of *en*, abandoned the office of *lagar*, and descended to the Underworld. She abandoned the E-ana in Unug, and descended to the Underworld. She abandoned the E-muc-kalama in Bad-tibira, and descended to the Underworld. She abandoned the Giguna in Zabalam, and descended to the Underworld. She abandoned the E-cara in Adab, and descended to the Underworld.

She abandoned the Barag-dur-jara in Nibru, and descended to the Underworld. She abandoned the Hursaj-kalama in Kic, and descended to the Underworld. She abandoned the E-Ulmac in Agade, and descended to the Underworld. She abandoned the Ibgal in Umma, and descended to the Underworld. She abandoned the E-Dilmuna in Urim, and descended to the Underworld. She abandoned the Amac-e-kug in Kisiga, and descended to the Underworld. She abandoned the E-ecdam-kug in Jirsu, and descended to the Underworld. She abandoned the E-sig-mece-du in Isin, and descended to the Underworld. She abandoned the Anzagar in Akcak, and descended to the Underworld. She abandoned the Nijin-jar-kug in Curuppag, and descended to the Underworld. She abandoned the E-cag-hula in Kazallu, and descended to the Underworld.

She took the seven divine powers. She collected the divine powers and grasped them in her hand. With the good divine powers, she went on her way. She put a turban, headgear for the open country, on her head. She took a wig for her forehead. She hung small lapis lazuli beads around her neck.

She placed twin egg-shaped beads on her breast. She covered her body with a *pala* dress, the garment of ladyship. She placed mascara which is called "Let a man come, let him come" on her eyes. She pulled the pectoral which is called "Come, man, come" over her breast. She placed a golden ring on her hand. She held the lapis lazuli measuring rod and measuring line in her hand.

Inana travelled towards the Underworld. Her minister Nincubura travelled behind her.

Holy Inana said to Nincubura: "Come, my faithful minister of E-ana, my minister who speaks fair words, my escort who speaks trustworthy words.

"On this day I will descend to the Underworld. When I have arrived in the Underworld, make a lament for me on the ruin mounds. Beat the drum for me in the sanctuary. Make the rounds of the houses of the gods for me.

"Lacerate your eyes for me, lacerate your nose for me. Lacerate your ears for me, in public. In private, lacerate your buttocks for me. Like a pauper, clothe yourself in a single garment and all alone set your foot in the E-kur, the house of Enlil.

"When you have entered the E-kur, the house of Enlil, lament before Enlil: 'Father Enlil, don't let anyone kill your daughter in the Underworld. Don't let your precious metal be alloyed there with the dirt of the Underworld. Don't let your precious lapis lazuli be split there with the mason's stone. Don't let your boxwood be chopped up there with the carpenter's wood. Don't let young lady Inana be killed in the Underworld.'

"If Enlil does not help you in this matter, go to Urim. In the E-mud-kura at Urim, when you have entered the E-kic-nu-jal, the house of Nanna, lament before Nanna: 'Father Nanna, don't let anyone kill your daughter in the Underworld. Don't let your precious metal be alloyed there with the dirt of the Underworld. Don't let your precious lapis lazuli be split there with the mason's stone. Don't let your boxwood be chopped up there with the carpenter's wood. Don't let young lady Inana be killed in the Underworld.'

"And if Nanna does not help you in this matter, go to Eridug. In Eridug, when you have entered the house of Enki, lament before Enki: 'Father Enki, don't let anyone kill your daughter in the Underworld. Don't let your precious metal be alloyed there with the dirt of the Underworld. Don't let your precious lapis lazuli be split there with the mason's stone. Don't let your boxwood be chopped up there with the carpenter's wood. Don't let young lady Inana be killed in the Underworld.'

"Father Enki, the lord of great wisdom, knows about the life-giving plant and the life-giving water. He is the one who will restore me to life."

When Inana travelled on towards the Underworld, her minister Nincubura travelled on behind her. She said to her minister Nincubura: "Go now, my Nincubura, and pay attention. Don't neglect the instructions I gave you."

When Inana arrived at the palace Ganzer, she pushed aggressively on the door of the Underworld. She shouted aggressively at the gate of the Underworld: "Open up, doorman, open up. Open up, Neti, open up. I am all alone and I want to come in."

Neti, the chief doorman of the Underworld, answered holy Inana: "Who are you?"

"I am Inana going to the east."

"If you are Inana going to the east, why have you travelled to the land of no return? How did you set your heart on the road whose traveller never returns?"

Holy Inana answered him: "Because lord Gud-gal-ana, the husband of my elder sister holy Erec-ki-gala, has died; in order to have his funeral rites observed, she offers generous libations at his wake – that is the reason."

Neti, the chief doorman of the Underworld, answered holy Inana: "Stay here, Inana. I will speak to my mistress. I will speak to my mistress Erec-ki-gala and tell her what you have said."

Neti, the chief doorman of the Underworld, entered the house of his mistress Erec-ki-gala and said: "My mistress, there is a lone girl outside. It is Inana, your sister, and she has arrived at the palace Ganzer. She pushed aggressively on the door of the Underworld.

She shouted aggressively at the gate of the Underworld. She has abandoned E-ana and has descended to the Underworld.

"She has taken the seven divine powers. She has collected the divine powers and grasped them in her hand. She has come on her way with all the good divine powers. She has put a turban, headgear for the open country, on her head. She has taken a wig for her forehead. She has hung small lapis lazuli beads around her neck.

"She has placed twin egg-shaped beads on her breast. She has covered her body with the *pala* dress of ladyship. She has placed mascara which is called "Let a man come" on her eyes. She has pulled the pectoral which is called "Come, man, come" over her breast. She has placed a golden ring on her hand. She is holding the lapis lazuli measuring rod and measuring line in her hand."

When she heard this, Erec-ki-gala slapped the side of her thigh. She bit her lip and took the words to heart. She said to Neti, her chief doorman: "Come Neti, my chief doorman of the Underworld, don't neglect the instructions I will give you. Let the seven gates of the Underworld be bolted. Then let each door of the palace Ganzer be opened separately. As for her, after she has entered, and crouched down and had her clothes removed, they will be carried away."

Neti, the chief doorman of the Underworld, paid attention to the instructions of his mistress. He bolted the seven gates of the Underworld. Then he opened each of the doors of the palace Ganzer separately. He said to holy Inana: "Come on, Inana, and enter."

And when Inana entered, the lapis lazuli measuring rod and measuring line were removed from her hand; when she entered the first gate, the turban, headgear for the open country, was removed from her head. "What is this?"

"Be satisfied, Inana, a divine power of the Underworld has been fulfilled. Inana, you must not open your mouth against the rites of the Underworld."

When she entered the second gate, the small lapis lazuli beads were removed from her neck. "What is this?"

"Be satisfied, Inana, a divine power of the Underworld has been fulfilled. Inana, you must not open your mouth against the rites of the Underworld."

When she entered the third gate, the twin egg-shaped beads were removed from her breast. "What is this?"

"Be satisfied, Inana, a divine power of the Underworld has been fulfilled. Inana, you must not open your mouth against the rites of the Underworld."

When she entered the fourth gate, the "Come, man, come" pectoral was removed from her breast. "What is this?"

"Be satisfied, Inana, a divine power of the Underworld has been fulfilled. Inana, you must not open your mouth against the rites of the Underworld."

When she entered the fifth gate, the golden ring was removed from her hand. "What is this?"

"Be satisfied, Inana, a divine power of the Underworld has been fulfilled. Inana, you must not open your mouth against the rites of the Underworld."

When she entered the sixth gate, the lapis lazuli measuring rod and measuring line were removed from her hand. "What is this?"

"Be satisfied, Inana, a divine power of the Underworld has been fulfilled. Inana, you must not open your mouth against the rites of the Underworld."

When she entered the seventh gate, the *pala* dress, the garment of ladyship, was removed from her body. "What is this?"

"Be satisfied, Inana, a divine power of the Underworld has been fulfilled. Inana, you must not open your mouth against the rites of the Underworld."

After she had crouched down and had her clothes removed, they were carried away. Then she made her sister Erec-ki-gala rise from her throne, and instead she sat on her throne. The Anuna, the seven judges, rendered their decision against her. They looked at her – it was the look of death. They spoke to her – it was the speech of anger. They shouted at her – it was the shout of heavy guilt. The afflicted woman was turned into a corpse. And the corpse was hung on a hook.

After three days and three nights had passed, her minister Nincubura, her minister who speaks fair words, her escort who speaks trustworthy words, carried out the instructions of her mistress.

She made a lament for her in her ruined (houses). She beat the drum for her in the sanctuaries. She made the rounds of the houses of the gods for her. She lacerated her eyes for her; she lacerated her nose. In private she lacerated her buttocks for her. Like a pauper, she clothed herself in a single garment, and all alone she set her foot in the E-kur, the house of Enlil.

When she had entered the E-kur, the house of Enlil, she lamented before Enlil: "Father Enlil, don't let anyone kill your daughter in the Underworld. Don't let your precious metal be alloyed there with the dirt of the Underworld. Don't let your precious lapis lazuli be split there with the mason's stone. Don't let your boxwood be chopped up there with the carpenter's wood. Don't let young lady Inana be killed in the Underworld."

In his rage father Enlil answered Nincubura: "My daughter craved the great heaven and she craved the great below as well. Inana craved the great heaven and she craved the great below as well. The divine powers of the Underworld are divine powers which should not be craved, for whoever gets them must remain in the Underworld. Who, having got to that place, could then expect to come up again?"

Thus father Enlil did not help in this matter, so she went to Urim. In the E-mud-kura at Urim, when she had entered the E-kic-nu-jal, the house of Nanna, she lamented before Nanna: "Father

Nanna, don't let your daughter be killed in the Underworld. Don't let your precious metal be alloyed there with the dirt of the Underworld. Don't let your precious lapis lazuli be split there with the mason's stone. Don't let your boxwood be chopped up there with the carpenter's wood. Don't let young lady Inana be killed in the Underworld."

In his rage father Nanna answered Nincubura: "My daughter craved the great heaven and she craved the great below as well. Inana craved the great heaven and she craved the great below as well. The divine powers of the Underworld are divine powers which should not be craved, for whoever gets them must remain in the Underworld. Who, having got to that place, could then expect to come up again?"

Thus father Nanna did not help her in this matter, so she went to Eridug. In Eridug, when she had entered the house of Enki, she lamented before Enki: "Father Enki, don't let anyone kill your daughter in the Underworld. Don't let your precious metal be alloyed there with the dirt of the Underworld. Don't let your precious lapis lazuli be split there with the mason's stone. Don't let your boxwood be chopped up there with the carpenter's wood. Don't let young lady Inana be killed in the Underworld."

Father Enki answered Nincubura: "What has my daughter done? She has me worried. What has Inana done? She has me worried. What has the mistress of all the lands done? She has me worried. What has the hierodule of An done? She has me worried." Thus father Enki helped her in this matter. He removed some dirt from the tip of his fingernail and created the *kur-jara*. He removed some dirt from the tip of his other fingernail and created the *gala-tura*. To the *kur-jara* he gave the life-giving plant. To the *gala-tura* he gave the life-giving water.

Then father Enki spoke out to the *gala-tura* and the *kur-jara*: "Go and direct your steps to the Underworld. Flit past the door like flies. Slip through the door pivots like phantoms. The mother who gave birth, Erec-ki-gala, on account of her children, is lying there. Her holy shoulders are not covered by a linen cloth. Her breasts are not full like a *cagan* vessel. Her nails are like a pickaxe (?) upon her. The hair on her head is bunched up as if it were leeks.

"When she says, 'Oh my heart', you are to say, 'You are troubled, our mistress, oh your heart'. When she says, 'Oh my liver', you are to say, 'You are troubled, our mistress, oh your liver'. (She will then ask:) 'Who are you? Speaking to you from my heart to your heart, from my liver to your liver – if you are gods, let me talk with you; if you are mortals, may a destiny be decreed for you.' Make her swear this by heaven and earth...

"They will offer you a riverful of water – don't accept it. They will offer you a field with its grain – don't accept it. But say to her: 'Give us the corpse hanging on the hook.' (She will answer:) 'That is the corpse of your queen.' Say to her: 'Whether it is that of our king, whether it is that of our queen, give it to us.' She will give you the corpse hanging on the hook. One of you sprinkle on it the life-giving plant and the other the life-giving water. Thus let Inana arise."

The *gala-tura* and the *kur-jara* paid attention to the instructions of Enki. They flitted through the door like flies. They slipped through the door pivots like phantoms. The mother who gave birth, Erec-ki-gala, because of her children, was lying there. Her holy shoulders were not covered by a linen cloth. Her breasts were not full like a *cagan* vessel. Her nails were like a pickaxe (?) upon her. The hair on her head was bunched up as if it were leeks.

When she said, "Oh my heart", they said to her, "You are troubled, our mistress, oh your heart". When she said, "Oh my liver", they said to her, "You are troubled, our mistress, oh your liver."

(Then she asked:) "Who are you? I tell you from my heart to your heart, from my liver to your liver – if you are gods, I will talk with you; if you are mortals, may a destiny be decreed for you." They made her swear this by heaven and earth. They...

They were offered a river with its water – they did not accept it. They were offered a field with its grain – they did not accept it. They said to her: "Give us the corpse hanging on the hook."

Holy Erec-ki-gala answered the *gala-tura* and the *kur-jara*: "The corpse is that of your queen."

They said to her: "Whether it is that of our king or that of our queen, give it to us." They were given the corpse hanging on the hook. One of them sprinkled on it the life-giving plant and the other the life-giving water. And thus Inana arose.

Erec-ki-gala said to the *gala-tura* and the *kur-jara*: "Bring your queen...your...has been seized." Inana, because of Enki's instructions, was about to ascend from the Underworld.

But as Inana was about to ascend from the Underworld, the Anuna seized her. "Who has ever ascended from the Underworld, has ascended unscathed from the Underworld? If Inana is to ascend from the Underworld, let her provide a substitute for herself."

So when Inana left the Underworld, the one in front of her, though not a minister, held a sceptre in his hand; the one behind her, though not an escort, carried a mace at his hip, while the small demons, like a reed enclosure, and the big demons, like the reeds of a fence, restrained her on all sides.

Those who accompanied her, those who accompanied Inana, know no food, know no drink, eat no flour offering and drink no libation. They accept no pleasant gifts. They never enjoy the pleasures of the marital embrace, never have any sweet children to kiss. They tear away the wife from a man's embrace. They snatch the son from a man's knee. They make the bride leave the house of her father-in-law. They crush no bitter garlic. They eat no fish, they eat no leeks. They, it was, who accompanied Inana.

After Inana had ascended from the Underworld, Nincubura threw herself at her feet at the door of the Ganzer. She had sat in the dust and clothed herself in a filthy garment. The demons said to holy Inana: "Inana, proceed to your city; we will take her back."

Holy Inana answered the demons: "This is my minister of fair words, my escort of trustworthy words. She did not forget my instructions. She did not neglect the orders I gave her. She made a lament for me on the ruin mounds. She beat the drum for me in the sanctuaries. She made the rounds of the gods' houses for me. She lacerated her eyes for me, lacerated her nose for me. She lacerated her ears for me in public. In private, she lacerated her buttocks for me. Like a pauper, she clothed herself in a single garment.

"All alone she directed her steps to the E-kur, to the house of Enlil, and to Urim, to the house of Nanna, and to Eridug, to the house of Enki. She wept before Enki. She brought me back to life. How could I turn her over to you? Let us go on. Let us go on to the Sig-kur-caga in Umma."

At the Sig-kur-caga in Umma, Cara, in his own city, threw himself at her feet. He had sat in the dust and dressed himself in a filthy garment. The demons said to holy Inana: "Inana, proceed to your city, we will take him back."

Holy Inana answered the demons: "Cara is my singer, my manicurist and my hairdresser. How could I turn him over to you? Let us go on. Let us go on to the E-muc-kalama in Bad-tibira."

At the E-muc-kalama in Bad-tibira, Lulal, in his own city, threw himself at her feet. He had sat in the dust and clothed himself in a filthy garment. The demons said to holy Inana: "Inana, proceed to your city, we will take him back."

Holy Inana answered the demons: "Outstanding Lulal follows me at my right and my left. How could I turn him over to you? Let us go on. Let us go on to the great apple tree in the plain of Kulaba."

They followed her to the great apple tree in the plain of Kulaba. There was Dumuzid clothed in a magnificent garment and seated magnificently on a throne. The demons seized him there by his thighs. The seven of them poured the milk from his churns. The seven of them shook their heads like…. They would not let the shepherd play the pipe and flute before her (?).

She looked at him; it was the look of death. She spoke to him (?), it was the speech of anger. She shouted at him (?), it was the shout of heavy guilt: "How much longer? Take him away." Holy Inana gave Dumuzid the shepherd into their hands.

Those who had accompanied her, who had come for Dumuzid, know no food, know no drink, eat no flour offering, drink no libation. They never enjoy the pleasures of the marital embrace, never have any sweet children to kiss. They snatch the son from a man's knee. They make the bride leave the house of her father-in-law.

Dumuzid let out a wail and turned very pale. The lad raised his hands to heaven, to Utu: "Utu, you are my brother-in-law. I am your relation by marriage. I brought butter to your mother's house. I brought milk to Ningal's house. Turn my hands into snake's hands and turn my feet into snake's feet, so I can escape my demons, let them not keep hold of me."

Utu accepted his tears. Dumuzid's demons could not keep hold of him. Utu turned Dumuzid's hands into snake's hands. He turned his feet into snake's feet. Dumuzid escaped his demons. Like a *sajkal* snake he…. They seized…Holy Inana…her heart.

Holy Inana wept bitterly for her husband...

She tore at her hair like esparto grass; she ripped it out like esparto grass. "You wives who lie in your men's embrace, where is my precious husband? You children who lie in your men's embrace, where is my precious child? Where is my man? Where...? Where is my man? Where...?"

A fly spoke to holy Inana: "If I show you where your man is, what will be my reward?" Holy Inana answered the fly: "If you show me where my man is, I will give you this gift: I will cover..."

The fly helped (?) holy Inana. The young lady Inana decreed the destiny of the fly: "In the beer-house and the tavern (?), may there...for you. You will live (?) like the sons of the wise." Now Inana decreed this fate and thus it came to be.

...was weeping. She came up to the sister (?) and...by the hand: "Now, alas, my.... You for half the year and your sister for half the year: when you are demanded, on that day you will stay, when your sister is demanded, on that day you will be released." Thus holy Inana gave Dumuzid as a substitute...

Holy Erec-ki-gala – sweet is your praise.

Ningishzida's Journey to the Netherworld

"Arise and get on board; arise, we are about to sail; arise and get on board!" – Woe, weep for the bright daylight, as the barge is steered away! – "I am a young man! Let me not be covered against my wishes by a cabin, as if with a blanket, as if with a blanket!"

Stretching out a hand to the barge, to the young man being steered away on the barge, stretching out a hand to my young man Damu being taken away on the barge, stretching out a hand to Ictaran of the bright visage being taken away on the barge, stretching out a hand to Alla, master of the battle-net, being taken away on the barge, stretching out a hand to Lugal-cud-e being taken away on the barge, stretching out a hand to Ninjiczida being taken away on the barge – his younger sister was crying in lament to him in the boat's cabin.

His older sister removed the cover (?) from the boat's cabin. "Let me sail away with you, let me sail away with you, brother, let me sail away with you."

She was crying a lament to him at the boat's bow: "Brother, let me sail away with you. Let me...for you in your boat's stern, brother, let me sail away with you. The *gudu* priest sits in the cabin at your boat's stern." She was crying a lament to him: "Let me sail away with you, my brother, let me sail away with you." [...]

The evil demon who was in their midst called out to Lugal-ki-suna: "Lugal-ki-suna, look at your sister!"

Having looked at his sister, Lugal-ki-suna said to her: "He sails with me, he sails with me. Why should you sail to the Underworld? Lady, the demon sails with me. Why should you sail to the Underworld? The thresher sails with me. Why should you sail to the Underworld? The man who has bound my hands sails with me. Why should you sail? The man who has tied my arms sails with me. Why should you sail?

"The river of the Netherworld produces no water, no water is drunk from it. Why should you sail? The fields of the Netherworld produce no grain, no flour is eaten from it. Why should you sail? The sheep of the Netherworld produce no wool, and no cloth is woven from it. Why should you sail? As for me, even if my mother digs as if for a canal, I shall not be able to drink the water meant for me. The waters of springtime will not be poured for me as they are for the tamarisks; I shall not sit in the shade intended for me. The dates I should bear like a date palm will not reveal (?) their beauty for me. I am a field threshed by my demon – you would scream at it. He has put manacles on my hands – you would scream at it. He has put a neck-stock on my neck – you would scream at it."

Ama-cilama (Ninjiczida's sister) said to Ninjiczida: "The ill-intentioned demon may accept something – there should be a limit to it for you. My brother, your demon may accept something, there should be a limit to it for you. For him let me…from my hand the…there should be a limit to it for you. For him let me…from my hand the…there should be a limit to it for you. For him let me…from my hips the dainty lapis lazuli beads, there should be a limit to it for you. For him let me…from my hips the… my lapis lazuli beads, there should be a limit to it for you.

"You are a beloved…there should be a limit to it for you. How they treat you, how they treat you! – there should be a limit to it for you. My brother, how they treat you, how haughtily they treat you! – there should be a limit to it for you. 'I am hungry, but the bread has slipped away from me!' – there should be a limit to it for you. 'I am thirsty, but the water has slipped away from me!' – there should be a limit to it for you."

The evil demon who was in their midst, the clever demon, that great demon who was in their midst, called out to the man at the boat's bow and to the man at the boat's stern: "Don't let the mooring stake be pulled out, don't let the mooring stake be pulled out, so that she may come on board to her brother, that this lady may come on board the barge."

When Ama-cilama had gone on board the barge, a cry approached the heavens, a cry approached the earth, that great demon set up an enveloping cry before him on the river: "Urim, at my cry to the heavens lock your houses, lock your houses, city, lock your houses! Shrine Urim, lock your houses, city, lock your houses! Against your lord who has left the *jipar*, city, lock your houses!" […]

He...to the empty river, the rejoicing (?) river (addressing *Ama-cilama*): "You shall not draw near to this house...to the place of Ereckigala. My mother...out of her love." (addressing the demon) "As for you, you may be a great demon...your hand against the Netherworld's office of throne-bearer.

"My king will no longer shed tears in his eyes. The drum will... his joy in tears. Come! May the fowler utter a lament for you in his well-stocked house, lord, may he utter a lament for you. How he has been humiliated! May the young fisherman utter a lament for you in his well-stocked house, lord, may he utter a lament for you. How he has been humiliated! May the mother of the dead *gudu* priest utter a lament for you in her empty *jipar*, utter a lament for you, lord, may she utter a lament for you. How he has been humiliated! May the mother high priestess utter a lament for you who have left the *jipar*, lord, may she utter a lament for you. How he has been humiliated!

"My king, bathe with water your head that has rolled in the dust...in sandals your feet defiled from the defiled place." The king bathed with water his head that had rolled in the dust...in sandals his feet defiled from the defiled place. "Not drawing near to this house...your throne...to you, 'Sit down'. May your bed...to you, 'Lie down'." He ate food in his mouth, he drank choice wine.

Great holy one, Ereckigala, praising you is sweet.

The Death of Ur-Namma

...entire land...struck, the palace was devastated...panic spread rapidly among the dwellings of the black-headed people...abandoned places...in Sumer...the cities were destroyed in their entirety; the people were seized with panic. Evil came upon Urim and made the trustworthy shepherd pass away. It made Ur-Namma, the trustworthy shepherd, pass away; it made the trustworthy shepherd pass away.

Because An had altered his holy words completely...became empty, and because, deceitfully, Enlil had completely changed the fate he decreed, Ninmah began a lament in her.... Enki shut (?) the great door of Eridug. Nudimmud withdrew into his bedchamber and lay down fasting. At his zenith, Nanna frowned at the...words of An. Utu did not come forth in the sky, and the day was full of sorrow.

The mother, miserable because of her son, the mother of the king, holy Ninsun, was crying: "Oh my heart!" Because of the fate decreed for Ur-Namma, because it made the trustworthy shepherd pass away, she was weeping bitterly in the broad square, which is otherwise a place of entertainment. Sweet sleep did not come to the people whose happing...they passed their time in lamentation over the trustworthy shepherd who had been snatched away.

As the early flood was filling the canals, their canal-inspector was already silenced (?); the mottled barley grown on the arable lands, the life of the land, was inundated. To the farmer, the fertile fields planted (?) by him yielded little. Enkimdu, the lord of levees and ditches, took away the levees and ditches from Urim...

As the intelligence and...of the Land were lost, fine food became scarce. The plains did not grow lush grass anymore, they grew the grass of mourning. The cows...their...cattle-pen has been destroyed. The calves...their cows bleated bitterly.

The wise shepherd...does not give orders anymore...in battle and combat. The king, the advocate of Sumer, the ornament of the assembly, Ur-Namma, the advocate of Sumer, the ornament of the assembly, the leader of Sumer...lies sick. His hands which used to grasp cannot grasp anymore; he lies sick. His feet...cannot step anymore, he lies sick...

The trustworthy shepherd, king, the sword of Sumer, Ur-Namma, the king of the Land, was taken to the...house. He was taken to Urim; the king of the Land was brought into the...house. The proud one lay in his palace. Ur-Namma, he who was beloved by the troops, could not raise his neck anymore. The wise one...lay down; silence descended. As he, who was the vigour of the Land, had fallen, the Land became demolished like a mountain; like a cypress forest it was stripped, its appearance changed. As if he were a boxwood tree, they put axes against him in his joyous dwelling place. As if he were a sappy cedar tree, he was uprooted in the palace where he used to sleep (?). His spouse...resting place...was covered by a storm; it embraced it like a wife her sweetheart (?). His appointed time had arrived, and he passed away in his prime.

His (?) pleasing sacrifices were no longer accepted; they were treated as dirty (?). The Anuna gods refused his gifts. [...] Because of what Enlil ordered, there was no more rising up; his beloved men lost their wise one. Strangers turned into (?).... How iniquitously Ur-Namma was abandoned, like a broken jar! His...with grandeur like (?) thick clouds (?). He does not...anymore, and he does not reach out for...Ur-Namma, the son of Ninsun, was brought to Arali, the... of the Land, in his prime. The soldiers accompanying the king shed tears: their boat (*i.e.* Ur-Namma) was sunk in a land as foreign to them as Dilmun...was cut. It was stripped of the oars, punting poles and rudder which it had...its bolt was broken off...was put aside; it stood (?) in saltpetre. His donkeys were to be found with the king; they were buried with him. His donkeys were to be found with Ur-Namma; they were buried with him. As he crossed over the...of the Land, the Land was deprived of its ornament. The journey to the Netherworld is a desolate route. Because of the king, the chariots were covered over, the roads were thrown into disorder, no one could go up and down on them. Because of Ur-Namma, the chariots were covered over, the roads were thrown into disorder, no one could go up and down on them.

He presented gifts to the seven chief porters of the Netherworld. As the famous kings who had died and the dead *icib* priests, *lumah* priests, and *nindijir* priestesses, all chosen by extispicy, announced the king's coming to the people, a tumult arose in the Netherworld. As they announced Ur-Namma's coming to the people, a tumult arose in the Netherworld. The king slaughtered numerous bulls and sheep, Ur-Namma seated the people at a huge banquet. The food of the Netherworld is bitter, the water of the Netherworld is brackish. The trustworthy shepherd knew well the rites of the Netherworld, so the king presented the offerings of the Netherworld, Ur-Namma presented the offerings of the Netherworld: as many faultless bulls, faultless kids, and fattened sheep as could be brought.

To Nergal, the Enlil of the Netherworld, in his palace, the shepherd Ur-Namma offered a mace, a large bow with quiver and arrows, an artfully made…dagger, and a multi-coloured leather bag for wearing at the hip.

To Gilgamec, the king of the Netherworld, in his palace, the shepherd Ur-Namma offered a spear, a leather bag for a saddle-hook, a heavenly lion-headed *imitum* mace, a shield resting on the ground, a heroic weapon, and a battle-axe, an implement beloved of Ereckigala.

To Ereckigala, the mother of Ninazu, in her palace, the shepherd Ur-Namma offered a…which he filled with oil, a *cajan* bowl of perfect make, a heavy garment, a long-fleeced garment, a queenly *pala* robe…the divine powers of the Netherworld.

To Dumuzid, the beloved husband of Inana, in his palace, the shepherd Ur-Namma offered a...sheep...mountain...a lordly golden sceptre...a shining hand.

To Namtar, who decrees all the fates, in his palace, the shepherd Ur-Namma offered perfectly wrought jewellery, a golden ring cast (?) as a...barge, pure cornelian stone fit to be worn on the breasts of the gods.

To Hucbisag, the wife of Namtar, in her palace, the shepherd Ur-Namma offered a chest (?) with a lapis lazuli handle, containing (?) everything that is essential in the Underworld, a silver hair clasp adorned with lapis lazuli, and a comb of womanly fashion.

To the valiant warrior Ninjiczida, in his palace, the shepherd Ur-Namma offered a chariot with...wheels sparkling with gold... donkeys, thoroughbreds...donkeys with dappled thighs... followed...by a shepherd and a herdsman.

To Dimpimekug, who stands by his side, he gave a lapis lazuli seal hanging from a pin, and a gold and silver toggle-pin with a bison's head.

To his spouse, Ninazimua, the august scribe, denizen of Arali, in her palace, the shepherd Ur-Namma offered a headdress with the august ear-pieces (?) of a sage, made of alabaster, a...stylus, the hallmark of the scribe, a surveyor's gleaming line, and the measuring rod... [...]

After the king had presented properly the offerings of the Netherworld, after Ur-Namma had presented properly the offerings of the Netherworld, the...seated Ur-Namma on a great dais of the Netherworld and set up a dwelling place for him in the Netherworld. At the command of Ereckigala all the soldiers who had been killed by weapons and all the men who had been found guilty were given into the king's hands. Ur-Namma was...so with Gilgamec, his beloved brother, he will issue the judgments of the Netherworld and render the decisions of the Netherworld.

After seven days, ten days had passed, lamenting for Sumer overwhelmed my king, lamenting for Sumer overwhelmed Ur-Namma. My king's heart was full of tears, he…bitterly that he could not complete the wall of Urim; that he could no longer enjoy the new palace he had built; that he, the shepherd, could no longer… his household (?); that he could no longer bring pleasure to his wife with his embrace; that he could not bring up his sons on his knees; that he would never see in their prime the beauty of their little sisters who had not yet grown up.

The trustworthy shepherd…a heart-rending lament for himself: "I, who have been treated like this, served the gods well, set up chapels for them. I have created evident abundance for the Anuna gods. I have laid treasures on their beds strewn with fresh herbs. Yet no god stood by me and soothed my heart. Because of them, anything that could have been a favourable portent for me was as far away from me as the heavens, the…. What is my reward for my eagerness to serve during the days? My days have been finished for serving them sleeplessly during the night! Now, just as the rain pouring down from heaven cannot turn back, alas, nor can I turn back to brick-built Urim.

"Alas, my wife has become a widow (?)! She spends the days in tears and bitter laments. My strength has ebbed away…. The hand of fate…bitterly me, the hero. Like a wild bull…I cannot…. Like a mighty bull…Like an offshoot…. Like an ass…. I died…my…wife… She spends the days in tears and bitter laments. Her kind protective god has left her; her kind protective goddess does not care for her anymore. Ninsun no longer rests her august arm firmly on her head.

Nanna, lord Acimbabbar, no longer leads (?) her by the hand. Enki, the lord of Eridug, does not.... Her...has been silenced (?), she can no longer answer. She is cast adrift like a boat in a raging storm; the mooring pole has not been strong enough for her. Like a wild ass lured (?) into a perilous pit she has been treated heavy-handedly. Like a lion fallen into a pitfall, a guard has been set up for her. Like a dog kept in a cage, she is silenced. Utu...does not pay heed to the cries, "Oh, my king," overwhelming her.

"My *tigi*, *adab*, flute and *zamzam* songs have been turned into laments because of me. The instruments of the house of music have been propped against the wall. Because I have been made to...on a heap of soil (?) instead of my throne whose beauty was endless; because I have been made to lie down in the open, desolate steppe instead of my bed, the sleeping place whose...was endless, alas, my wife and my children are in tears and wailing. My people whom I used to command (?) sing like lamentation and dirge singers because of her (?). While I was so treated, foremost Inana, the warlike lady, was not present at my verdict. Enlil had sent her as a messenger to all the foreign lands concerning very important matters."

When she had turned her gaze away from there, Inana humbly entered the shining E-kur, she...at Enlil's fierce brow. (Then Enlil said:) "Great lady of the E-ana, once someone has bowed down, he cannot...anymore; the trustworthy shepherd left E-ana, you cannot see him anymore." [...] Then Inana, the fierce storm, the eldest child of Suen...made the heavens tremble, made the earth shake.

Inana destroyed cattle-pens, devastated sheepfolds, saying: "I want to hurl insults at An, the king of the gods. Who can change the matter, if Enlil elevates someone? Who can change the import of the august words uttered by An, the king? If there are divine ordinances imposed on the Land, but they are not observed, there will be no abundance at the gods' place of sunrise. My holy *jipar*, the shrine E-ana, has been barred up like (?) a mountain. If only my shepherd could enter before me in it in his prime – I will not enter it otherwise! If only my strong one could grow for me like grass and herbs in the desert. If only he could hold steady for me like a river boat at its calm mooring." This is how Inana…a lament over him… Lord Ninjiczida…Ur-Namma, my…who was killed…

Among tears and laments…decreed a fate for Ur-Namma: "Ur-Namma…your august name will be called upon. From the south to the uplands…the holy sceptre. Sumer…to your palace. The people will admire…the canals which you have dug, the…which you have… the large and grand arable tracts which you have…the reed-beds which you have drained, the wide barley fields which you…and the fortresses and settlements which you have…Ur-Namma, they will call upon…your name. Lord Nunamnir, surpassing…will drive away the evil spirits…"

After shepherd Ur-Namma…Nanna, lord Acimbabbar…Enki, the king of Eridug…devastated sheepfolds…holy…lion born on high… renders just judgments…lord Ninjiczida be praised! My king… among tears and laments…among tears and laments.

The Ancient Egyptian Doctrine of the Immortality of the Soul

Alfred Wiedemann

In most religions the gods of life are distinct from the gods of death, but such a distinction scarcely existed at all in Egypt. There the same beings who were supposed to determine the fate of man in this world were supposed to determine it also in the world to come; only in the case of certain deities sometimes the one and sometimes the other side of the divine activity was brought into special prominence. The exercise of their different functions by the gods was not in accordance with any fixed underlying principle, was not any essential outcome of their characters, but rather a matter of their caprice and inclination. In course of time the Egyptian idea of these functions changed, and was variously apprehended in different places. It seems to us at first as though the relation of the gods to the life beyond had nearly everywhere been regarded as more important than their relation to this life. But this impression is owing to the fact that our material for the study of the Egyptian religion is almost exclusively derived from tombs and funerary temples, while the number of Egyptian monuments unconnected with the cult of the dead is comparatively small.

On this account it has been supposed that both in their religion and in their public life the Egyptians turned all their thoughts towards death and what lay beyond it. But a close examination of the monuments has proved that they had as full an enjoyment of the life here as other nations of antiquity, and that they are not to be regarded as a stiff and spiritless race of men whose thoughts were pedantically turned towards the contemplation of the next world.

Had this been the case, the Egyptians would have come to hold a pessimistic view of the life here and hereafter something like that prevailing in India, and have striven to escape from the monotony and dullness of existence by seeking some means to end it. But this is the reverse of what happened in the valley of the Nile. The most ardent wish of its inhabitants was to remain on earth as long as possible, to attain to the age of one hundred and ten years, and to continue to lead after death the same life which they had been wont to lead while here. They pictured the afterlife in the most material fashion; they could imagine no fairer existence than that which they led on the banks of the Nile. How simple and at the same time how complicated were their conceptions can best be shown by some account of their ideas on the immortality of the soul and its constitution as a combination of separate parts set forth in ancient Egyptian documents.

When once a man was dead, when his heart had ceased to beat and warmth had left his body, a lifeless hull was all that remained of him upon earth. The first duty of the survivors was to preserve this from destruction, and to that end it was handed over to a guild whose duty it was to carry out its embalmment under priestly supervision. This was done according to old and strictly established rules. The internal and more corruptible parts were taken away, and the rest of the body – *i.e.*, the bony framework and its covering

– was soaked in natron and asphalt, smeared with sweet-smelling unguents, and made incorruptible. The inside of the body was filled with linen bandaging and asphalt, among which were placed all kinds of amulets symbolizing immortality – heart-shaped vases, snake-heads in carnelian, scarabaei, and little glazed-ware figures of divinities. By their mystic power these amulets were intended to further and assist the preservation of the corpse, for which physical provision had already been made by embalmment. In about seventy days, when the work of embalmment was completed, the body was wrapped in linen bandages, placed in a coffin, and so returned to the family.

The friends and relatives of the deceased then carried the dead in solemn procession across the river to his last resting-place, which he had provided for himself in the hills forming the western boundary of the valley of the Nile. Mourning-women accompanied the procession with their wailing; priests burnt incense and intoned prayers, and other priests made offerings and performed mysterious ceremonies both during the procession and at the entrance to the tomb. The mummy was then lowered into the vault, which was closed and walled up, further offerings were made, and afterwards the mourners partook of the funeral feast in the antechamber of the tomb. Harpers were there who sang of the dead man and of his worth, and exhorted his relations to forget their grief and again to rejoice in life, so long as it should be granted unto them to enjoy the light of the sun; for when life is past, man knows not what shall follow it; beyond the grave is darkness and long sleep. Gayer and gayer grew the banquet, often degenerating into an orgy; when at length all the guests had withdrawn, the tomb was closed, and the dead was left alone. Afterwards it was only on certain feast days that the relatives made pilgrimages to the city of the dead, sometimes alone and sometimes accompanied by priests. On these occasions they again entered the antechamber of the tomb, and there offered prayers to the dead, or brought him offerings, either in the shape of real foods and drinks, or else under the symbolic forms of little clay models of oxen, geese, cakes of bread, and the like. Otherwise the tomb remained unvisited. How it there fared with the dead could only be learned from the doctrines and mysteries of religion; to descend into the vault and disturb the peace of the mummy was accounted a heavy crime against both gods and men.

And yet how much an Egyptian could have wished to look behind the sealed walls of the sepulchral chamber and see what secret and mysterious things there befell the dead! For their existence had not terminated with death; their earthly being only had come to an end, but they themselves had entered on a new, a higher and an eternal life. The constituent parts, whose union in the man had made a human life possible, separated at the moment of his death into those which were immortal and those which were mortal. But while the latter formed a unity, and constituted the corruptible body only, on which the above-mentioned rites of embalmment were practised, each of the former were distinct even when in combination. These "living, indestructible" parts of a man, which together almost correspond to our idea of the soul, had found their common home in his living body; but on leaving it at his death, each set out alone to find its own way to the gods. If all succeeded in doing so, and it was further proved that the deceased had been good and upright, they again became one with him, and so entered into the company of the blessed, or even of the gods.

The most important of all these component parts was the so-called Ka, the divine counterpart of the deceased, holding the same relation to him as a word to the conception which it expresses, or a statue to the living man. It was his individuality as embodied in the man's name; the picture of him which was, or might have been, called up in the minds of those who knew him at the mention of that name. Among other races similar thoughts have given rise to higher ideas, and led to a philosophic explanation of the distinction between personalities and persons, such as that contained in the Platonic Ideas. But the Egyptian was incapable of abstract thought, and was reduced to forming a purely concrete conception of this individuality, which is strangely impressive by reason of its thorough sensuousness. He endowed it with a material form completely corresponding to that of the man, exactly resembling him, his second self, his Double, his Doppelgänger.

Many scenes, dating from 12 BC and onwards, represent different kings appearing before divinities, while behind the king stands his Ka, as a little man with the king's features, or as a staff with two hands, and surmounted by certain symbols of royalty, or by the king's head. In these scenes the Personality accompanies the Person, following him as a shadow follows a man.

But even as early as the time of Amenophis III, about 1500 BC, the Egyptians had carried the idea still further, and had completely dissevered the Personality from the Person, the king being frequently represented as appearing before his own Personality, which bears the insignia of divinity, the staff of command, and the symbol of life, the ānkh. To it the king presents offerings of every kind and prefers his petition for gifts of the gods; in exchange His Personality replies, "I give unto thee all Life, all Stability, all Power, all Health, and all Joy (enlargement of heart); I subdue for thee the peoples of Nubia (Khent), so that thou mayest cut off their heads." In bas-reliefs of the same period which represent the birth of Amenophis III, his Ka is born at the same time as the king, and both are presented to Amen Rā, as two boys exactly alike, and blessed by him. About this time the kings began to build temples to their own Personalities, and appointed priests to them; and from time to time the sovereign would visit his temple to implore from himself his own protection, and still greater gifts. So long as the king walked the earth, so long his "living Ka, lord of Upper and Lower Egypt, tarried in his dwelling, in the Abode of Splendour (Pa Dûat)"; for his Ka was himself, independent of him, superior to him, and yet his counterpart and bound up with him.

The disjunction of the Personality from the Person was not, however, rigorously and systematically insisted upon; the two were indeed separate, but were so far one as to come into being only through and with each other. A man lived no longer than his Ka remained with him, and it never left him until the moment of his death. But there was this difference in their reciprocal relations: the Ka could live without the body, but the body could not live without the Ka. Yet this does not imply that the Ka was a higher, a spiritual being; it was material in just the same way as the body itself, needing food and drink for its wellbeing, and suffering hunger and thirst if these were denied it. In this respect its lot was the common lot of Egyptian gods; they also required bodily sustenance, and were sorely put to it if offerings failed them and their food and drink were unsupplied.

After a man's death his Ka became his Personality proper; prayers and offerings were made to the gods that they might grant bread and wine, meat and milk, and all good things needful for the sustenance of a god to the Ka of the deceased. Offerings were also made to the Ka itself, and it was believed that from time to time it visited the tomb in order to accept the food there provided for it. On such occasions it became incorporate in the mummy, which began to live and grow (rûd), or renew itself as do plants and trees (renp), and became, as the texts occasionally express it, "the living Ka in its coffin." The rich founded endowments whose revenues were to be expended to all time in providing their Kas with food offerings, and bequeathed certain sums for the maintenance of priests to attend to this; large staffs of officials were kept up to provide the necessaries of life for the Personalities of the dead. The Ka was represented by statues of the dead man which were placed within his tomb, and sometimes in temples also by gracious permission of the sovereign. Wherever one of these statues stood, there might the Ka sojourn and take part in Feasts of Offerings and the pleasures of earthly life; there even seems to have been a belief that it might be imprisoned in a statue by means of certain magic formulae. Royal statues in the temples were destined to the use of the royal Kas, the many statues of the same king in one temple being apparently all intended for his own Ka service.

Soul and Body
Ancient Egyptian Scribe

This extract is from the Papyrus of Ani, an example of a manuscript from the *Book of the Dead*, intended to help the deceased in their afterlife:

The chapter of causing the soul to be united to its body in the Underworld – the Osiris Ani, triumphant, saith:

"Hail, thou god Anniu (*i.e.*, Bringer)! Hail, thou god Pehrer (*i.e.*, Runner), who dwellest in thy hall! (Hail,) great God! Grant thou that my soul may come unto me from wheresoever it may be. If (it) would tarry, then let my soul be brought unto me from wheresoever it may be, for thou shalt find the Eye of Horus standing by thee like unto those beings who are like unto Osiris, and who never lie down in death. Let not the Osiris Ani, triumphant, lie down in death among those who lie down in Annu, the land wherein souls are joined unto their bodies even in thousands. Let me have possession of my *ba* (soul), and of my *khu*, and let me triumph therewith in every place wheresoever it may be. (Observe these things which (I) speak, for it hath staves with it); observe then, O ye divine guardians of heaven, my soul (wheresoever it may be). If it would tarry, do thou make my soul to look upon my body, for thou shalt find the Eye of Horus standing by thee like those (beings who are like unto Osiris).

"Hail, ye gods, who tow along the boat of the lord of millions of years, who bring (it) above the Underworld and who make it to travel over Nut, who make souls to enter into (their) spiritual bodies, whose hands are filled with your ropes and who clutch your weapons tight, destroy ye the Enemy; thus shall the boat of the sun be glad and the great God shall set out on his journey in peace. And behold, grant ye that the soul of Osiris Ani, triumphant, may come forth before the gods and that it may be triumphant along with you in the eastern part of the sky to follow unto the place where it was yesterday; (and that it may have) peace, peace in Amentet. May it look upon its material body, may it rest upon its spiritual body; and may its body neither perish nor suffer corruption for ever."

(These) words are to be said over a soul of gold inlaid with precious stones and placed on the breast of Osiris.

The Daughter of the Prince of Bakhtan and the Possessing Spirit

Ancient Egyptian Scribe

Horus, mighty bull, crowned with diadems, and established as firmly in his royalties as the god Atumu; Horus triumphant over Nubîti, mighty with the sword, destroyer of the barbarians, the king of both Egypts, Uasimarîya-Satapanrîya, son of the Sun, Rîyamasâsu Maîamânu, beloved of Amonrâ lord of Karnak and of the cycle of the gods lords of Thebes; the good god, son of Amon, born of Maût, begotten by Harmakhis, the glorious child of the universal Lord, begotten by the god, husband of his own mother, king of Egypt, prince of the desert tribes, sovereign who rules the barbarians, when scarcely issued from his mother's womb he directed wars, and he commanded valour while still in the egg like a bull who thrusts before – for this king is a bull, a god who comes out on the day of fighting, like Montu, and who is very valiant like the son of Nuît.

Now, when His Majesty was in Naharaina, according to his rule of every year, the princes of every land came, bending beneath the weight of offerings that they brought to the souls of His Majesty, and the fortresses brought their tribute, gold silver, lapis lazuli, malachite, and all the scented woods of Arabia on their back, and marching in file one behind the other; behold the prince of Bakhtan caused his tribute to be brought, and put his eldest daughter at the head of the train, to salute His Majesty, and to ask life of him. Because she was a very beautiful woman, pleasing to His Majesty more than anything, behold, he gave her the title of Great Royal Spouse, Nafrurîya, and when he returned to Egypt, she accomplished all the rites of a royal spouse.

And it happened in the year XV, the 22nd of the month Payni, that His Majesty was a Thebes the mighty, the queen of cities, engaged in doing that whereby he praised his father Amonrâ, lord of Karnak, at his fine festival of southern Thebes, his favourite dwelling, where the god has been since the creation; behold, one came to say to His Majesty, "There is a messenger from the prince of Bakhtan, who comes with many gifts for the Royal Spouse." Brought before His Majesty with his gifts, he said, while saluting His Majesty, "Glory to thee, Sun of foreign nations, thou by whom we live," and when he had said his adoration before His Majesty, he began again to speak to His Majesty. "I come to thee, Sire my lord, on account of Bintrashît, the youngest sister of the royal spouse, Nafrurîya, for a malady pervades her limbs. Let Thy Majesty send a sage to see her." Then the king said, "Bring me the scribes of the *Double House of Life* who are attached to the palace." As soon as they had come, His Majesty said, "Behold, I have sent for you that you may hear this saying: Send me from among you one who is skilled in his heart, a scribe learned with his fingers." When the royal scribe, Thotemhabi, had come into the presence of His Majesty, His Majesty commanded him to repair to Bakhtan with the messenger. As soon as the sage had arrived at Bakhtan, he found Bintrashît in the state of one possessed, and he found the ghost that possessed her an enemy hard to fight. The prince of Bakhtan therefore sent a second message to His Majesty, saying, "Sire my lord, let Thy Majesty command a god to be brought to fight the spirit."

When the messenger arrived in the presence of His Majesty, in year XXIII, the 1st of Pakhons, the day of the feast of Amon, while His Majesty was at Thebes, behold, His Majesty spake again, in the presence of Khonsu in Thebes, god of good counsel, saying, "Excellent lord, I am again before thee on account of the daughter of the prince of Bakhtan." Then Khonsu in Thebes, god of good counsel, was transported to Khonsu who rules destinies, the great god who drives away foreigners, and His Majesty said, facing Khonsu in Thebes, god of good counsel, "Excellent lord, may it please thee to turn thy face to Khonsu who rules destinies, great god who drives away foreigners; he will be taken to Bakhtan." And the god nodded with his head greatly twice. Then His Majesty said, "Give him thy virtue, that I may cause the majesty of this god to go to Bakhtan to deliver the daughter of the prince of Bakhtan." And Khonsu in Thebes, god of good counsel, nodded with his head greatly, twice, and he made the transmission of magic virtue to Khonsu who rules destinies in Thebes, four times. His Majesty commanded that Khonsu who rules destinies in Thebes should be sent on a great bark escorted by five smaller boats, by chariots, and many horses marching on the right and on the left. When this god arrived at Bakhtan, in the space of a year and five months, behold the prince of Bakhtan came with his soldiers and his generals before Khonsu who rules destinies, and threw himself on his belly, saying, "Thou comest to us, thou dost join with us, according to the orders of the king of the two Egypts, Uasimarîya-Satapanrîya."

Behold as soon as the god had gone to the place where Bintrashît was, and had made the magic passes for the daughter of the prince of Bakhtan, she became well immediately, and the spirit who was with her said in presence of Khonsu who rules destinies in Thebes, "Come in peace, great god who drives away foreigners, Bakhtan is thy town, its people are thy slaves, and I myself, I am thy slave. I will go, therefore, to the place from whence I came, in order to give satisfaction to thy heart on account of the matter which brings thee, but let Thy Majesty command that a feast day be celebrated for me and for the prince of Bakhtan." The god made an approving nod of the head to his prophet, to say, "Let the prince of Bakhtan make a great offering before this ghost." Now, while this was happening between Khonsu, who rules destinies in Thebes, and the spirit, the prince of Bakhtan was there with his army stricken with terror. And when they had made a great offering before Khonsu who rules destinies in Thebes, and before the ghost, from the prince of Bakhtan, while celebrating a feast day in their honour, the spirit departed in peace whithersoever it pleased him, according to the command of Khonsu who rules destinies in Thebes.

The prince of Bakhtan rejoiced greatly, as well as all the people of Bakhtan, and he communed with his heard, saying, "Since this god has been given to Bakhtan, I will not send him back to Egypt." Now after this god had remained three years and nine months at Bakhtan, when the prince of Bakhtan was laid down on his bed, he saw in a dream this god issuing from his shrine in the form of a sparrow-hawk of gold which flew towards Egypt; when he awoke he was shivering greatly. He then said to the prophet of Khonsu who rules destinies in Thebes, "This god who has dwelt with us, he wills to return to Egypt; let his chariot go to Egypt." The prince of

Bakhtan granted that this god should depart for Egypt, and he gave him numerous presents of all good things, and also a strong escort of soldiers and horses. When they had arrived at Thebes, Khonsu who rules destinies in Thebes repaired to the temple of Khonsu in Thebes, the good counsellor; he placed the gifts that the prince of Bkahtan had given him of all good things in the presence of Khonsu in Thebes, the good counsellor, he kept nothing for himself. Now, Khonsu the good counsellor in Thebes returned to his temple in peace, in the year XXIII, the 19th Mechir, of the King Uasimarîya-Satapanrîya, living for ever, like the Sun.

Fragments of a Ghost Story (Khonsemhab and the Ghost)

Ancient Egyptian Scribe,
presented by Gaston Maspero

These fragments have come down to us on four potsherds, one of which is now at the Louvre, and another at the Vienna Museum; the two others are in the Egyptian Museum in Florence. [...]

It is impossible to discover what the leading idea of the story may have been. Several personages appear in it: a Theban high priest of Amon, Khonsûmhabi [Khonsemhab], three unnamed men, and a ghost who employs very good language to tell the story of his former life. [...] The high priest, Khonsûmhabi, appears to be entirely occupied with finding a suitable site for his tomb:

> *He sent one of his subordinates to the place of the tomb of the king of Upper and Lower Egypt Râhotpu, l. h. s.* [l. h. s. is an abbreviation of the formula, *Life, health, strength*, which always follows the name of a king or a royal title], *and with him the men under the orders of the high priest of Amonrâ, king of the gods, three men, four men in all; he embarked with them, he steered, he led them to the*

*place indicated, near the tomb of the king Râhotpu, l. h. s.
They went to it with her, and they went inside; she adored
twenty-five...in the royal...country, then they came to the
riverbank, and they sailed to Khonsûmhabi, the high priest
of Amonrâ, king of the gods, and they found him who sang
the praises of the god in the temple of the city of Amon.*

*He said to them, "Let us rejoice, for I have come,
and I have found the place favourable for establishing thy
dwelling to perpetuity," and they seated themselves before
her, and she passed a happy day, and her heart was given
to joy. Then he said to them, "Be ready tomorrow morning
when the solar disc issues from the two horizons." He
commanded the lieutenant of the temple of Amon to find
lodgement for those people, he told each of them what he
had to do, and he caused them to return to sleep in the city
in the evening. He established...*

In the fragments at Florence, the high priest found himself face
to face chatting with the ghost, and perhaps this was while
digging out the more ancient tomb, the owners of which entered
into conversation with him, as the mummies of Nenoferkephtah
talked with Prince Setne Khamwas. At the point where we take
up the text again, one of the mummies seems to be relating the
story of his earthly life to the first prophet of Amon:

*I grew, and I did not see the rays of the sun, I did
not breathe the air, but darkness was before me every day,
and no one came to find me." The spirit said to him, "For
me, when I was still living on earth, I was the treasurer of*

*king Râhotpu, l. h. s., I was also his infantry lieutenant.
Then I passed before men and behind the gods, and I died
in the year XIV, during the months of Shomu, of the king
Manhapurîya, l. h. s. He gave me my four casings, and my
sarcophagus of alabaster; he caused to be done for me all
that is done for a man of quality, he gave me offerings…"*

All that follows is very obscure. The ghost seems to complain of
some accident that has happened to himself or to his tomb, but I
cannot clearly make out what is the subject of his dissatisfaction.
Perhaps, like Nenoferkephtah in the story of Setne Khamwas,
he simply wished to have his wife, his children, or someone
whom he had loved, to dwell with him. When he has finished
his speech, his visitor speaks in his turn:

*The first prophet of Amonrâ, king of the gods,
Khonsûmhabi said to him, "Oh, give me excellent counsel
as to what I should do, and I will have it done for thee, or
at least grant that five men and five slaves may be given
me, in all then persons, to bring me water, and then I
will give corn every day, and that will enrich me, and a
libation of water shall be brought me every day." The spirit,
Nuîtbusokhnu, said to him, "What hast thou done? If the
wood is not left in the sun, it will not remain dried, it is not
a stone worn with age that is brought…"*

The prophet of Amon appears to ask some favour from the
ghost; which, on his part, the ghost does not appear disposed
to grant him, notwithstanding the promises made by his visitor.

The conversation on this theme lasted a considerable time, and I think we find it continued on the Vienna ostracon. Khonsûmhabi enquires to which family one of his interlocutors belonged, and his very natural curiosity was amply satisfied:

> *The spirit said to him, "X...is the name of my father, X...the name of the father of my father, and X...the name of my mother." The high priest Khonsûmhabi said to him, "But then I know thee well. This eternal house in which thou art, it is I who had it made for thee; it is I who caused thee to be buried, in the day when thou didst return to earth; it is I who had done for thee that which should be done for him who is of high rank. But behold I am in poverty, an evil wind of winter has breathed famine over the country, and I am no longer happy. My heart does not touch (joy), because the Nile..." Thus said Khonsûmhabi, and after that Khonsûmhabi remained there, weeping, for a long time, not eating, not drinking, not...*

The text is so interrupted by lacunae that I cannot hope to have interpreted it correctly throughout. Even had it been complete, the difficulty would have been scarcely less great. I do not know whether the fashion among Egyptian ghosts was to render their language obscure at pleasure; this one does not seem to have attempted to make himself clear. His remarks are brusquely broken off in the middle of a phrase, and unless Golénischeff discovers some other fragments on a potsherd in a museum, I see scarcely any chance that we shall ever know the remainder of the story.

The Adventure of Setne Khamwas with the Mummies

Ziharpto

At one time there was a king named Usimares, l. h. s., and this king had a son named Setne Khamwas, and the foster-brother of Setne Khamwas was called Inarôs by name. And Setne Khamwas was well instructed in all things. He passed his time wandering about the necropolis of Memphis, to read there the books of the sacred writings and the books of the *Double House of Life*, and the writings that are carved on the stelae and on the walls of the temples; he knew the virtues of amulets and talismans, he understood how to compose them and to draw up powerful writings, for he was a magician who had no equal in the land of Egypt.

Now, one day, when he was walking in the open court of the temple of Ptah, reading the inscriptions, behold, a man of noble bearing who was there began to laugh. Setne said to him, "Wherefore dost thou laugh at me?" The noble said, "I do not laugh at thee, but can I refrain from laughing when thou dost decipher the writings here which possess no power? If thou desirest truly to read an efficacious writing, come with me. I will cause thee to go to the place where the book is that Thoth wrote with his own hand, and which will put thee immediately below the gods. The two formulae that are written there, if thou recites the first of them, thou shalt charm the heaven, the earth, the world of the night, the mountains, the waters; thou shalt understand what all the birds of heaven and the reptiles say, as many as there are. Thou shalt behold the fish, for a divine power will bring them to the surface of the water. If thou readest the second formula, even when thou art in the tomb, thou shalt resume the form thou hadst on earth; thou shalt also behold the sun rising in the heavens, and his cycle of gods, also the moon in the form that she has when she appears." Setne said, "By my life! Let it be told me what thou dost wish for, and I will do it for thee; but lead me to the place where the book is." The noble said to Setne, "The book in question is not mine, it is in the midst of the necropolis, in the tomb of Nenoferkephtah, son of the King Merenephthis, l. h. s. Beware indeed of taking this book from him, for he will make thee bring it back, a forked stick and a staff in thy hand, a lighted brazier on thy head." From the hour when the noble spake to Setne, he knew no longer in what part of the world he was; he went before the king, and he said before the king all the words that the noble had said to him. The king said to him, "What dost thou desire?" He said to the king, "Permit me to go down into the tomb of Nenoferkephtah, son of the King Merenphthis, l. h. s.; I will take Inarôs, my foster-brother, with me, and I shall bring back that book." He went to the necropolis of Memphis with Inarôs, his foster-brother. He spent three days and three nights searching among the tombs which are in the necropolis of Memphis, reading the stelae of the *Double House of Life*, reciting the inscriptions they bore. On the third day he recognized the place where Nenoferkephtah was laid. When they had recognized the place where Nenoferkephtah was laid, Setne recited a writing over him; a gap opened in the ground, and Setne went down to the place where the book was. [...]

When he entered, behold, it was as light as if the sun shone there, for the light came from the book and lighted all around. And Nenoferkephtah was not alone in the tomb, but his wife Ahuri, and Maîhêt his son, were with him; for though their bodies reposed at Coptos, their double was with him by virtue of the book of Thoth. And when Setne entered the tomb, Ahuri stood up and said to him, "Thou, who art thou?" He said, "I am Setne Khamwas, son of the King Usimares, l. h. s.; I am come to have that book of Thoth, that I perceive between thee and Nenoferkephtah. Give it me, for if not I will take it from thee by force." Ahuri said, "I pray thee, be not in haste, but listen first to all the misfortunes that came to me because of this book of which thou sayest, 'Let it be given to me.' Do not say that, for on account of it we were deprived of the time we had to remain on earth.

"I am named Ahuri, daughter of the King Merenephthis, l. h. s., and he whom thou seest here with me is my brother Nenoferkephtah. We were born of the same father and the same mother, and our parents had no other children than ourselves. When I was of age to marry, I was taken before the king at the time of diversion with he king; I was much adorned and I was considered beautiful. The king said, 'Behold, Ahuri, our daughter, is already grown, and the time has come to marry her. To whom shall we marry Ahuri, our daughter?' Now I loved Nenoferkephtah, my brother, exceedingly, and I desired no other husband than he. I told this to my mother; she went to find the King Merenephthis, she said to him, 'Ahuri, our daughter, loves Nenoferkephtah, her eldest brother; let us marry them one tot the other according to custom.' When the King had heard all the words that my mother had said, he said, 'Thou hast had but two children, and wouldest thou marry them one to the other? Would it not be better to marry Ahuri to the son of a general of infantry, and Nenoferkephtah to the daughter of another general of infantry?' She said, 'Dos thou wrangle with me? Even if I have no children after those two children, is it not the law to marry them one to the other? – I shall marry Nenoferkephttah to the daughter of a commander of troops, and Ahuri to the son of another commander of troops, and may this turn to good for our family.' As this was the time to make festival before Pharaoh, behold, one came to fetch me, one led me to the festival; I was very troubled, and I had no longer the manner of the previous day. Now Pharaoh said to me, 'Is it not thou who didst send me those foolish words, "Marry me to Nenoferkephtah my eldest brother"?' I said to him, 'Well, let me be married to the son of a general of infantry, and let Nenoferkephtah be married to the daughter of another general of infantry, and may this turn to good for our family.' I laughed, Pharaoh laughed. Pharaoh said to the major-domo of the royal house, 'Let Ahuri be taken to the house of Nenoferkephtah this very night; let all manner of fine presents be taken with her.' They took me as spouse to the house of Nenoferkephtah, and Pharaoh commanded that a great dowry of gold and silver should be taken to me, and all the servants of the royal house presented them to me. Nenoferkephtah spent a happy day with me; he received all the servants of the royal house, and he slept with me that very night, and he found me a virgin, and he knew me again and again, for each of us loved the other. And when the time of my monthly purifications was come, lo, I had no purifications to make. One went to announce it to Pharaoh, and his heart rejoiced greatly thereat, and he had all manner of precious things of the property of the royal house taken, and he had very beautiful gifts of gold, of silver, of fine linen, brought to me. And when the time came that I should be delivered, I brought forth this little child who is before thee. The name of Maîhêt was given him, and it was inscribed on the register of the *Double House of Life*.

And many days after that, Nenoferkephtah, my brother, seemed only to be on earth to walk about in the necropolis of Memphis, reading the writings that are in the tombs of the Pharaohs, and the stelae of the scribes of the *Double House of Life*, as well as the writings that are inscribed on them, for he was greatly interested in writings. After that there was a procession in honour of the god Ptah, and Nenoferkephtah entered the temple to pray. Now while he walked behind the procession, deciphering the writings that are on the chapels of the gods, an old man saw him and laughed. Nenoferkephtah said to him, 'Where fore dost thou laugh at me?' The priest said, 'I am not laughing at thee; but can I refrain from laughing when thou readest here writings that have no power? If thou verily desirest to read a writing, come to me. I will cause thee to go to a place where the book is that Thoth wrote with his hand himself, when he came here below with the gods. The two formulae that are written there, if thou recitest the first thou shalt charm the heavens, the earth, the world of the night, the mountains, the waters; thou shalt understand that which the birds of the heaven and the reptiles say, as many as they are; thou shalt see the fish of the deep, for a divine power will rest on the water above them. If thou readest the second formula, even after thou art in the tomb, thou shalt resume the form that thou hadst on earth; also thou shalt see the sun rising in the heavens, with his cycle of gods, and the moon in the form she has when she appears.' Nenoferkephtah said to the priest, 'By the life of the King, let me be told what good thing thou dost wish for, and I will cause it to be given to thee if thou wilt lead me to the place where the book is.' The priest said to Nenoferkephtah, 'If thou desirest that I should send thee to the place where the book is thou shalt give me a hundred pieces of silver for my burial, and thou shalt cause the two coffins of a wealthy priest to be made for me.' Nenoferkephtah called a page and commanded him that the hundred pieces of silver should be given to the priest, also he caused the two coffins to be made that the desired; in short, he did all that the priest had said. The priest said to Nenoferkephtah, 'The book in question is in the midst of the sea of Coptos in an iron coffer. The iron coffer is in a bronze coffer; the bronze coffer is in a coffer of cinnamon wood; the coffer of cinnamon wood is in a coffer of ivory and ebony; the coffer of ivory and ebony is in a coffer of silver; the coffer of silver is in a coffer of gold, and the book is in that. And there is a schene of reptiles round the coffer in which is the book, and there is an immortal serpent rolled round the coffer in question.'

"From the hour that the priest spoke to Nenoferkephtah he knew not in what part of the world he was. He came out of the temple; he spake with me of all that had happened to him; he said to me, 'I go to Coptos, I will bring back that book, and after that I will not again leave the country of the north.' But I rose up against the priest, saying, 'Beware of Amon for thyself, because of that which thou hast said to Nenoferkephtah; for thou hast brought me disputing, thou has brought me war; and the country of the Thebaid, I find it hostile to my happiness.' I raised my hand to Nenoferkephttah that they should not go to Coptos, but he did not listen to me; he went before Pharaoh, and he spake before Pharaoh all the words that the priest had said to him. Pharaoh said to him, 'What is the desire of thy heart?' He said to him, 'Let the royal cange be given to me fully equipped. I shall take Ahuri, my sister, and Maîhêt, her little child, to the south with me; I shall bring back the book, and I shall not leave this place again.' The cange fully equipped was given to him; we embarked on it, we made the voyage, we arrived at Coptos. When this was told to the priests of Isis of Coptos, and to the superior of the priests of Isis, behold they came down to us; they came without delay before Nenoferkephtah, and their wives came down before me. We disembarked, and we went to the temple of Isis, and of Harpocrates. Nenoferkephtah caused a bull to be brought, a goose, and wine; he presented an offering and a libation before Isis of Coptos, and Harpocrates. We were then conducted to a house which was very beautiful, and full of all manner of good things. Nenoferkephtah spent five days diverting himself with the priests of Isis of Coptos, while the wives of the priests of Isis of Coptos diverted themselves with me. When the morning of the following day came Nenoferkephtah caused a large quantity of pure wax to be brought before hum; he made of it a bark filled with its rowers and sailors, he recited a spell over them, he brought them to life, he gave them breath, he threw them into the water, he filled the royal cange with sand, he said farewell to me, he embarked, and I placed myself on the sea of Coptos, saying, 'I know what will happen to him.'

"He said, 'Rowers, row for me, to the place where the book is,' and they rowed for him, by night as by day. When he had arrived there in three days, he threw sand in front of him, and a chasm opened in the river. When he had found a schene of serpents, of scorpions, and of all manner of reptiles round the coffer where the book was, and when he had beheld an eternal serpent round the coffer itself, he recited a spell over the schene of serpents, scorpions, and reptiles who were round the coffer, and if rendered them motionless. He came to the place where the eternal serpent was; he attacked him, he slew him. The serpent came to life, and took his form again. He attacked the serpent a second time; he slew him. The serpent came to life again. He attacked the serpent a third time; he cut him in two pieces, he put sand between piece and piece; the serpent died, and he did not again take his previous form. Nenoferkephtah went to the place where the coffer was, and he recognized that it was an iron coffer. He opened it and he found a bronze coffer. He opened it and found a cinnamon-wood coffer. He opened it and found an ivory and ebony coffer. He opened it and found a silver coffer. He opened it and found a gold coffer. He opened it and found that the book was inside. He drew the book in question out of the gold coffer, and recited a formula of that which was written in it; he enchanted the heaven, the earth, the world of the night, the mountains, the waters; he understood all that was spoken by the birds of the heaven, the fish of the waters, the beasts of the mountain. He recited the other formula of the writing, and he beheld the sun as it mounted the sky with his cycle of gods, the moon rising, the stars in their form; he beheld the fish of the deep, for a divine force rested on the water above them. He recited a spell over the water, and it made it return to its former shape, he re-embarked; he said to the rowers, 'Row for me to the place where Ahuri is.' They rowed for him, by night as by day. When he arrived at the place where I was, in three days, he found me sitting near the sea of Coptos. I was not drinking nor eating; I was doing nothing in the world; I was like a person arrived at the *Good Dwelling*. I said to Nenoferkephtah, 'By the life of the King! Grant that I see this book for which you have taken all this trouble.' He put the book in my hand, I read one formula of the writing which was there; I enchanted the heaven, the earth, the world of the night, the mountains, the waters; I understood all that was spoken by the birds of the heaven, the fish of the deep, and the quadrupeds. I recited the other formula of the writing. I beheld the sun which appeared in the heaven with his cycle of gods, I beheld the moon rising. And all the stars of heaven in their form; I beheld the fish of the water, for there was a divine force which rested on the water above them. As I could not write, I said to Nenoferkephtah, my eldest brother, who was an accomplished scribe and a very learned man; he caused a piece of virgin papyrus to be brought, he wrote therein all the words that were in the book, he soaked it in beer, he dissolved the whole in water. When he saw that it had all dissolved, he drank, and he knew all that was in the writing.

"We returned to Coptos the same day, and we made merry before Isis of Coptos and Harpocrates. We embarked, we set off. We reached the north of Coptos, the distance of a schene. Now behold, Thoth had learnt all that had happened to Nenoferkephtah with regard to this book, and Thoth did not delay to plead before Râ, saying, 'Know that my right and my law are with Nenoferkephtah, son of the King Merenephthis, l. h. s. He has penetrated into my abode, he has pillaged it, he has taken my coffer with my book of incantations, he has slain my guardian who watched over the coffer.' One said to him, 'He is thine, he and all his, all of them.' One sent down a divine force from heaven saying, 'Nenoferkephtah shall not arrive safe and sound at Memphis, he and whoever is with him.' At this same hour Maîhêt, the young child, came out from under the awning of the cange of Pharaoh. He fell in the river, and while he praised Râ, all who were on board uttered a cry. Nenoferkephtah came out from below the cabin; he recited a spell over the child, and brought him up again, for there was a divine force which rested on the water above him. He recited a spell over him, he made him tell all that had happened to him, and the accusation that Thoth had brought before Râ. We returned to Coptos with him, we had him carried to the *Good Dwelling*, we waited to see that care was taken of him, we had him embalmed as beseemed a great one, we laid him in his coffin in the cemetery of Coptos. Nenoferkephtah, my brother, said, 'Let us go; do not let us delay to return until the king has heard what has happened to us, and his heart is troubled on this account.' We embarked, we parted, we were not long in arriving at the north of Coptos, the distance of a schene. At the place where the little child Maîhêt had tumbled into the river, I came out from below the awning of the cange of Pharaoh, I fell into the river, and while I praised Râ all who were on board uttered a cry. It was told to Nenoferkephtah, and he came out from below the awning of the cange of Pharaoh. He recited a spell over me, and he brought me up again, for there was a divine force which rested on the water above me. He took me out of the river, he read a spell over me, he made me tell all that had happened to me, and the accusation that Thoth had brought before Râ. He returned to Coptos with me, he had me carried to the *Good Dwelling*, he waited to see that care was taken of me, he had me embalmed as beseemed a very great personage, he had me laid in the tomb where Maîhêt, the little child, was already laid. He embarked, he set out, he was not long in arriving at the north of Coptos, the distance of a schene, at the place where we had fallen into the river. He communed with his heart, saying, 'Would it not be better to go to Coptos, and take up my abode with them? If, on the contrary, I return at once to Memphis, and Pharaoh questions me on the subject of his children, what could I say to him? Could I say thus to him: 'I took thy children with me to the nome of Thebes; I have killed them, and I live. I returned to Memphis still living.' He caused a piece of royal fine linen that belonged to him to be brought, he made of it a magic band, he tied the book with it, he put it on his breast, and fixed it there firmly. Neoferkephtah came out from below the awning of the cange of Pharaoh, he fell into the water, and while he praised Râ all who were on board uttered a cry, saying, 'Oh, what great mourning, what lamentable mourning! Is he not gone, the excellent scribe, the learned man who had no equal!'

"The cange of Pharaoh went on its way, before anyone in the world knew in what place Nenoferkephtah was. When it arrived at Memphis one informed Pharaoh, and Pharaoh came down in front of the cange. He was wearing a mourning cloak, and all the garrison of Memphis wore mourning cloaks, as well as the priests of Ptah, the high priest of Ptah, and all the people who surround Pharaoh. And lo! they beheld Nenoferkephtah, who was fixed on to the rudder-oars of the cange of Pharaoh by his knowledge as an excellent scribe. They raised him, they saw the book on his breast, and Pharaoh said, 'Let the book that is on his breast be taken away.' The couriers of Pharaoh, as well as the priests of Ptah and the high priest of Ptah, said before the king, 'Oh, our great lord – may he have the duration of Râ! – he is an excellent scribe and a very learned man, this Nenoferkephtah!' Pharaoh had him placed in the *Good Dwelling* for the space of sixteen days, clothed with stuffs for the space of thirty-five days, laid out for the space of seventy days, and then he was laid in his tomb among the *Dwellings of Repose*.

"I have told thee all the sorrows that came to us on account of this book, of which thou sayest, 'Let it be given me.' Thou hast no right to it; for, on account of it, the time we had to remain on the earth was taken from us."

Setne said, "Ahuri, give me that book that I see between thee and Nenoferkephtah; if not, I will take it from thee by force." Nenoferkephtah raised himself on the bed and said, "Art thou not Setne, to whom that woman has told all those misfortunes that thou hast not yet experienced? Art thou capable of obtaining this book by the power of an excellent scribe, or by thy skill in playing against me? Let us two play for it." Setne said, "Agreed." Then they brought the *board* before them, with its *dogs*, and they two played. Nenoferkephtah won a game from Setne; he recited his magic over him, he placed over him the playing-board which was before him, and he caused him to sink into the ground up to the legs. He did the same with the second game; he won from Setne, and he caused him to sink into the ground up to the waist. He did the same with the third game, and he caused Setne to sink into the ground up to the ears. After that, Setne attacked Nenoferkephtah with his hand; Setne called Inarôs, his foster-brother, saying, "Do not delay to go up on to the earth; tell all that has happened to me before Pharaoh; bring me the talismans of my father Ptah, as well as my books of magic." He went up without delay on the ground; he recounted before Pharaoh all that had happened to Setne, and Pharaoh said, "Take him the talismans of his father as well as his books of incantations." Inarôs went down without delay into the tomb; he placed the talismans on the body of Setne, and he at once rose to the earth. Setne stretched out his hand towards the book and seized it; and when Setne came up out of the tomb, the light went before him and darkness came behind him. Ahuri wept after him, saying, "Glory to thee, oh darkness! Glory to thee, oh light! All of it is departed, all that was in our tomb." Nenoferkephtah said to Ahuri, "Do not afflict thyself. I shall make him bring back this book

in due time, a forked stick in his hand, a lighted brazier on his head."
Setne went up out of the tomb, and he closed it behind him as it was
before. Setne went before Pharaoh, and he recounted to Pharaoh
all that had happened to him on account of the book. Pharaoh said
to Setne, "Replace this book in the tomb of Nenoferkephtah, like a
wise man; if not, he will force thee to take it back, a forked stick in
thy hand, a lighted brazier on thy head." But Setne did not listen to
him; he had no other occupation in the world than to spread out
the roll and to read it, it mattered not to whom.

After that it happened one day, when Setne was walking on the
forecourt of the temple of Ptah, he saw a woman, very beautiful, for
there was no woman who equalled her in beauty; she had much
gold upon her, and there were young girls who walked behind her,
and with her were servants to the number of fifty-two. From the
hour that Setne beheld her, he no longer knew the part of the world
in which he was. Setne called his page, saying, "Do not delay to go
to the place where that woman is and learn who she is." The young
page made no delay in going to the place where the woman was.
He addressed the maid-servant who walked behind her, and he
questioned her, saying, "What person is that?" She said to him, "She
is Tbubui, daughter of the prophet of Bastît, lady of Ankhutaûi, who
now goes to make her prayer before Ptah, the great god." When
the young man had returned to Setne, he recounted all the words
that she had said to him without exception. Setne said to the young
man, "Go and say thus to the maid-servant, 'Setne Khamwas, son
of the Pharaoh Usimares, it is who sends me, saying, "I will give
thee ten pieces of gold that thou mayest pass an hour with me. If
there is necessity to have recourse to violence, he will do it, and
he will take thee to a hidden place, where no one in the world will

find thee." When the young man had returned to the place where Tbubui was, he addressed the maid-servant, and spake with her, but she exclaimed against his words, as though it were an insult to speak them. Tbubui said to the young man, "Cease to speak to that wretched girl; come and speak to me." The young man approached the place where Tbubui was; he said to her, "I will give thee ten pieces of gold if thou wilt pass an hour with Setne Khamwas, the son of Pharaoh Usimares. If there is necessity to have recourse to violence, he will do so, and will take thee to a hidden place where no one in the world will find thee." Tbubui said, "Go, say to Setne, 'I am a hierodule, I am no mean person; if thou dost desire to have thy pleasure of me, and no one in the world shall know it, and I shall not have acted like a woman of the streets.'" When the page had returned to Setne, he repeated to him all the words that she had said without exception, and he said, "Lo, I am satisfied." But all who were with Setne began to curse.

Setne caused a boat to be fetched, he embarked, and delayed not to arrive at Bubastis. He went to the west of the town, until he came to a house that was very high; it had a wall all around it, it had a garden on the north side, there was a flight of steps in front of it. Setne inquired, saying, "Whose is this house?" They said to him, "It is the house of Tbubui." Setne entered the grounds, and he marvelled at the pavilion situated in the garden while they told Tbubui; she came down, she took the hand of Setne, and she said to him, "By my life! The journey to the house of the priest of Bastît, lady of Ankhutaûi, at which thou art arrived, is very pleasant to me. Come up with me." Setne went up by the stairway of the house with Tbubui. He found the upper storey of the house sanded and powered with sand and powder of real lapis lazuli and real turquoise. There were several beds there, spread with stuffs of royal linen, and also many cups of gold on a stand. They filled a golden cup with wine, and placed it in the had of Setne, and Tbubui said to him, "Will it please thee to rest thyself?" He said to her, "That is not what I wish to do." They put scented wood on the fire, they brought perfumes of the kind that are supplied to Pharaoh, and Setne made a happy day with Tbubui, for he had never before seen her equal. Then Setne said to Tbubui, "Let us accomplish that for which we have come here." She said to him, "Thou shalt arrive at thy house, that where thou art. But for me, I am a hierodule, I am no mean person. If thou desirest to have thy pleasure of me, thou shall make me a contract of sustenance, and a contract of money on all the things and on all the goods that are thine." He said to her, "Let the scribe of the school be brought." He was brought immediately, and Setne caused to be made in favour of Tbubui a contract for maintenance, and he made her in writing a dowry of all his things, all the goods that were his. An hour passed; one came to say this to Setne, "Thy children are below." He said, "Let them be brought up." Tbubui arose, she put on a robe of fine linen and Setne beheld all her limbs through it, and his desire increased yet more than before. Setne said to Tbubui, "Let us accomplish now that for which I came." She said to him, "Thou shalt arrive at thy house, that where thou art. But for me, I am a hierodule, I am no mean person. If thou desirest to have thy pleasure of me, thou wilt cause thy children to subscribe to my writing, that they may not seek a quarrel with my children on the subject of thy possessions." Setne had his children fetched and made them subscribe to the writing. Setne said to Tbubui, "Let me now accomplish that for which I came." She said to him, "Thou shalt arrive at thy house, that where thou art. But for me, I am a hierodule, I am no mean person. If thou dost desire to have thy pleasure of me, thou shalt cause thy children to be slain, so that they may not seek a quarrel with my children on account of thy possessions." Setne said, "Let the crime be committed on them of which the desire has entered thy heart." She caused the children of Setne to be slain before him, she had them thrown out below the window, to the dogs and cats, and they ate their flesh, and he heard them while he was drinking with Tbubui. Setne said to Tbubui, "Let us accomplish that for which we have come here, for all that thou hast said before me has been done for thee." She said to him, "Come into this chamber." Setne entered the chamber, he lay down on a bed of ivory and ebony, in order that his love might be rewarded, and Tbubui lay down by the side of Setne. He stretched out his hand to touch her; she opened her mouth widely and uttered a loud cry.

When Setne came to himself he was in a place of a furnace without any clothing on his back. After an hour Setne perceived a very big man standing on a platform, with quite a number of attendants beneath his feet, for he had the semblance of a Pharaoh. Setne was about to raise himself, but he could not arise for shame, for he had no clothing on his back. This Pharaoh said, "Setne, what is the state in which you are?" He said, "It is Nenoferkephtah who has had all this done to me." This Pharaoh said, "Go to Memphis; thy children, lo! They wish for thee. Lo! they are standing before Pharaoh." Setne spake before this Pharaoh, "My great lord the king – mayest thou have the duration of Râ – how can I arrive at Memphis if I have no raiment in the world on my back?" This Pharaoh called a page who was standing near him and commanded him to give a garment to Setne. This Pharaoh said, "Setne, go to Memphis. Thy children, behold they live, behold they are standing before the king." Setne went to Memphis; he embraced his children with joy, because they were in life. Pharaoh said, "Is it not drunkenness that has caused thee to do all that?" Setne related all that had happened to him with Tbubui and Nenoferkephtah. Pharaoh said, "Setne, I have before come to thin aid, saying, 'They will slay thee, if thou dost not return that book to the place where thou didst take it for thyself, but thou hast not listened to me up to this hour.' Now take back the book to Nenoferkephtah, a forked staff in thy hand and a lighted brazier on thy head." Setne went out before Pharaoh, a fork and a staff in his hand and a lighted brazier on his head, and he descended into the tomb where Nenoferkephtah was. Ahuri said to him, "Setne, it is Ptah the great god who brings thee here safe and sound." Nenoferkephtah laughed, saying, "This is what I said to thee before." Setne began to talk with Nenoferkephtah, and he perceived that while they talked the sun was altogether in the tomb. Ahuri and Nenoferkephtah talked much with Setne. Setne said, "Nenoferkephtah, is it not something humiliating that thou askest?" Nenoferkephtah said, "Thou knowest this by knowledge, that Ahuri and Maîhêt, her child, are at Coptos, and also in this tomb, by the art of a skilful scribe. Let it be commanded to thee to take the trouble to go to Coptos and bring them hither."

Setne went up out of the tomb; he went before Pharaoh, he related before Pharaoh all that Nenoferkephtah had said to him. Pharaoh said, "Setne, go to Coptos and bring back Ahuri and Maîhêt her child." He said before Pharaoh, "Let the cange of Pharaoh and its crew be given me." The cange of Pharaoh and its crew were given him; he embarked, he started, he did not delay to arrive at Coptos. One told the priests of Isis, of Coptos, and the high priest of Isis; behold, they came down to him, they came down to the bank. He disembarked, he went to the temple of Isis of Coptos, and Harpocrates. He caused a bull, a goose, and some wine to be brought; he made a burnt offering and a libation before Isis of Coptos and Harpocrates. He went to the cemetery of Coptos with the priests of Isis and the high priest of Isis. They spent three days and three nights searching among the tombs that are in the necropolis of Coptos, moving the stelae of the scribes of the *Double House of Life*, deciphering the inscriptions on them; they did not find the chambers where Ahuri and Maîhêt her child reposed. Nenoferkephtah knew that they did not find the chambers where Ahuri and Maîhêt her child reposed. He manifested himself under the form of an old man, a priest very advanced in years, he presented himself before Setne.

Setne saw him; Setne said, "Thou seemest to be a man advanced in years, dost thou not know the house where Ahuri and Maîhêt her child repose?" The old man said to Setne, "The father of the father of my father said to the father of my father, 'The chambers where Ahuri and Maîhêt her child repose are below the southern corner of the house of the priest...'" Setne said to the old man, "Perchance the priest...hath injured thee, and therefore it is that thou wouldest destroy his house." The old man said to Setne, "Let a good watch be kept on me while the house of the priest...is destroyed, and if it happens that Ahuri and Maîhêt her child are not found under the southern corner of the house of the priest...let me be treated as a criminal." A good watch was kept over the old man; the chamber where Ahuri and Maîhêt her child reposed was found below the southern angle of the house of the priest...Setne caused these great personages to be carried to the cange of Pharaoh, and he then had the house of the priest...rebuilt as it was before. Nenoferkephtah made known to Setne that it was he who had come to Coptos, to discover for him the chamber where Ahuri and Maîhêt her child reposed.

Setne embarked on the cange of Pharaoh. He made the voyage, he did not delay to arrive at Memphis, and all the escort who were with him. One told Pharaoh, and Pharaoh came down before the cange of Pharaoh. He caused the great personages to be carried to the tomb where Nenoferkephtah was, and he had the upper chamber all sealed as before.

This complete writing, wherein is related the history of Setne Khamwas and Nenoferkephtah, also of Ahuri his wife and Maîhêt his son, has been written by the scribe Ziharpto, the year 5, in the month of Tybi.

Greek and Roman Stories of Haunting

Collected by Lacy Collison-Morley

Tales of spirits are abundant in the wealth of literature that has survived from the cultures of ancient Greece and Rome, as well as numerous ghostly legends handed down orally and recorded generations and centuries later. The following pieces exemplify the deep immersion of the Greek and Roman consciousness in the supernatural.

The Mostellaria

In the *Mostellaria*, Plautus uses a ghost as a recognized piece of supernatural machinery. The regulation father of Roman comedy has gone away on a journey, and in the meantime the son has, as usual, almost reached the end of his father's fortune. The father comes back unexpectedly, and the son turns in despair to his faithful slave, Tranio, for help. Tranio is equal to the occasion, and undertakes to frighten the inconvenient parent away again. He gives an account of an apparition that has been seen, and has announced that it is the ghost of a stranger from overseas, who has been dead for six years.

"Here must I dwell," it had declared, "for the gods of the lower world will not receive me, seeing that I died before my time. My host murdered me, his guest, villain that he was, for the gold that I carried, and secretly buried me, without funeral rites, in this house. Be gone hence, therefore, for it is accursed and unholy ground." This story is enough for the father. He takes the advice, and does not return till Tranio and his dutiful son are quite ready for him.

Spirits on the Battlefield

Great battlefields are everywhere believed to be haunted. Tacitus relates how, when Titus was besieging Jerusalem, armies were seen fighting in the sky; and at a much later date, after a great battle against Attila and the Huns, under the walls of Rome, the ghosts of the dead fought for three days and three nights, and the clash of their arms was distinctly heard. Marathon is no exception to the rule. Pausanias says that any night you may hear horses neighing and men fighting there. To go on purpose to see the sight never brought good to any man; but with him who unwittingly lights upon it the spirits are not angry. He adds that the people of Marathon worship the men who fell in the battle as heroes; and who could be more worthy of such honour than they? The battle itself was not without its marvellous side. Epizelus, the Athenian, used to relate how a huge hoplite, whose beard over-shadowed all his shield, stood over against him in the thick of the fight. The apparition passed him by and killed the man next him, but Epizelus came out of the battle blind, and remained so for the rest of his life. Plutarch also relates of a place in Boeotia where a battle had been fought, that there is a stream running by, and that people imagine that they hear panting horses in the roaring waters.

The Ghost of Protesilaus

But the strangest account of the habitual haunting of great battlefields is to be found in Philostratus's *Heroica*, which represents the spirits of the Homeric heroes as still closely connected with Troy and its neighbourhood. How far the stories are based on local tradition it is impossible to say; they are told by a vine-dresser, who declares that he lives under the protection of Protesilaus. At one time he was in danger of being violently ousted from all his property, when the ghost of Protesilaus appeared to the would-be despoiler in a vision, and struck him blind. The great man was so terrified at this event that he carried his depredations no further; and the vine-dresser has since continued to cultivate what remained of his property under the protection of the hero, with whom he lives on most intimate terms. Protesilaus often appears to him while he is at work and has long talks with him, and he keeps off wild beasts and disease from the land.

Not only Protesilaus, but also his men, and, in fact, virtually all of the "giants of the mighty bone and bold emprise" who fought round Troy, can be seen on the plain at night, clad like warriors, with nodding plumes. The inhabitants are keenly interested in these apparitions, and well they may be, as so much depends upon them. If the heroes are covered with dust, a drought is impending; if with sweat, they foreshadow rain. Blood upon their arms means a plague; but if they show themselves without any distinguishing mark, all will be well.

Sightings of Ajax

Though the heroes are dead, they cannot be insulted with impunity. Ajax was popularly believed, owing to the form taken by his madness, to be especially responsible for any misfortune that might befall flocks and herds. On one occasion some shepherds, who had had bad luck with their cattle, surrounded his tomb and abused him, bringing up all the weak points in his earthly career recorded by Homer. At last they went too far for his patience, and a terrible voice was heard in the tomb and the clash of armour. The offenders fled in terror, but came to no harm.

On another occasion some strangers were playing at draughts near his shrine, when Ajax appeared and begged them to stop, as the game reminded him of Palamedes.

Sightings of Hector

Hector was a far more dangerous person. Maximus of Tyre says that the people of Ilium often see him bounding over the plain at dead of night in flashing armour – a truly Homeric picture. Maximus cannot, indeed, boast of having seen Hector, though he also has had his visions vouchsafed him. He had seen Castor and Pollux, like twin stars, above his ship, steering it through a storm. Aesculapius also he has seen – not in a dream, by Hercules, but with his waking eyes. But to return to Hector. Philostratus says that one day an unfortunate boy insulted him in the same way in which the shepherds had treated Ajax. Homer, however, did not satisfy this boy, and as a parting shaft he declared that the statue in Ilium did not really represent Hector, but Achilles. Nothing happened immediately, but not long afterwards, while the boy was driving a team of ponies, Hector appeared in the form of a warrior in a brook which was, as a rule, so small as not even to have a name. He was heard shouting in a foreign tongue as he pursued the boy in the stream, finally overtaking and drowning him with his ponies. The bodies were never afterwards recovered.

Tales of the White Isle

Then we hear the story of the White Isle. Helen and Achilles fell in love with one another, though they had never met – the one hidden in Egypt, the other fighting before Troy. There was no place near Troy suited for their eternal life together, so Thetis appealed to Poseidon to give them an island home of their own. Poseidon consented, and the White Isle rose up in the Black Sea, near the mouth of the Danube. There Achilles and Helen, the manliest of men and the most feminine of women, first met and first embraced; and Poseidon himself, and Amphitrite, and all the Nereids, and as many river gods and spirits as dwell near the Euxine and Maeotis, came to the wedding. The island is thickly covered with white trees and with elms, which grow in regular order round the shrine; and on it there dwell certain white birds, fragrant of the salt sea, which Achilles is said to have tamed to his will, so that they keep the glades cool, fanning them with their wings and scattering spray as they fly along the ground, scarce rising above it. To men sailing over the broad bosom of the sea the island is holy when they disembark, for it lies like a hospitable home to their ships. But neither those who sail thither, nor the Greeks and barbarians living round the Black Sea, may build a house upon it; and all who anchor and sacrifice there must go on board at sunset. No man may pass the night upon the isle, and no woman may even land there. If the wind is favourable, ships must sail away; if not, they must put out and anchor in the bay and sleep on board. For at night men say that Achilles and Helen drink together, and sing of each other's love, and of the war, and of Homer. Now that his battles are over, Achilles cultivates the gift of song he had received from Calliope. Their voices ring out clear and godlike over the water, and the sailors sit trembling with emotion as they listen. Those who had anchored there declared that they had heard the neighing of horses, and the clash of arms, and shouts such as are raised in battle.

Maximus of Tyre also describes the island, and tells how sailors have often seen a fair-haired youth dancing a war-dance in golden armour upon it; and how once, when one of them unwittingly slept there, Achilles woke him, and took him to his tent and entertained him. Patroclus poured the wine and Achilles played the lyre, while Thetis herself is said to have been present with a choir of other deities.

If they anchor to the north or the south of the island, and a breeze springs up that makes the harbours dangerous, Achilles warns them, and bids them change their anchorage and avoid the wind. Sailors relate how, "when they first behold the island, they embrace each other and burst into tears of joy. Then they put in and kiss the land, and go to the temple to pray and to sacrifice to Achilles." Victims stand ready of their own accord at the altar, according to the size of the ship and the number of those on board.

Pausanias also mentions the White Isle. On one occasion, Leonymus, while leading the people of Croton against the Italian Locrians, attacked the spot where he was informed that Ajax Oïleus, on whom the people of Locris had called for help, was posted in the van. According to Conon, who, by the way, calls the hero Autoleon, when the people of Croton went to war, they also left a vacant space for Ajax in the forefront of their line. However this may be, Leonymus was wounded in the breast, and as the wound refused to heal and weakened him considerably, he applied to Delphi for advice. The god told him to sail to the White Isle, where Ajax would heal him of his wound. Thither, therefore, he went, and was duly healed. On his return he described what he had seen – how that Achilles was now married to Helen; and it was Leonymus who told Stesichorus that his blindness was due to Helen's wrath, and thus induced him to write the *Palinode*.

Achilles himself is once said to have appeared to a trader who frequently visited the island. They talked of Troy, and then the hero gave him wine, and bade him sail away and fetch him a certain Trojan maiden who was the slave of a citizen of Ilium. The trader was surprised at the request, and ventured to ask why he wanted a Trojan slave. Achilles replied that it was because she was of the same race as Hector and his ancestors, and of the blood of the sons of Priam and Dardanus. The trader thought that Achilles was in love with the girl, whom he duly brought with him on his next visit to the island. Achilles thanked him, and bade him keep her on board the ship, doubtless because women were not allowed to land. In the evening he was entertained by Achilles and Helen, and his host gave him a large sum of money, promising to make him his guest-friend and to bring luck to his ship and his business. At daybreak Achilles dismissed him, telling him to leave the girl on the shore. When they had gone about a furlong from the island, a horrible cry from the maiden reached their ears, and they saw Achilles tearing her to pieces, rending her limb from limb.

Greek and Roman Tales of Necromancy
Collected by Lacy Collison-Morley

Saul and the Witch of Endor

The belief that it was possible to call up the souls of the dead by means of spells was almost universal in antiquity. We know that even Saul, who had himself cut off those that had familiar spirits and the wizards out of the land, disguised himself and went with two others to consult the Witch of Endor; that she called up the spirit of Samuel at his request; that Samuel asked Saul, "Why hast thou disquieted me, to bring me up?" and then prophesied his ruin and death at the hands of the Philistines at Mount Gilboa.

Portals to the Underworld

There were always certain spots hallowed by tradition as particularly favourable to intercourse with the dead, or even as being actual entrances to the lower world. For instance, at Heraclea in Pontus there was a famous οςψυχομαντειον [*psychomanteion*], or place where the souls of the dead could be conjured up and consulted, as Hercules was believed to have dragged Cerberus up to earth here.

Other places supposed to be connected with this myth had a similar legend attached to them, as also did all places where Pluto was thought to have carried off Persephone. Thus we hear of entrances to Hades at Eleusis, at Colonus, at Enna in Sicily, and finally at the lovely pool of Cyane, up the Anapus River, near Syracuse, one of the few streams in which the papyrus still flourishes. Lakes and seas also were frequently believed to be entrances to Hades.

The existence of sulphurous fumes easily gave rise to a belief that certain places were in direct communication with the lower world. This was the case at Cumae where Aeneas consulted the Sybil, and at Colonus; while at Hierapolis in Phrygia there was a famous "Plutonium," which could only be safely approached by the priests of Cybele. It was situated under a temple of Apollo, a real entrance to Hades; and it is doubtless to this that Cicero refers when he speaks of the deadly "Plutonia" he had seen in Asia. These "Plutonia" or "Charonia" are, in fact, places where mephitic vapours exist, like the Grotto del Cane and other spots in the neighbourhood of Naples and Pozzuoli. The priests must either have become used to the fumes, or have learnt some means of counteracting them; otherwise their lives can hardly have been more pleasant than that of the unfortunate dog which used to be exhibited in the Naples grotto, though the control of these very realistic entrances to the kingdom of Pluto must have been a very profitable business, well worth a little personal inconvenience. Others are mentioned by Strabo at Magnesia and Myus, and there was one at Cyllene, in Arcadia.

In addition to these there were numerous special temples or places where the souls of the dead, which were universally thought to possess a knowledge of the future, could be called up and consulted – *e.g.*, the temple at Phigalia, in Arcadia, used by Pausanias, the Spartan commander;

or the νεκυομαντέιον [*nekyomanteion*], the oracle of the dead, by the River Acheron, in Threspotia, to which Periander, the famous tyrant of Corinth, had recourse; and it was here, according to Pausanias, that Orpheus went down to the lower world in search of Eurydice.

Recalling to Life

Lucian tells us that it was only with Pluto's permission that the dead could return to life, and they were invariably accompanied by Mercury. Consequently, both these gods were regularly invoked in the prayers and spells used on such occasions. Only the souls of those recently dead were, as a rule, called up, for it was naturally held that they would feel greater interest in the world they had just left, and in the friends and relations still alive, to whom they were really attached. Not that it was impossible to evoke the ghosts of those long dead, if it was desired. Even Orpheus and Cecrops were not beyond reach of call, and Apollonius of Tyana claimed to have raised the shade of Achilles.

Oracles of the Dead

All oracles were originally sacred to Persephone and Pluto, and relied largely on necromancy, a snake being the emblem of prophetic power. Hence, when Apollo, the god of light, claimed possession of the oracles as the conqueror of darkness, the snake was twined round his tripod as an emblem, and his priestess was called Pythia. When Alexander set up his famous oracle, as described by Lucian, the first step taken in establishing its reputation was the finding of a live snake in an egg in a lake. The find had, of course, been previously arranged by Alexander and his confederates.

We still possess accounts of the working of these oracles of the dead, especially of the one connected with the Lake of Avernus, near Naples. Cicero describes how, from this lake, "shades, the spirits of the dead, are summoned in the dense gloom of the mouth of Acheron with salt blood"; and Strabo quotes the early Greek historian Ephorus as relating how, even in his day, "the priests that raise the dead from Avernus live in underground dwellings, communicating with each other by subterranean passages, through which they led those who wished to consult the oracle hidden in the bowels of the earth." "Not far from the lake of Avernus," says Maximus of Tyre, "was an oracular cave, which took its name from the calling up of the dead. Those who came to consult the oracle, after repeating the sacred formula and offering libations and slaying victims, called upon the spirit of the friend or relation they wished to consult. Then it appeared, an unsubstantial shade, difficult both to see and to recognize, yet endowed with a human voice and skilled in prophecy. When it had answered the questions put to it, it vanished." One is at once struck with the similarity of this account to those of the spiritualistic séances of the famous Eusapia in the same part of the world, not so very long ago. In most cases those consulting the oracle would probably be satisfied with hearing the voice of the dead man, or with a vision of him in sleep, so that some knowledge of ventriloquism or power of hypnotism or suggestion would often be ample stock-in-trade for those in charge.

Speaking with Spirits

This consulting of the dead must have been very common in antiquity. Both Plato and Euripides mention it; and the belief that the dead have a knowledge of the future, which seems to be ingrained in human nature, gave these oracles great power. Thus, Cicero tells us that Appius often consulted "soul-oracles" (psychomantia), and also mentions a man having recourse to one when his son was seriously ill. The poets have, of course, made free use of this supposed prophetic power of the dead. The shade of Polydorus, for instance, speaks the prologue of the Hecuba, while the appearance of the dead Creusa in the *Aeneid* is known to everyone. In the *Persae*, Aeschylus makes the shade of Darius ignorant of all that has happened since his death, and is thus able to introduce his famous description of the battle of Salamis; but Darius, nevertheless, possesses a knowledge of the future, and can therefore give us an equally vivid account of the battle of Plataea, which had not yet taken place. The shade of Clytemnestra in the *Eumenides*, however, does not prophesy.

Gabienus's Ghost

Pliny mentions the belief that the dead had prophetic powers, but declares that they could not always be relied on, as the following instance proves. During the Sicilian war, Gabienus, the bravest man in Caesar's fleet, was captured by Sextus Pompeius, and beheaded by his orders. For a whole day the corpse lay upon the shore, the head almost severed from the body. Then, towards evening, a large crowd assembled, attracted by his groans and prayers; and he begged Sextus Pompeius either to come to him himself or to send some of his friends; for he had returned from the dead, and had something to tell him. Pompeius sent friends, and Gabienus informed them that Pompeius's cause found favour with the gods below, and was the right cause, and that he was bidden to announce that all would end as he wished. To prove the truth of what he said, he announced that he would die immediately, as he actually did.

A Prediction from the Undead

Lucan describes how Sextus Pompeius went to consult Erichtho, one of the famous Thessalian witches, as to the prospects of his father's success against Caesar, during the campaign that ended in the disastrous defeat at Pharsalia. It is decided that a dead man must be called back to life, and Erichtho goes out to where a recent skirmish has taken place, and chooses the body of a man whose throat had been cut, which was lying there unburied. She drags it back to her cave, and fills its breast with warm blood. She has chosen a man recently dead, because his words are more likely to be clear and distinct, which might not be the case with one long accustomed to the world below. She then washes it, uses various magic herbs and potions, and prays to the gods of the lower world. At last she sees the shade of the man, whose lifeless body lies stretched before her, standing close by and gazing upon the limbs it had left and the hated bonds of its former prison. Furious at the delay and the slow working of her spells, she seizes a live serpent and lashes the corpse with it. Even the last boon of death, the power of dying, is denied the poor wretch. Slowly the life returns to the body, and Erichtho promises that if the man speaks the truth she will bury him so effectually that no spells will ever be able to call him back to life again. He is weak and faint, like a dying man, but finally tells her all she wishes to know, and dies once again. She fulfills her promise and burns the body, using every kind of magic spell to make it impossible for anyone to trouble the shade again. Indeed, it seems to have been unusual to summon a shade from the lower world more than once, except in the case of very famous persons. This kind of magic was nearly always carried on at night. Statius has also given us a long and characteristically elaborate account of the calling up of the shade of Laius by Eteocles and Tiresias.

An Account of Reanimation

Apuleius, in his truly astounding account of Thessaly in his day, gives a detailed description of the process of calling back a corpse to life. "The prophet then took a certain herb and laid it thrice upon the mouth of the dead man, placing another upon the breast. Then, turning himself to the east with a silent prayer for the help of the holy sun, he drew the attention of the audience to the great miracle he was performing. Gradually the breast of the corpse began to swell in the act of breathing, the arteries to pulsate, and the body to be filled with life. Finally the dead man sat up and asked why he had been brought back to life and not left in peace."

Caracalla's Visions

Caracalla, besides his bodily illnesses, was obviously insane and often troubled with delusions, imagining that he was being driven out by his father and also by his brother Geta, whom he had murdered in his mother's arms, and that they pursued him with drawn swords in their hands. At last, as a desperate resource, he endeavoured to find a cure by means of necromancy, and called up, among others, the shade of his father, Septimius Severus, as well as that of Commodus. But they all refused to speak to him, with the exception of Commodus; and it was even rumoured that the shade of Severus was accompanied by that of the murdered Geta, though it had not been evoked by Caracalla. Nor had Commodus any comfort for him. He only terrified the suffering Emperor the more by his ominous words.

The Return of Achilles

Philostratus has described for us a famous interview which Apollonius of Tyana maintained that he had had with the shade of Achilles. The philosopher related that it was not by digging a trench nor by shedding the blood of rams, like Odysseus, that he raised the ghost of Achilles; but by prayers such as the Indians are said to make to their heroes. In his prayer to Achilles he said that, unlike most men, he did not believe that the great warrior was dead, anymore than his master Pythagoras had done; and he begged him to show himself. Then there was a slight earthquake shock, and a beautiful youth stood before him, nine feet in height, wearing a Thessalian cloak. He did not look like a boaster, as some men had thought him, and his expression, if grim, was not unpleasant. No words could describe his beauty, which surpassed anything imaginable. Meanwhile he had grown to be twenty feet high, and his beauty increased in proportion. His hair he had never cut. Apollonius was allowed to ask him five questions, and accordingly asked for information on five of the most knotty points in the history of the Trojan War – whether Helen was really in Troy, why Homer never mentions Palamedes, etc. Achilles answered him fully and correctly in each instance. Then suddenly the cock crew, and, like Hamlet's father, he vanished from Apollonius's sight.

Greek and Roman Visions of the Dead in Sleep

Collected by Lacy Collison-Morley

Quintilian's Tenth Declamation

The most interesting passage that has come down to us, dealing with the whole question of the power of the dead to appear to those whom they love in dreams, is undoubtedly Quintilian's Tenth Declamation. The fact that the greatest teacher of rhetoric of his day actually chose it as a subject for one of his model speeches shows how important a part it must have played in the feelings of educated Romans of the time. The story is as follows.

A mother was plunged in grief at the loss of her favourite son, when, on the night of the funeral, which had been long delayed at her earnest request, the boy appeared to her in a vision, and remained with her all night, kissing her and fondling her as if he were alive. He did not leave her till daybreak. "All that survives of a son," says Quintilian, "will remain in close communion with his mother when he dies." In her unselfishness, she begs her son not to withhold the comfort which he has brought to her from his father. But the father, when he hears the story, does not at all relish the idea of a visit from his son's ghost, and is, in fact, terrified at the prospect. He says nothing to the mother, who had moved the gods of the world above no less than those of the world below by the violence of her grief and the importunity of her prayers, but at once sends for a sorcerer. As soon as he arrives, the sorcerer is taken to the family tomb, which has its place in the city of the dead that stretches along the highway from the town gate. The magic spell is wound about the grave, and the urn is finally sealed with the dread words, until at last the hapless boy has become, in very truth, a lifeless shade. Finally, we are told, the sorcerer threw himself upon the urn itself and breathed his spells into the very bones and ashes. This at least he admitted, as he looked up: "The spirit resists. Spells are not enough. We must close the grave completely and bind the stones together with iron." His suggestions are carried out, and at last he declares that all has been accomplished successfully. "Now he is really dead. He cannot appear or come out. This night will prove the truth of my words." The boy never afterwards appeared, either to his mother or to anyone else.

The mother is beside herself with grief. Her son's spirit, which had successfully baffled the gods of the lower world in its desire to visit her, is now, thanks to these foreign spells, dashing itself against the top of the grave, unable to understand the weight that has been placed upon it to keep it from escaping. Not only do the spells shut the boy in – he might possibly have broken through these – but the iron bands and solid fastenings have once again brought him face to face with death. This very realistic, if rather material, picture of a human soul mewed up for ever in the grave gives us a clear idea of the popular belief in Rome about the future life, and enables us to realize the full meaning of the inscription, "Sit tibi terra levis" (May the earth press lightly upon thee), which is so common upon Roman tombs as often to be abbreviated to "S.T.T.L."

The speech is supposed to be delivered in an action for cruelty brought by the wife against her husband, and in the course of it the father is spoken of as a parricide for what he has done. He defends himself by saying that he took the steps which are the cause of the action for his wife's peace of mind. To this plea it is answered that the ghost of a son could never frighten a mother, though other spirits, if unknown to her, might conceivably do so.

In the course of the speech we are told that the spirit, when freed from the body, bathes itself in fire and makes for its home among the stars, where other fates await it. Then it remembers the body in which it once dwelt. Hence the dead return to visit those who once were dear to them on earth, and become oracles, and give us timely warnings, and are conscious of the victims we offer them, and welcome the honours paid them at their tombs.

The Declamation ends, like most Roman speeches, with an appeal: in this case to the sorcerer and the husband to remove the spells; especially to the sorcerer, who has power to torture the gods above and the spirits of the dead; who, by the terror of his midnight cries, can move the deepest caves, can shake the very foundations of the earth. "You are able both to call up the spirits that serve you and to act as their cruel and ruthless gaoler. Listen for once to a mother's prayers, and let them soften your heart."

Vengeance from Beyond the Grave

Then we have the story of Thrasyllus, as told by Apuleius, which is thoroughly modern in its romantic tone. He was in love with the wife of his friend, Tlepolemus, whom he treacherously murdered while out hunting. His crime is not discovered, and he begins to press his suit for her hand to her parents almost immediately. The widow's grief is heart-rending. She refuses food and altogether neglects herself, hoping that the gods will hear her prayer and allow her to rejoin her husband. At last, however, she is persuaded by her parents, at Thrasyllus's instance, to give ordinary care to her own health. But she passes her days before the likeness of the deceased, which she has had made in the image of that of the god Liber, paying it divine honours and finding her one comfort in thus fomenting her own sufferings.

When she hears of Thrasyllus's suit, she rejects it with scorn and horror; and then at night her dead husband appears to her and describes exactly what happened, and begs her to avenge him. She requires no urging, and almost immediately decides on the course that her vengeance shall take. She has Thrasyllus informed that she cannot come to any definite decision till her year of mourning is over. Meanwhile, however, she consents to receive his visits at night, and promises to arrange for her old nurse to let him in. Overjoyed at his success, Thrasyllus comes at the hour appointed, and is duly admitted by the old nurse. The house is in complete darkness, but he is given a cup of wine and left to himself. The wine has been drugged, however, and he sinks into a deep slumber. Then Tlepolemus's widow comes and triumphs over her enemy, who has fallen so easily into her hands. She will not kill him as he killed her husband. "Neither the peace of death nor the joy of life shall be yours," she exclaims. "You shall wander like a restless shade between Orcus and the light of day.... The blood of your eyes I shall offer up at the tomb of my beloved Tlepolemus, and with them I shall propitiate his blessed spirit." At these words she takes a pin from her hair and blinds him. Then she rushes through the streets, with a sword in her hand to frighten anyone who might try to stop her, to her husband's tomb, where, after telling all her story, she slays herself.

Thither Thrasyllus followed her, declaring that he dedicated himself to the Manes of his own free will. He carefully shut the tomb upon himself, and starved himself to death.

Cleonice

This is by far the best of the stories in which we find a vision of the dead in sleep playing an important part; but there is also the well-known tale of the Byzantine maiden Cleonice. She was of high birth, but had the misfortune to attract the attention of the Spartan Pausanias, who was in command of the united Greek fleet at the Hellespont after the battle of Plataea. Like many Spartans, when first brought into contact with real luxury after his frugal upbringing at home, he completely lost his mental balance, and grew intoxicated with the splendour of his position, endeavouring to imitate the Persians in their manners, and even aspiring, it is said, to become tyrant of the whole of Greece. Cleonice was brutally torn from her parents and brought to his room at night. He was asleep at the time, and being awakened by the noise, he imagined that someone had broken into his room with the object of murdering him, and snatched up a sword and killed her. After this her ghost appeared to him every night, bidding him "go to the fate which pride and lust prepare." He is said to have visited a temple at Heraclea, where he had her spirit called up and implored her pardon. She duly appeared, and told him that "he would soon be delivered from all his troubles after his return to Sparta" – an ambiguous way of prophesying his death, which occurred soon afterwards. She was certainly avenged in the manner of it.

The Culex

A shepherd falls asleep in the shade by a cool fountain, just as he would do in Southern Italy today, for his rest after the midday meal. Suddenly a snake, the horrors of which are described with a vividness that is truly Virgilian, appears upon the scene and prepares to strike the shepherd. A passing gnat, the hero of the poem, sees the danger, and wakes the shepherd by stinging him in the eye. He springs up angrily, brushes it off with his hand, and dashes it lifeless to the ground. Then, to his horror, he sees the snake, and promptly kills it with the branch of a tree.

While he lies asleep that night, the ghost of the gnat appears to him in a dream, and bitterly reproaches him for the cruel death with which it has been rewarded for its heroic services. Charon has now claimed it for his own. It goes on to give a lurid description of the horrors of Tartarus, and contrasts its hard lot with that of the shepherd. When he wakes, the shepherd is filled with remorse for his conduct and is also, perhaps, afraid of being continually haunted by the ghost of his tiny benefactor. He therefore sets to work to raise a mound in honour of the gnat, facing it with marble. Round it he plants all kinds of flowers, especially violets and roses, the flowers usually offered to the dead, and cuts on a marble slab the following inscription: "Little gnat, the shepherd dedicates to thee thy meed of a tomb in return for the life thou gavest him."

Vision of a Goddess

There is also an interesting story of Pindar, told by Pausanias. In his old age the great poet dreamt that Persephone appeared to him and told him that she alone of all the goddesses had not been celebrated in song by him, but that he should pay the debt when he came to her. Shortly after this he died. There was, however, a relation of his, a woman then far advanced in years, who had practised the singing of most of his hymns. To her Pindar appeared in a dream and sang the hymn to Proserpine, which she wrote down from memory when she awoke.

Greek and Roman Apparitions of the Dead

Collected by Lacy Collison-Morley

Philopseudus

Among the tall stories in Lucian's *Philopseudus* is an amusing account of a man whose wife, whom he loved dearly, appeared to him after she had been dead for twenty days. He had given her a splendid funeral, and had burnt everything she possessed with her. One day, as he was sitting quietly reading *Phaedo*, she suddenly appeared to him, to the terror of his son. As soon as he saw her he embraced her tearfully, a fact which seems to show that she was of a more substantial build than the large majority of ghosts of the ancient world; but she strictly forbade him to make any sound whatever. She then explained that she had come to upbraid the unfortunate man for having neglected to burn one of her golden slippers with her at the funeral. It had fallen behind the chest, she explained, and had been forgotten and not placed upon the pyre with the other. While they were talking, a confounded little Maltese puppy suddenly began to bark from under the bed, when she vanished. But the slipper was found exactly where she had described, and was duly burnt on the following day. The story is refreshingly human.

Afterlife Fashion

Periander, the tyrant of Corinth, on one occasion wished to consult his wife's spirit upon a very important matter; but she replied, as she had doubtless often done when alive, that she would not answer his questions till she had some decent clothes to wear. Periander waited for a great festival, when he knew that all the women of Corinth would be assembled in their best, and then gave orders that they should one and all strip themselves. He burnt the clothes on a huge pyre in his wife's honour; and one can imagine his satisfaction at feeling that he had at last settled the question for ever. He applied to his wife once more with a clear conscience, when she gave him an unmistakable sign that she was speaking the truth, and answered his questions as he desired.

Phantom Emperors

The spirits of the worst of the Roman Emperors were, as we should expect, especially restless. [...]

Nero, in fact, had a romantic charm about him, in spite of, or perhaps because of, the wild recklessness of his life; and he possessed the redeeming feature of artistic taste. Like Francis I of France, or our own Charles II, he was irresistible with the ladies, and must have been the darling of all the housemaids of Rome. People long refused to believe in his death, and for many years it was confidently affirmed that he would appear again. His ghost was long believed to walk in Rome, and the church of Santa Maria del Popolo is said to have been built as late as 1099 by Pope Paschalis II on the site of the tombs of the Domitii, where Nero was buried, near the modern Porta del Popolo, where the Via Flaminia entered the city, in order to lay his restless shade.

Caligula also appeared shortly after his death, and frequently disturbed the keepers of the Lamian Gardens, for his body had been hastily buried there without due ceremony. Not till his sisters, who really loved him, in spite of his many faults, had returned from exile were the funeral rites properly performed, after which his ghost gave no more trouble.

On the night of the day of Galba's murder, the Emperor Otho was heard groaning in his room by his attendants. They rushed in, and found him lying in front of his bed, endeavouring to propitiate Galba's ghost, by whom he declared that he saw himself being driven out and expelled. Otho was a strange mixture of superstition and scepticism, for when he started on his last fatal expedition he treated the unfavourable omens with contempt. By this time, however, he may have become desperate.

Moreover, irreligious people are notoriously superstitious, and at this period it would be very difficult to say just where religion ended and superstition began.

Mythological Ghosts

We have one or two ghost stories connected with early Greek mythology. Cillas, the charioteer of Pelops, though Troezenius gives his name as Sphaerus, died on the way to Pisa, and appeared to Pelops by night, begging that he might be duly buried. Pelops took pity on him and burnt his body with all ceremony, raised a huge mound in his honour, and built a chapel to the Cillean Apollo near it. He also named a town after him. Strabo even says that there was a mound in Cillas's honour at

Crisa in the Troad. This dutiful attention did not go unrewarded. Cillas appeared to Pelops again, and thanked him for all he had done, and to Cillas also he is said to have owed the information by which he was able to overthrow Oenomaus in the famous chariot race which won him the hand of Hippodamia. Pelops's shameless ingratitude to Oenomaus's charioteer, Myrtilus, who had removed the pin of his master's chariot, and thus caused his defeat and death in order to help Pelops, on the promise of the half of the kingdom, is hardly in accordance with his treatment of Cillas, though it is thoroughly Greek. However, on the theory that a man who betrays one master will probably betray another, especially if he is to be rewarded for his treachery with as much as half a kingdom, Pelops was right in considering that Myrtilus was best out of the way; and he can hardly have foreseen the curse that was to fall upon his family in consequence.

With this story we may compare the well-known tale of the poet Simonides, who found an unknown corpse on the shore, and honoured it with burial. Soon afterwards he happened to be on the point of starting on a voyage, when the man whom he had buried appeared to him in a dream, and warned him on no account to go by the ship he had chosen, as it would undoubtedly be wrecked. Impressed by the vision, the poet remained behind, and the ship went down soon afterwards, with all on board. Simonides expressed his gratitude in a poem describing the event, and in several epigrams. Libanius even goes so far as to place the scene of the event at Tarentum, where he was preparing to take ship for Sicily.

Pausanias has a story of one of Ulysses' crew. Ulysses' ship was driven about by the winds from one city to another in Sicily and Italy, and in the course of these wanderings it touched at Tecmessa. Here one of the sailors got drunk and ravished a maiden, and was stoned to death in consequence by the indignant people of the town. Ulysses did not trouble about what had occurred, and sailed away. Soon, however, the ghost of the murdered man became a source of serious annoyance to the people of the place, killing the inhabitants of the town, regardless of age and sex. Finally, matters came to such a pass that the town was abandoned. But the Pythian priestess bade the people return to Tecmessa and appease the hero by building him a temple and precinct of his own, and giving him every year the fairest maiden of the town to wife. They took this advice, and there was no more trouble from the ghost. It chanced, however, that Euthymus came to Tecmessa just when the people were paying the dead sailor the annual honours. Learning how matters stood, he asked to be allowed to go into the temple and see the maiden. At their meeting he was first touched with pity, and then immediately fell desperately in love with her. The girl swore to be his, if he would save her. Euthymus put on his armour and awaited the attack of the monster. He had the best of the fight, and the ghost, driven from its home, plunged into the sea. The wedding was, of course, celebrated with great splendour, and nothing more was heard of the spirit of the drunken sailor. The story is obviously to be classed with that of Ariadne.

Murder at an Inn

The god-fearing Aelian seeks to show that Providence watches over a good man and brings his murderers to justice by a story taken from Chrysippus. A traveller put up at an inn in Megara, wearing a belt full of gold. The innkeeper discovered that he had the money about him, and murdered him at night, having arranged to carry his body outside the gates in a dung-cart. But meanwhile the murdered man appeared to a citizen of the town and told him what had happened. The man was impressed by the vision. Investigations were made, and the murderer was caught exactly where the ghost had indicated, and was duly punished.

Aristeas

Aristeas of Proconesus, a man of high birth, died quite suddenly in a fulling establishment in his native town. The owner locked the building and went to inform his relatives, when a man from Cyzicus, hearing the news, denied it, saying that Aristeas had met him on the way thither and talked to him; and when the relatives came, prepared to remove the body, they found no Aristeas, either alive or dead. Altogether, he seems to have been a remarkable person. He disappeared for seven years, and then appeared in Proconesus and wrote an epic poem called *Arimispea*, which was well known in Herodotus's day. Two hundred and forty years later he was seen again, this time at Metapontum, and bade the citizens build a shrine to Apollo, and near it erect a statue to himself, as Apollo would come to them alone of the Italian Greeks, and he would be seen following in the form of a raven. The townsmen were troubled at the apparition, and consulted the Delphic oracle, which confirmed all that Aristeas had said; and Apollo received his temple and Aristeas his statue in the marketplace.

Apollonius tells virtually the same story, except that in his version Aristeas was seen giving a lesson in literature by a number of persons in Sicily at the very hour he died in Proconesus. He says that Aristeas appeared at intervals for a number of years after his death. The elder Pliny also speaks of Aristeas, saying that at Proconesus his soul was seen to leave his body in the form of a raven, though he regards the tale as in all probability a fabrication.

The Undead Patient

The doctor in Lucian's *Philopseudus* (*c.* 26) declares that he knew a man who rose from the dead twenty days after he was buried, and that he attended him after his resurrection. But when asked how it was the body did not decompose or the man die of hunger, he has no answer to give.

Digging a Canal

Dio Cassius describes how, when Nero wished to cut a canal through the Isthmus of Corinth, blood spurted up in front of those who first touched the earth, groans and cries were heard, and a number of ghosts appeared. Not till Nero took a pickaxe and began to work himself, to encourage the men, was any real progress made.

Astral Projection

Pliny quotes an interesting account, from Hermotimus of Clazomenae, of a man whose soul was in the habit of leaving his body and wandering abroad, as was proved by the fact that he would often describe events which had happened at a distance, and could only be known to an actual eyewitness. His body meanwhile lay like that of a man in a trance or half dead. One day, however, some enemies of his took the body while in this state and burnt it, thus, to use Pliny's phrase, leaving the soul no sheath to which it could return.

An Incident in Aetolia

Phlegon of Tralles was a freedman of the Emperor Hadrian. His work is not of great merit. The following is a favourable specimen of his stories. A monstrous child was born in Aetolia, after the death of its father, Polycrates. At a public meeting, where it was proposed to do away with it, the father suddenly appeared, and begged that the child might be given him. An attempt was made to seize the father, but he snatched up the child, tore it to pieces, and devoured all but the head. When it was proposed to consult the Delphic oracle on the matter, the head prophesied to the crowd from where it lay on the ground.

Greek and Roman Warning Apparitions

Collected by Lacy Collison-Morley

Tales of Towering Women

As we should expect, there are a number of instances of warning apparitions in antiquity; and it is interesting to note that the majority of these are gigantic women endowed with a gift of prophecy.

Thus the younger Pliny tells us how Quintus Curtius Rufus, who was on the staff of the Governor of Africa, was walking one day in a colonnade after sunset, when a gigantic woman appeared before him. She announced that she was Africa, and was able to predict the future, and told him that he would go to Rome, hold office there, return to the province with the highest authority, and there die. Her prophecy was fulfilled to the letter, and as he landed in Africa for the last time the same figure is reported to have met him.

So, again, at the time of the conspiracy of Callippus, Dion was meditating one evening before the porch of his house, when he turned round and saw a gigantic female figure, in the form of a Fury, at the end of the corridor, sweeping the floor with a broom. The vision terrified him, and soon afterwards his only son committed suicide and he himself was murdered by the conspirators.

A similar dramatic story is related of Drusus during his German campaigns. While engaged in operations against the Alemanni, he was preparing to cross the Elbe, when a gigantic woman barred the way, exclaiming, "Insatiate Drusus, whither wilt thou go? Thou art not fated to see all things. Depart hence, for the end of thy life and of thy deeds is at hand." Drusus was much troubled by this warning, and instantly obeyed the words of the apparition; but he died before reaching the Rhine.

We meet with the same phenomenon again in Dio Cassius, among the prodigies preceding the death of Macrinus, when "a dreadful gigantic woman, seen of several, declared that all that had happened was as nothing compared with what they were soon to endure" – a prophecy which was amply fulfilled by the reign of Heliogabalus.

But the most gigantic of all these gigantic women was, as we should only expect from his marvellous power of seeing ghosts, the one who appeared to Eucrates in the *Philopseudus*. Eucrates has seen over a thousand ghosts in his time, and is now quite used to them, though at first he found them rather upsetting; but he had been given a ring and a charm by an Arab, which enabled him to deal with anything supernatural that came in his way. The ring was made from the iron of a cross on which a criminal had been executed, and doubtless had the same value in Eucrates' eyes that a piece of the rope with which a man has been hung possesses in the eyes of a gambler today. On this particular occasion he had left his men at work in the vineyard, and was resting quietly at midday, when his dog began to bark. At first he thought it was only a favourite boy of his indulging in a little hunting with some friends; but on looking up he saw in front of him a woman at least three hundred feet high, with a sword thirty feet long.

Her lower extremities were like those of a dragon, and snakes were coiling round her neck and shoulders. Eucrates was not in the least alarmed, but turned the seal of his ring, when a vast chasm opened in the earth, into which she disappeared. This seems rather to have astonished Eucrates; but he plucked up courage, caught hold of a tree that stood near the edge, and looked over, when he saw all the lower world lying spread before him, including the mead of asphodel, where the shades of the blessed were reclining at ease with their friends and relations, arranged according to clans and tribes. Among these he recognized his own father, dressed in the clothes in which he was buried; and it must have been comforting to the son to have such good evidence that his parent was safely installed in the Elysian Fields. In a few moments the chasm closed.

Trajan's Hero

Dio Cassius relates how Trajan was saved in the great earthquake that destroyed nearly the whole of Antioch by a phantom, which appeared to him suddenly, and warned him to leave his house by the window. A similar story is told of the poet Simonides, who was warned by a spectre that his house was going to fall, and thus enabled to make his escape in time.

The Phantom Hairdresser

Pliny the Younger tells us how a slave of his, named Marcus, imagined that he saw someone cutting his hair during the night. When he awoke, the vision proved to have been a true one, for his hair lay all round him. Soon afterwards the same thing happened again. His brother, who slept with him, saw nothing; but Marcus declared that two people came in by the windows, dressed in white, and, after cutting his hair, disappeared. "Nothing astonishing happened," adds Pliny, "except that I was not prosecuted, as I undoubtedly should have been, had Domitian lived; for this happened during his principate. Perhaps the cutting of my slave's hair was a sign of my approaching doom, for accused people cut their hair," as a sign of mourning. One may be allowed to wonder whether, after all, a fondness for practical joking is not even older than the age of the younger Pliny.

The Statue

In this case we are told of a little statue of Aesculapius, which stood in the house of the narrator of the story, and at the feet of which a number of pence had been placed as offerings, while other coins, some of them silver, were fastened to the thighs with wax. There were also silver plates which had been vowed or offered by those who had been cured of fever by the god. The offerings and tablets are just such as might be found in a Catholic church in the south of Europe today; but the coins, in our more practical modern world, would have found their way into the coffers of the church. One would like to know what was the ultimate destination of these particular coins – whether they were to be sent as contributions to one of the temples of Aesculapius, which were the centre of the medical world at this period, and had elaborate hospitals attached to them, about which we learn so much from Aristides.

In this case they were merely a source of temptation to an unfortunate Libyan groom, who stole them one night, intending to make his escape. But he had not studied the habits of the statue, which, we are told, habitually got down from its pedestal every night; and in this case such was the power of the god that he kept the man wandering about all night, unable to leave the court, where he was found with the money in the morning, and soundly flogged. The god, however, considered that he had been let off much too easily; and he was mysteriously flogged every night, as the weals upon him showed, till he ultimately died of the punishment.

The Nine Maidens

Aelian has a charming story of Philemon, the comic poet. He was still, apparently, in the full vigour of his powers when he had a vision of nine maidens leaving his house in the Piraeus and bidding him farewell. When he awoke, he told his slave the story, and set to work to finish a play with which he was then busy. After completing it to his satisfaction, he wrapped himself in his cloak and lay down upon his bed. His slave came in, and, thinking he was asleep, went to wake him, when he found that he was dead. Aelian challenges the unbelieving Epicureans to deny that the nine maidens were the nine Muses, leaving a house which was so soon to be polluted by death.

A Supernatural Crossing

But there is a story connected with the crossing of the Rubicon by Caesar that certainly deserves to be better known than it is. It is only fitting that an event fraught with such momentous consequences should have a supernatural setting of some kind;

and Suetonius relates that while Caesar was still hesitating whether he should declare himself an enemy of his country by crossing the little river that bounded his province at the head of an army, a man of heroic size and beauty suddenly appeared, playing upon a reed-pipe. Some of the troops, several trumpeters among them, ran up to listen, when the man seized a trumpet, blew a loud blast upon it, and began to cross the Rubicon. Caesar at once decided to advance, and the men followed him with redoubled enthusiasm after what they had just seen.

Philinnion and Machates

Phlegon of Tralles,
collected by Lacy Collison-Morley

Philinnion was the daughter of Demostratus and Charito. She had been married to Craterus, Alexander's famous General, but had died six months after her marriage. As we learn that she was desperately in love with Machates, a foreign friend from Pella who had come to see Demostratus, the misery of her position may possibly have caused her death. But her love conquered death itself, and she returned to life again six months after she had died, and lived with Machates, visiting him for several nights. "One day an old nurse went to the guest-chamber, and as the lamp was burning, she saw a woman sitting by Machates. Scarcely able to contain herself at this extraordinary occurrence, she ran to the girl's mother, calling: 'Charito! Demostratus!' and bade them get up and go with her to their daughter, for by the grace of the gods she had appeared alive, and was with the stranger in the guest-chamber.

"On hearing this extraordinary story, Charito was at first overcome by it and by the nurse's excitement; but she soon recovered herself, and burst into tears at the mention of her daughter, telling the old woman she was out of her senses, and ordering her out of the room.

The nurse was indignant at this treatment, and boldly declared that she was not out of her senses, but that Charito was unwilling to see her daughter because she was afraid. At last Charito consented to go to the door of the guest-chamber, but as it was now quite two hours since she had heard the news, she arrived too late, and found them both asleep. The mother bent over the woman's figure, and thought she recognized her daughter's features and clothes. Not feeling sure, as it was dark, she decided to keep quiet for the present, meaning to get up early and catch the woman. If she failed, she would ask Machates for a full explanation, as he would never tell her a lie in a case so important. So she left the room without saying anything.

"But early on the following morning, either because the gods so willed it or because she was moved by some divine impulse, the woman went away without being observed. When she came to him, Charito was angry with the young man in consequence, and clung to his knees, and conjured him to speak the truth and hide nothing from her. At first he was greatly distressed, and could hardly be brought to admit that the girl's name was Philinnion. Then he described her first coming and the violence of her passion, and told how she had said that she was there without her parents' knowledge. The better to establish the truth of his story, he opened a coffer and took out the things she had left behind her – a ring of gold which she had given him, and a belt which she had left on the previous night. When Charito beheld all these convincing proofs, she uttered a piercing cry, and rent her clothes and her cloak, and tore her coif from her head, and began to mourn for her daughter afresh in the midst of her friends. Machates was deeply distressed on seeing what had happened, and how they were all mourning, as if for her second funeral. He begged them to be comforted, and promised them that they should see her if she appeared. Charito yielded, but bade him be careful how he fulfilled his promise.

"When night fell and the hour drew near at which Philinnion usually appeared, they were on the watch for her. She came, as was her custom, and sat down upon the bed. Machates made no pretence, for he was genuinely anxious to sift the matter to the bottom, and secretly sent some slaves to call her parents. He himself could hardly believe that the woman who came to him so regularly at the same hour was really dead, and when she ate and drank with him, he began to suspect what had been suggested to him – namely, that some grave robbers had violated the tomb and sold the clothes and the gold ornaments to her father.

"Demostratus and Charito hastened to come at once, and when they saw her, they were at first speechless with amazement. Then, with cries of joy, they threw themselves upon their daughter. But Philinnion remained cold. 'Father and mother,' she said, 'cruel indeed have ye been in that ye grudged my living with the stranger for three days in my father's house, for it brought harm to no one. But ye shall pay for your meddling with sorrow. I must return to the place appointed for me, though I came not hither without the will of Heaven.' With these words she fell down dead, and her body lay stretched upon the bed. Her parents threw themselves upon her, and the house was filled with confusion and sorrow, for the blow was heavy indeed; but the event was strange, and soon became known throughout the town, and finally reached my ears.

"During the night I kept back the crowds that gathered round the house, taking care that there should be no disturbance as the news spread. At early dawn the theatre was full. After a long discussion it was decided that we should go and open the tomb, to see whether the body was still on the bier, or whether we should find the place empty, for the woman had hardly been dead six months. When we opened the vault where all her family was buried, the bodies were seen lying on the other biers; but on the one where Philinnion had been placed, we found only the iron ring which had belonged to her lover and the gilt drinking-cup Machates had given her on the first day. In utter amazement, we went straight to Demostratus's house to see whether the body was still there. We beheld it lying on the ground, and then went in a large crowd to the place of assembly, for the whole event was of great importance and absolutely past belief. Great was the confusion, and no one could tell what to do, when Hyllus, who is not only considered the best diviner among us, but is also a great authority on the interpretation of the flight of birds, and is generally well versed in his art, got up and said that the woman must be buried outside the boundaries of the city, for it was unlawful that she should be laid to rest within them; and that Hermes Chthonius and the Eumenides should be propitiated, and that all pollution would thus be removed. He ordered the temples to be re-consecrated and the usual rites to be performed in honour of the gods below. As for the King, in this affair, he privately told me to sacrifice to Hermes, and to Zeus Xenius, and to Ares, and to perform these duties with the utmost care. We have done as he suggested.

"The stranger Machates, who was visited by the ghost, has committed suicide in despair.

"Now, if you think it right that I should give the King an account of all this, let me know, and I will send some of those who gave me the various details."

The Visit to the Dead
Homer

In this passage from Homer's *The Odyssey*, Ulysses (the Roman name for Odysseus) recounts to the Phaeacians the tale of his journey to the Underworld, which he undertook in order to speak with the ghost of the prophet Teiresias regarding his journey homeward after the Trojan War.

"Then, when we had got down to the seashore, we drew our ship into the water and got her mast and sails into her; we also put the sheep on board and took our places, weeping and in great distress of mind. Circe, that great and cunning goddess, sent us a fair wind that blew dead aft and staid steadily with us keeping our sails all the time well filled; so we did whatever wanted doing to the ship's gear and let her go as the wind and helmsman headed her. All day long her sails were full as she held her course over the sea, but when the sun went down and darkness was over all the earth, we got into the deep waters of the river Oceanus, where lie the land and city of the Cimmerians who live enshrouded in mist and darkness which the rays of the sun never pierce neither at his rising nor as he goes down again out of the heavens, but the poor wretches live in one long melancholy night. When we got there we beached the ship, took the sheep out of her, and went along by the waters of Oceanus till we came to the place of which Circe had told us.

"Here Perimedes and Eurylochus held the victims, while I drew my sword and dug the trench a cubit each way. I made a drink-offering to all the dead, first with honey and milk, then with wine, and thirdly with water, and I sprinkled white barley meal over the whole, praying earnestly to the poor feckless ghosts, and promising them that when I got back to Ithaca I would sacrifice a barren heifer for them, the best I had, and would load the pyre with good things. I also particularly promised that Teiresias should have a black sheep to himself, the best in all my flocks. When I had prayed sufficiently to the dead, I cut the throats of the two sheep and let the blood run into the trench, whereon the ghosts came trooping up from Erebus – brides, young bachelors, old men worn out with toil, maids who had been crossed in love, and brave men who had been killed in battle, with their armour still smirched with blood; they came from every quarter and flitted round the trench with a strange kind of screaming sound that made me turn pale with fear. When I saw them coming I told the men to be quick and flay the carcasses of the two dead sheep and make burnt offerings of them, and at the same time to repeat prayers to Hades and to Proserpine; but I sat where I was with my sword drawn and would not let the poor feckless ghosts come near the blood till Teiresias should have answered my questions.

"The first ghost that came was that of my comrade Elpenor, for he had not yet been laid beneath the earth. We had left his body unwaked and unburied in Circe's house, for we had had too much else to do. I was very sorry for him, and cried when I saw him:

'Elpenor,' said I, 'how did you come down here into this gloom and darkness? You have got here on foot quicker than I have with my ship.'

"'Sir,' he answered with a groan, 'it was all bad luck, and my own unspeakable drunkenness. I was lying asleep on the top of Circe's house, and never thought of coming down again by the great staircase but fell right off the roof and broke my neck, so my soul came down to the house of Hades. And now I beseech you by all those whom you have left behind you, though they are not here, by your wife, by the father who brought you up when you were a child, and by Telemachus who is the one hope of your house, do what I shall now ask you. I know that when you leave this limbo you will again hold your ship for the Aeaean island. Do not go thence leaving me unwaked and unburied behind you, or I may bring heaven's anger upon you; but burn me with whatever armour I have, build a barrow for me on the seashore, that may tell people in days to come what a poor unlucky fellow I was, and plant over my grave the oar I used to row with when I was yet alive and with my messmates.' And I said, 'My poor fellow, I will do all that you have asked of me.'

"Thus, then, did we sit and hold sad talk with one another, I on the one side of the trench with my sword held over the blood, and the ghost of my comrade saying all this to me from the other side. Then came the ghost of my dead mother Anticlea, daughter to Autolycus. I had left her alive when I set out for Troy and was moved to tears when I saw her, but even so, for all my sorrow I would not let her come near the blood till I had asked my questions of Teiresias.

"Then came also the ghost of Theban Teiresias, with his golden sceptre in his hand. He knew me and said, 'Ulysses, noble son of Laertes, why, poor man, have you left the light of day and come down to visit the dead in this sad place? Stand back from the trench and withdraw your sword that I may drink of the blood and answer your questions truly.'

"So I drew back, and sheathed my sword, whereon when he had drank of the blood he began with his prophecy.

"'You want to know,' said he, 'about your return home, but heaven will make this hard for you. I do not think that you will escape the eye of Neptune, who still nurses his bitter grudge against you for having blinded his son. Still, after much suffering you may get home if you can restrain yourself and your companions when your ship reaches the Thrinacian island, where you will find the sheep and cattle belonging to the sun, who sees and gives ear to everything. If you leave these flocks unharmed and think of nothing but of getting home, you may yet after much hardship reach Ithaca; but if you harm them, then I forewarn you of the destruction both of your ship and of your men. Even though you may yourself escape, you will return in bad plight, after losing all your men, in another man's ship, and you will find trouble in your house, which will be overrun by high-handed people, who are devouring your substance under the pretext of paying court and making presents to your wife.

"'When you get home you will take your revenge on these suitors; and after you have killed them by force or fraud in your own house, you must take a well-made oar and carry it on and on, till you come to a country where the people have never heard of the sea and do not even mix salt with their food, nor do they know anything about ships, and oars that are as the wings of a ship. I will give you this certain token which cannot escape your notice. A wayfarer will meet you and will say it must be a winnowing shovel that you have got upon your shoulder; on this you must fix the oar in the ground and sacrifice a ram, a bull, and a boar to Neptune. Then go home and offer hecatombs to all the gods in heaven one after the other. As for yourself, death shall come to you from the sea, and your life shall ebb away very gently when you are full of years and peace of mind, and your people shall bless you. All that I have said will come true.'

"'This,' I answered, 'must be as it may please heaven, but tell me and tell me and tell me true, I see my poor mother's ghost close by us; she is sitting by the blood without saying a word, and though I am her own son she does not remember me and speak to me; tell me, Sir, how I can make her know me.'

"'That,' said he, 'I can soon do. Any ghost that you let taste of the blood will talk with you like a reasonable being, but if you do not let them have any blood they will go away again.'

"On this the ghost of Teiresias went back to the house of Hades, for his prophesyings had now been spoken, but I sat still where I was until my mother came up and tasted the blood. Then she knew me at once and spoke fondly to me, saying, 'My son, how did you come down to this abode of darkness while you are still alive? It is a hard thing for the living to see these places, for between us and them there are great and terrible waters, and there is Oceanus, which no man can cross on foot, but he must have a good ship to take him. Are you all this time trying to find your way home from Troy, and have you never yet got back to Ithaca nor seen your wife in your own house?'

"'Mother,' said I, 'I was forced to come here to consult the ghost of the Theban prophet Teiresias. I have never yet been near the Achaean land nor set foot on my native country, and I have had nothing but one long series of misfortunes from the very first day that I set out with Agamemnon for Ilius, the land of noble steeds, to fight the Trojans. But tell me, and tell me true, in what way did you die? Did you have a long illness, or did heaven vouchsafe you a gentle easy passage to eternity? Tell me also about my father, and the son whom I left behind me; is my property still in their hands, or has someone else got hold of it, who thinks that I shall not return to claim it? Tell me again what my wife intends doing, and in what mind she is; does she live with my son and guard my estate securely, or has she made the best match she could and married again?'

"My mother answered, 'Your wife still remains in your house, but she is in great distress of mind and spends her whole time in tears both night and day. No one as yet has got possession of your fine property, and Telemachus still holds your lands undisturbed. He has to entertain largely, as of course he must, considering his position as a magistrate, and how everyone invites him; your father remains at his old place in the country and never goes near the town. He has no comfortable bed nor bedding; in the winter he sleeps on the floor in front of the fire with the men and goes about all in rags, but in summer, when the warm weather comes on again, he lies out in the vineyard on a bed of vine leaves thrown any how upon the ground. He grieves continually about your never having come home, and suffers more and more as he grows older. As for my own end it was in this wise: heaven did not take me swiftly and painlessly in my own house, nor was I attacked by any illness such as those that generally wear people out and kill them, but my longing to know what you were doing and the force of my affection for you – this it was that was the death of me.'

"Then I tried to find some way of embracing my poor mother's ghost. Thrice I sprang towards her and tried to clasp her in my arms, but each time she flitted from my embrace as it were a dream or phantom, and being touched to the quick I said to her, 'Mother, why do you not stay still when I would embrace you? If we could throw our arms around one another we might find sad comfort in the sharing of our sorrows even in the house of Hades; does Proserpine want to lay a still further load of grief upon me by mocking me with a phantom only?'

"'My son,' she answered, 'most ill-fated of all mankind, it is not Proserpine that is beguiling you, but all people are like this when they are dead. The sinews no longer hold the flesh and bones together; these perish in the fierceness of consuming fire as soon as life has left the body, and the soul flits away as though it were a dream. Now, however, go back to the light of day as soon as you can, and note all these things that you may tell them to your wife hereafter.'

"Thus did we converse, and anon Proserpine sent up the ghosts of the wives and daughters of all the most famous men. They gathered in crowds about the blood, and I considered how I might question them severally. In the end I deemed that it would be best to draw the keen blade that hung by my sturdy thigh, and keep them from all drinking the blood at once. So they came up one after the other, and each one as I questioned her told me her race and lineage.

"The first I saw was Tyro. She was daughter of Salmoneus and wife of Cretheus the son of Aeolus. She fell in love with the river Enipeus, who is much the most beautiful river in the whole world. Once when she was taking a walk by his side as usual, Neptune, disguised as her lover, lay with her at the mouth of the river, and a huge blue wave arched itself like a mountain over them to hide both woman and god, whereon he loosed her virgin girdle and laid her in a deep slumber. When the god had accomplished the deed of love, he took her hand in his own and said, 'Tyro, rejoice in all good will; the embraces of the gods are not fruitless, and you will have fine twins about this time twelve months. Take great care of them. I am Neptune, so now go home, but hold your tongue and do not tell anyone.'

"Then he dived under the sea, and she in due course bore Pelias and Neleus, who both of them served Jove with all their might. Pelias was a great breeder of sheep and lived in Iolcus, but the other lived in Pylos. The rest of her children were by Cretheus, namely, Aeson, Pheres, and Amythaon, who was a mighty warrior and charioteer.

"Next to her I saw Antiope, daughter to Asopus, who could boast of having slept in the arms of even Jove himself, and who bore him two sons Amphion and Zethus. These founded Thebes with its seven gates, and built a wall all round it; for strong though they were, they could not hold Thebes till they had walled it.

"Then I saw Alcmena, the wife of Amphitryon, who also bore to Jove indomitable Hercules; and Megara who was daughter to great King Creon, and married the redoubtable son of Amphitryon.

"I also saw fair Epicaste mother of King Oedipodes whose awful lot it was to marry her own son without suspecting it. He married her after having killed his father, but the gods proclaimed the whole story to the world; whereon he remained king of Thebes, in great grief for the spite the gods had borne him; but Epicaste went to the house of the mighty jailor Hades, having hanged herself for grief, and the avenging spirits haunted him as for an outraged mother – to his ruing bitterly thereafter.

"Then I saw Chloris, whom Neleus married for her beauty, having given priceless presents for her. She was youngest daughter to Amphion son of Iasus and king of Minyan Orchomenus, and was Queen in Pylos. She bore Nestor, Chromius, and Periclymenus, and she also bore that marvellously lovely woman Pero, who was wooed by all the country round; but Neleus would only give her to him who should raid the cattle of Iphicles from the grazing grounds of Phylace, and this was a hard task. The only man who would undertake to raid them was a certain excellent seer, but the will of heaven was against him, for the rangers of the cattle caught him and put him in prison; nevertheless, when a full year had passed and the same season came round again, Iphicles set him at liberty, after he had expounded all the oracles of heaven. Thus, then, was the will of Jove accomplished.

"And I saw Leda the wife of Tyndarus, who bore him two famous sons, Castor breaker of horses, and Pollux the mighty boxer. Both these heroes are lying under the earth, though they are still alive, for by a special dispensation of Jove, they die and come to life again, each one of them every other day throughout all time, and they have the rank of gods.

"After her I saw Iphimedeia wife of Aloeus who boasted the embrace of Neptune. She bore two sons Otus and Ephialtes, but both were short lived. They were the finest children that were ever born in this world, and the best looking, Orion only excepted; for at nine years old they were nine fathoms high, and measured nine cubits round the chest. They threatened to make war with the gods in Olympus, and tried to set Mount Ossa on the top of Mount Olympus, and Mount Pelion on the top of Ossa, that they might scale heaven itself, and they would have done it too if they had been grown up, but Apollo, son of Leto, killed both of them, before they had got so much as a sign of hair upon their cheeks or chin.

"Then I saw Phaedra, and Procris, and fair Ariadne daughter of the magician Minos, whom Theseus was carrying off from Crete to Athens, but he did not enjoy her, for before he could do so Diana killed her in the island of Dia on account of what Bacchus had said against her.

"I also saw Maera and Clymene and hateful Eriphyle, who sold her own husband for gold. But it would take me all night if I were to name every single one of the wives and daughters of heroes whom I saw, and it is time for me to go to bed, either on board ship with my crew, or here. As for my escort, heaven and yourselves will see to it."

Here he ended, and the guests sat all of them enthralled and speechless throughout the covered cloister. Then Arete said to them:

"What do you think of this man, O Phaeacians? Is he not tall and good-looking, and is he not clever? True, he is my own guest, but all of you share in the distinction. Do not be in a hurry to send him away, nor niggardly in the presents you make to one who is in such great need, for heaven has blessed all of you with great abundance."

Then spoke the aged hero Echeneus, who was one of the oldest men among them. "My friends," said he, "what our august queen has just said to us is both reasonable and to the purpose, therefore be persuaded by it; but the decision whether in word or deed rests ultimately with King Alcinous."

"The thing shall be done," exclaimed Alcinous, "as surely as I still live and reign over the Phaeacians. Our guest is indeed very anxious to get home, still we must persuade him to remain with us until tomorrow, by which time I shall be able to get together the whole sum that I mean to give him. As regards his escort it will be a matter for you all, and mine above all others as the chief person among you."

And Ulysses answered, "King Alcinous, if you were to bid me to stay here for a whole twelve months, and then speed me on my way, loaded with your noble gifts, I should obey you gladly and it would redound greatly to my advantage, for I should return fuller-handed to my own people, and should thus be more respected and beloved by all who see me when I get back to Ithaca."

"Ulysses," replied Alcinous, "not one of us who sees you has any idea that you are a charlatan or a swindler. I know there are many people going about who tell such plausible stories that it is very hard to see through them, but there is a style about your language which assures me of your good disposition. Moreover, you have told the story of your own misfortunes, and those of the Argives, as though you were a practiced bard; but tell me, and tell me true, whether you saw any of the mighty heroes who went to Troy at the same time with yourself, and perished there. The evenings are still at their longest, and it is not yet bedtime – go on, therefore, with your divine story, for I could stay here listening till tomorrow morning, so long as you will continue to tell us of your adventures."

"Alcinous," answered Ulysses, "there is a time for making speeches, and a time for going to bed; nevertheless, since you so desire, I will not refrain from telling you the still sadder tale of those of my comrades who did not fall fighting with the Trojans, but perished on their return, through the treachery of a wicked woman.

"When Proserpine had dismissed the female ghosts in all directions, the ghost of Agamemnon son of Atreus came sadly up to me, surrounded by those who had perished with him in the house of Aegisthus. As soon as he had tasted the blood, he knew me, and weeping bitterly stretched out his arms towards me to embrace me; but he had no strength nor substance anymore, and I too wept and pitied him as I beheld him. 'How did you come by your death,' said I, 'King Agamemnon? Did Neptune raise his winds and waves against you when you were at sea, or did your enemies make an end of you on the mainland when you were cattle-lifting or sheep-stealing, or while they were fighting in defence of their wives and city?'

"'Ulysses,' he answered, 'noble son of Laertes, I was not lost at sea in any storm of Neptune's raising, nor did my foes despatch me upon the mainland, but Aegisthus and my wicked wife were the death of me between them. He asked me to his house, feasted me, and then butchered me most miserably as though I were a fat beast in a slaughterhouse, while all around me my comrades were slain like sheep or pigs for the wedding breakfast, or picnic, or gorgeous banquet of some great nobleman. You must have seen numbers of men killed either in a general engagement, or in single combat, but you never saw anything so truly pitiable as the way in which we fell in that cloister, with the mixing bowl and the loaded tables lying all about, and the ground reeking with our blood. I heard Priam's daughter Cassandra scream as Clytemnestra killed her close beside me. I lay dying upon the earth with the sword in my body, and raised my hands to kill the slut of a murderess, but she slipped away from me; she would not even close my lips nor my eyes when I was dying, for there is nothing in this world so cruel and so shameless as a woman when she has fallen into such guilt as hers was. Fancy murdering her own husband! I thought I was going to be welcomed home by my children and my servants, but her abominable crime has brought disgrace on herself and all women who shall come after – even on the good ones.'

"And I said, 'In truth Jove has hated the house of Atreus from first to last in the matter of their women's counsels. See how many of us fell for Helen's sake, and now it seems that Clytemnestra hatched mischief against you too during your absence.'

"'Be sure, therefore,' continued Agamemnon, 'and not be too friendly even with your own wife. Do not tell her all that you know perfectly well yourself. Tell her a part only, and keep your own counsel about the rest. Not that your wife, Ulysses, is likely to murder you, for Penelope is a very admirable woman, and has an excellent nature. We left her a young bride with an infant at her breast when we set out for Troy. This child no doubt is now grown up happily to man's estate, and he and his father will have a joyful meeting and embrace one another as it is right they should do, whereas my wicked wife did not even allow me the happiness of looking upon my son, but killed me ere I could do so. Furthermore I say – and lay my saying to your heart – do not tell people when you are bringing your ship to Ithaca, but steal a march upon them, for after all this there is no trusting women. But now tell me, and tell me true, can you give me any news of my son Orestes? Is he in Orchomenus, or at Pylos, or is he at Sparta with Menelaus – for I presume that he is still living.'

"And I said, 'Agamemnon, why do you ask me? I do not know whether your son is alive or dead, and it is not right to talk when one does not know.'

"As we two sat weeping and talking thus sadly with one another, the ghost of Achilles came up to us with Patroclus, Antilochus, and Ajax who was the finest and goodliest man of all the Danaans after the son of Peleus. The fleet descendant of Aeacus knew me and spoke piteously, saying, 'Ulysses, noble son of Laertes, what deed of daring will you undertake next, that you venture down to the house of Hades among us silly dead, who are but the ghosts of them that can labour no more?'

"And I said, 'Achilles, son of Peleus, foremost champion of the Achaeans, I came to consult Teiresias, and see if he could advise me about my return home to Ithaca, for I have never yet been able to get near the Achaean land, nor to set foot in my own country, but have been in trouble all the time. As for you, Achilles, no one was ever yet so fortunate as you have been, nor ever will be, for you were adored by all us Argives as long as you were alive, and now that you are here you are a great prince among the dead. Do not, therefore, take it so much to heart even if you are dead.'

"'Say not a word,' he answered, 'in death's favour; I would rather be a paid servant in a poor man's house and be above ground than king of kings among the dead. But give me news about my son; is he gone to the wars and will he be a great soldier, or is this not so? Tell me also if you have heard anything about my father Peleus – does he still rule among the Myrmidons, or do they show him no respect throughout Hellas and Phthia now that he is old and his limbs fail him? Could I but stand by his side, in the light of day, with the same strength that I had when I killed the bravest of our foes upon the plain of Troy – could I but be as I then was and go even for a short time to my father's house, anyone who tried to do him violence or supersede him would soon rue it.'

"'I have heard nothing,' I answered, 'of Peleus, but I can tell you all about your son Neoptolemus, for I took him in my own ship from Scyros with the Achaeans. In our councils of war before Troy he was always first to speak, and his judgment was unerring. Nestor and I were the only two who could surpass him; and when it came to fighting on the plain of Troy, he would never remain with the body of his men, but would dash on far in front, foremost of them all in valour. Many a man did he kill in battle – I cannot name every single one of those whom he slew while fighting on the side of the Argives, but will only say how he killed that valiant hero Eurypylus son of Telephus, who was the handsomest man I ever saw except Memnon; many others also of the Ceteians fell around him by reason of a woman's bribes. Moreover, when all the bravest of the Argives went inside the horse that Epeus had made, and it was left to me to settle when we should either open the door of our ambuscade, or close it, though all the other leaders and chief men among the Danaans were drying their eyes and quaking in every limb, I never once saw him turn pale nor wipe a tear from his cheek; he was all the time urging me to break out from the horse – grasping the handle of his sword and his bronze-shod spear, and breathing fury against the foe. Yet when we had sacked the city of Priam he got his handsome share of the prize money and went on board (such is the fortune of war) without a wound upon him, neither from a thrown spear nor in close combat, for the rage of Mars is a matter of great chance.'

"When I had told him this, the ghost of Achilles strode off across a meadow full of asphodel, exulting over what I had said concerning the prowess of his son.

"The ghosts of other dead men stood near me and told me each his own melancholy tale; but that of Ajax son of Telamon alone held aloof – still angry with me for having won the cause in our dispute about the armour of Achilles. Thetis had offered it as a prize, but the Trojan prisoners and Minerva were the judges. Would that I had never gained the day in such a contest, for it cost the life of Ajax, who was foremost of all the Danaans after the son of Peleus, alike in stature and prowess.

"When I saw him I tried to pacify him and said, 'Ajax, will you not forget and forgive even in death, but must the judgment about that hateful armour still rankle with you? It cost us Argives dear enough to lose such a tower of strength as you were to us. We mourned you as much as we mourned Achilles son of Peleus himself, nor can the blame be laid on anything but on the spite which Jove bore against the Danaans, for it was this that made him counsel your destruction – come hither, therefore, bring your proud spirit into subjection, and hear what I can tell you.'

"He would not answer, but turned away to Erebus and to the other ghosts; nevertheless, I should have made him talk to me in spite of his being so angry, or I should have gone on talking to him, only that there were still others among the dead whom I desired to see.

"Then I saw Minos son of Jove with his golden sceptre in his hand sitting in judgment on the dead, and the ghosts were gathered sitting and standing round him in the spacious house of Hades, to learn his sentences upon them.

"After him I saw huge Orion in a meadow full of asphodel driving the ghosts of the wild beasts that he had killed upon the mountains, and he had a great bronze club in his hand, unbreakable for ever and ever.

"And I saw Tityus son of Gaia stretched upon the plain and covering some nine acres of ground. Two vultures on either side of him were digging their beaks into his liver, and he kept on trying to beat them off with his hands, but could not; for he had violated Jove's mistress Leto as she was going through Panopeus on her way to Pytho.

"I saw also the dreadful fate of Tantalus, who stood in a lake that reached his chin; he was dying to quench his thirst, but could never reach the water, for whenever the poor creature stooped to drink, it dried up and vanished, so that there was nothing but dry ground – parched by the spite of heaven. There were tall trees, moreover, that shed their fruit over his head – pears, pomegranates, apples, sweet figs and juicy olives, but whenever the poor creature stretched out his hand to take some, the wind tossed the branches back again to the clouds.

"And I saw Sisyphus at his endless task raising his prodigious stone with both his hands. With hands and feet he tried to roll it up to the top of the hill, but always, just before he could roll it over on to the other side, its weight would be too much for him, and the pitiless stone would come thundering down again on to the plain. Then he would begin trying to push it uphill again, and the sweat ran off him and the steam rose after him.

"After him I saw mighty Hercules, but it was his phantom only, for he is feasting ever with the immortal gods, and has lovely Hebe to wife, who is daughter of Jove and Juno. The ghosts were screaming round him like scared birds flying all whithers. He looked black as night with his bare bow in his hands and his arrow on the string, glaring around as though ever on the point of taking aim. About his breast there was a wondrous golden belt adorned in the most marvellous fashion with bears, wild boars, and lions with gleaming eyes; there was also war, battle, and death. The man who made that belt, do what he might, would never be able to make another like it. Hercules knew me at once when he saw me, and spoke piteously, saying, 'My poor Ulysses, noble son of Laertes, are you too leading the same sorry kind of life that I did when I was above ground? I was son of Jove, but I went through an infinity of suffering, for I became bondsman to one who was far beneath me – a low fellow who set me all manner of labours. He once sent me here to fetch the hellhound – for he did not think he could find anything harder for me than this, but I got the hound out of Hades and brought him to him, for Mercury and Minerva helped me.'

"On this Hercules went down again into the house of Hades, but I stayed where I was in case some other of the mighty dead should come to me. And I should have seen still other of them that are gone before, whom I would fain have seen – Theseus and Pirithous – glorious children of the gods, but so many thousands of ghosts came round me and uttered such appalling cries, that I was panic stricken lest Proserpine should send up from the house of Hades the head of that awful monster Gorgon. On this I hastened back to my ship and ordered my men to go on board at once and loose the hawsers; so they embarked and took their places, whereon the ship went down the stream of the river Oceanus."

The Liar
Lucian

Tychiades – Philocles, what is it that makes most men so fond of a lie? Can you explain it? Their delight in romancing themselves is only equalled by the earnest attention with which they receive other people's efforts in the same direction.

Philocles – Why, in some cases there is no lack of motives for lying – motives of self-interest.

Tychiades – Ah, but that is neither here nor there. I am not speaking of men who lie with an object. There is some excuse for that: indeed, it is sometimes to their credit, when they deceive their country's enemies, for instance, or when mendacity is but the medicine to heal their sickness. Odysseus, seeking to preserve his life and bring his companions safe home, was a liar of that kind. The men I mean are innocent of any ulterior motive: they prefer a lie to truth, simply on its own merits; they like lying, it is their favourite occupation; there is no necessity in the case. Now what good can they get out of it?

Philocles – Why, have you ever known anyone with such a strong natural turn for lying?

Tychiades – Any number of them.

Philocles – Then I can only say they must be fools, if they really prefer evil to good.

Tychiades – Oh, that is not it. I could point you out plenty of men of first-rate ability, sensible enough in all other respects, who have somehow picked up this vice of romancing. It makes me quite angry: what satisfaction can there be to men of their good qualities in deceiving themselves and their neighbours? There are instances among the ancients with which you must be more familiar than I. Look at Herodotus, or Ctesias of Cnidus; or, to go further back, take the poets – Homer himself: here are men of world-wide celebrity, perpetuating their mendacity in black and white; not content with deceiving their hearers, they must send their lies down to posterity, under the protection of the most admirable verse. Many a time I have blushed for them, as I read of the mutilation of Uranus, the fetters of Prometheus, the revolt of the Giants, the torments of Hell; enamoured Zeus taking the shape of bull or swan; women turning into birds and bears; Pegasuses, Chimaeras, Gorgons, Cyclopes, and the rest of it; monstrous medley! fit only to charm the imaginations of children for whom Mormo and Lamia have still their terrors. However, poets, I suppose, will be poets. But when it comes to national lies, when one finds whole cities bouncing collectively like one man, how is one to keep one's countenance? A Cretan will look you in the face, and tell you that yonder is Zeus's tomb. In Athens, you are informed that Erichthonius sprang out of the Earth, and that the first Athenians grew up from the soil like so many cabbages; and this story assumes quite a sober aspect when compared with that of the Sparti, for whom the Thebans claim descent from a dragon's teeth. If you presume to doubt these stories, if you choose to exert your common sense, and leave Triptolemus's winged aerial car, and Pan's Marathonian exploits, and Orithyia's mishap, to the stronger digestions of a Coroebus and a Margites, you are a fool and a blasphemer, for questioning such palpable truths. Such is the power of lies!

Philocles – I must say I think there is some excuse, Tychiades, both for your national liars and for the poets. The latter are quite right in throwing in a little mythology: it has a very pleasing effect, and is just the thing to secure the attention of their hearers. On the other hand, the Athenians and the Thebans and the rest are only trying to add to the lustre of their respective cities. Take away the legendary treasures of Greece, and you condemn the whole race of ciceroni to starvation: sightseers do not want the truth; they would not take it at a gift. However, I surrender to your ridicule anyone who has no such motive, and yet rejoices in lies.

Tychiades – Very well: now I have just been with the great Eucrates, who treated me to a whole string of old wives' tales. I came away in the middle of it; he was too much for me altogether; Furies could not have driven me out more effectually than his marvel-working tongue.

Philocles – What, Eucrates, of all credible witnesses? That venerably bearded sexagenarian, with his philosophic leanings? I could never have believed that he would lend his countenance to other people's lies, much less that *he* was capable of such things himself.

Tychiades – My dear sir, you should have heard the stuff he told me; the way in which he vouched for the truth of it all too, solemnly staking the lives of his children on his veracity! I stared at him in amazement, not knowing what to make of it: one moment I thought he must be out of his mind; the next I concluded he had been a humbug all along, an ape in a lion's skin. Oh, it was monstrous.

Philocles – Do tell me all about it; I am curious to see the quackery that shelters beneath so long a beard.

Tychiades – I often look in on Eucrates when I have time on my hands, but today I had gone there to see Leontichus; he is a friend of mine, you know, and I understood from his boy that he had gone off early to inquire after Eucrates' health, I had not heard that there was anything the matter with him, but this was an additional reason for paying him a visit. When I got there, Leontichus had just gone away, so Eucrates said; but he had a number of other visitors. There was Cleodemus the Peripatetic and Dinomachus the Stoic, and Ion. You know Ion? He is the man who fancies himself so much on his knowledge of Plato; if you take his word for it, he is the only man who has ever really got to the bottom of that philosopher's meaning, or is qualified to act as his interpreter. There is a company for you; Wisdom and Virtue personified, the *elite* of every school, most reverend gentlemen all of them; it almost frightened one. Then there was Antigonus the doctor, who I suppose attended in his professional capacity. Eucrates seemed to be better already: he had come to an understanding with the gout, which had now settled down in his feet again. He motioned me to a seat on the couch beside him. His voice sank to the proper invalid level when he saw me coming, but on my way in I had overheard him bellowing away most lustily. I made him the usual compliments – explained that this was the first I had heard of his illness, and that I had come to him post-haste – and sat down at his side, in very gingerly fashion, lest I should touch his feet. There had been a good deal of talk already about gout, and this was still going on; each man had his pet prescription to offer. Cleodemus was giving his. 'In the left hand take up the tooth of a field-mouse, which has been killed in the manner described, and attach it to the skin of a freshly flayed lion; then bind the skin about your legs, and the pain will instantly cease.' 'A lion's skin?' says Dinomachus; 'I understood it was an uncovered hind's. That sounds more likely: a hind has more pace, you see, and is particularly strong in the feet. A lion is a brave beast, I grant you; his fat, his right fore-paw, and his beard-bristles, are all very efficacious, if you know the proper incantation to use with each; but they would hardly be much use for gout.' 'Ah, yes; that is what I used to think for a long time: a hind was fast, so her skin must be the one for the purpose. But I know better now: a Libyan, who understands these things, tells me that lions are faster than stags; they must be, he says, because how else could they catch them? 'All agreed that the Libyan's argument was convincing. When I asked what good incantations could do, and how an internal complaint could be cured by external attachments, I only got laughed at for my pains; evidently they set me down as a simpleton, ignorant of the merest truisms, that no one in his senses would think of disputing. However, I thought doctor Antigonus seemed rather pleased at my question. I expect his professional advice had been slighted: he wanted to lower Eucrates' tone – cut down his wine, and put him on a vegetable diet. 'What, Tychiades,' says Cleodemus, with a faint grin,' you don't believe these remedies are good for anything?' 'I should have to be pretty far gone,' I replied, 'before I could admit that external things, which have no communication with the internal causes of disease, are going to work by means of incantations and stuff, and effect a cure merely by being hung on. You might take the skin of the Nemean lion himself, with a dozen of fieldmice tacked on, and you would do no good. Why, I have seen a live lion limping before now, hide and all complete.' 'Ah, you have a great deal to learn,' cried Dinomachus; 'you have never taken the trouble to inquire into the operation of these valuable remedies. It would not surprise me to hear you disputing the most palpable facts, such as the curing of tumours and intermittent fevers, the charming of reptiles, and so on; things that every old woman can effect in these days. And this being so, why should not the same principles be extended further?' 'Nail drives out nail,' I replied; 'you argue in a circle. How do I know that these cures are brought about by the means to which you attribute them? You have first to show inductively that it is in the course of nature for a fever or a tumour to take fright and bolt at the sound of holy names and foreign incantations; till then, your instances are no better than old wives' tales.' 'In other words, you do not believe in the existence of the Gods, since you maintain that cures cannot be wrought by the use of holy names?' 'Nay, say not so, my dear Dinomachus,' I answered; 'the Gods may exist, and these things may yet be lies. I respect the Gods: I see the cures performed by them, I see their beneficence at work in restoring the sick through the medium of the medical faculty and their drugs. Asclepius, and his sons after him, compounded soothing medicines and healed the sick – without the lion's-skin-and-field-mouse process.'

'Never mind Asclepius,' cried Ion. 'I will tell you of a strange thing that happened when I was a boy of fourteen or so. Someone came and told my father that Midas, his gardener, a sturdy fellow and a good workman, had been bitten that morning by an adder, and was now lying prostrate, mortification having set in the leg. He had been tying the vine branches to the trellis-work, when the reptile crept up and bit him on the great toe, getting off to its hole before he could catch it; and he was now in a terrible way. Before our informant had finished speaking, we saw Midas being carried up by his fellow servants on a stretcher: his whole body was swollen, livid and mortifying, and life appeared to be almost extinct. My father was very much troubled about it; but a friend of his who was there assured him there was no cause for uneasiness. 'I know of a Babylonian,' he said, 'what they call a Chaldaean; I will go and fetch him at once, and he will put the man right.' To make a long story short, the Babylonian came, and by means of an incantation expelled the venom from the body, and restored Midas to health; besides the incantation, however, he used a splinter of stone chipped from the monument of a virgin; this he applied to Midas's foot. And as if that were not enough (Midas, I may mention, actually picked up the stretcher on which he had been brought, and took it off with him into the vineyard! and it was all done by an incantation and a bit of stone), the Chaldaean followed it up with an exhibition nothing short of miraculous. Early in the morning he went into the field, pronounced seven names of sacred import, taken from an old book, purified the ground by going thrice round it with sulphur and burning torches, and thereby drove every single reptile off the estate! They came as if drawn by a spell: venomous toads and snakes of every description, asp and adder, cerastes and acontias; only one old serpent, disabled apparently by age, ignored the summons. The Chaldaean declared that the number was not complete, appointed the youngest of the snakes as his ambassador, and sent him to fetch the old serpent who presently arrived. Having got them all together, he blew upon them; and imagine our astonishment when every one of them was immediately consumed!'

'Ion,' said I, 'about that one who was so old: did the ambassador snake give him an arm, or had he a stick to lean on?' 'Ah, you will have your joke,' Cleodemus put in; 'I was an unbeliever myself once – worse than you; in fact I considered it absolutely impossible to give credit to such things. I held out for a long time, but all my scruples were overcome the first time I saw the Flying Stranger; a Hyperborean, he was; I have his own word for it. There was no more to be said after that: there was he travelling through the air in broad daylight,

walking on the water, or strolling through fire, perfectly at his ease!'
'What,' I exclaimed, 'you saw this Hyperborean actually flying and
walking on water?' 'I did; he wore brogues, as the Hyperboreans
usually do. I need not detain you with the everyday manifestations
of his power: how he would make people fall in love, call up spirits,
resuscitate corpses, bring down the Moon, and show you Hecate
herself, as large as life. But I will just tell you of a thing I saw him
do at Glaucias's. It was not long after Glaucias's father, Alexicles, had
died. Glaucias, on coming into the property, had fallen in love with
Chrysis, Demaenetus's daughter. I was teaching him philosophy
at the time, and if it had not been for this love affair he would have
thoroughly mastered the Peripatetic doctrines: at eighteen years old
that boy had been through his physics, and begun analysis. Well, he
was in a dreadful way, and told me all about his love troubles. It was
clearly my duty to introduce him to this Hyperborean wizard, which I
accordingly did; his preliminary fee, to cover the expenses of sacrifice,
was to be fifteen pounds, and he was to have another sixty pounds if
Glaucias succeeded with Chrysis. Well, as soon as the moon was full,
that being the time usually chosen for these enchantments, he dug a
trench in the courtyard of the house, and commenced operations, at
about midnight, by summoning Glaucias's father, who had now been
dead for seven months. The old man did not approve of his son's
passion, and was very angry at first; however, he was prevailed on to
give his consent. Hecate was next ordered to appear, with Cerberus
in her train, and the Moon was brought down, and went through a
variety of transformations; she appeared first in the form of a woman,
but presently she turned into a most magnificent ox, and after that
into a puppy. At length the Hyperborean moulded a clay Eros, and
ordered it to *go and fetch Chrysis*. Off went the image, and before

long there was a knock at the door, and there stood Chrysis. She came
in and threw her arms about Glaucias's neck; you would have said
she was dying for love of him; and she stayed on till at last we heard
cocks crowing. Away flew the Moon into Heaven, Hecate disappeared
underground, all the apparitions vanished, and we saw Chrysis out of
the house just about dawn – Now, Tychiades, if you had seen that, it
would have been enough to convince you that there was something
in incantations.'

'Exactly,' I replied. 'If I had seen it, I should have been convinced: as
it is, you must bear with me if I have not your eyes for the miraculous.
But as to Chrysis, I know her for a most inflammable lady. I do not
see what occasion there was for the clay ambassador and the Moon,
or for a wizard all the way from the land of the Hyperboreans; why,
Chrysis would go that distance herself for the sum of twenty shillings;
'tis a form of incantation she cannot resist. She is the exact opposite
of an apparition: apparitions, you tell me, take flight at the clash of
brass or iron, whereas if Chrysis hears the chink of silver, she flies
to the spot. By the way, I like your wizard: instead of making all the
wealthiest women in love with himself, and getting thousands out
of them, he condescends to pick up fifteen pounds by rendering
Glaucias irresistible.'

'This is sheer folly,' said Ion; 'you are determined not to believe
anyone. I shall be glad, now, to hear your views on the subject of
those who cure demoniacal possession; the effect of *their* exorcisms
is clear enough, and they have spirits to deal with. I need not enlarge
on the subject: look at that Syrian adept from Palestine: everyone
knows how time after time he has found a man thrown down on the
ground in a lunatic fit, foaming at the mouth and rolling his eyes;
and how he has got him on to his feet again and sent him away in his

right mind; and a handsome fee he takes for freeing men from such horrors. He stands over them as they lie, and asks the spirit whence it is. The patient says not a word, but the spirit in him makes answer, in Greek or in some foreign tongue as the case may be, stating where it comes from, and how it entered into him. Then with adjurations, and if need be with threats, the Syrian constrains it to come out of the man. I myself once saw one coming out: it was of a dark, smoky complexion.' 'Ah, that is nothing for you,' I replied; 'your eyes can discern those *ideas* which are set forth in the works of Plato, the founder of your school: now they make a very faint impression on the dull optics of us ordinary men.'

'Do you suppose,' asked Eucrates, 'that he is the only man who has seen such things? Plenty of people besides Ion have met with spirits, by night and by day. As for me, if I have seen one apparition, I have seen a thousand. I used not to like them at first, but I am accustomed to them now, and think nothing of it; especially since the Arab gave me my ring of gallows-iron, and taught me the incantation with all those names in it. But perhaps you will doubt my word too?' 'Doubt the word of Eucrates, the learned son of Dino? Never! least of all when he unbosoms himself in the liberty of his own house.' 'Well, what I am going to tell you about the statue was witnessed night after night by all my household, from the eldest to the youngest, and any one of them could tell you the story as well as myself.' 'What statue is this?' 'Have you never noticed as you came in that beautiful one in the court, by Demetrius the portrait sculptor?' 'Is that the one with the quoit – leaning forward for the throw, with his face turned back towards the hand that holds the quoit, and one knee bent, ready to rise as he lets it go?' 'Ah, that is a fine piece of work, too – a Myron; but I don't mean that, nor the beautiful Polyclitus next it, the Youth tying on the Fillet. No, forget all you pass on your right as you come in; the Tyrannicides of Critius and Nesiotes are on that side too – but did you never notice one just by the fountain? – bald, pot-bellied, half-naked; beard partly caught by the wind; protruding veins? That is the one I mean; it looks as if it must be a portrait, and is thought to be Pelichus, the Corinthian general.' 'Ah, to be sure, I have seen it,' I replied; 'it is to the right of the Cronus; the head is crowned with fillets and withered garlands, and the breast gilded.' 'Yes, I had that done, when he cured me of the tertian ague; I had been at Death's door with it.' 'Bravo, Pelichus!' I exclaimed; 'so he was a doctor too?' 'Not was, but is. Beware of trifling with him, or he may pay you a visit before long. Well do I know what virtue is in that statue with which you make so merry. Can you doubt that he who cures the ague may also inflict it at will?' 'I implore his favour,' I cried; 'may he be as merciful as he is mighty! And what are his other doings, to which all your household are witnesses?' 'At nightfall,' said Eucrates, 'he descends from his pedestal, and walks all round the house; one or other of us is continually meeting with him; sometimes he is singing. He has never done any harm to anyone: all we have to do when we see him is to step aside, and he passes on his way without molesting us. He is fond of taking a bath; you may hear him splashing about in the water all night long.' 'Perhaps,' I suggested, 'it is not Pelichus at all, but Talos the Cretan, the son of Minos? He was of bronze, and used to walk all round the island. Or if only he were made of wood instead of bronze, he might quite well be one of Daedalus's ingenious mechanisms – you say he plays truant from his pedestal just like them – and not the work of Demetrius at all.' 'Take care, Tychiades; you will be sorry for this some day. I have not forgotten what happened to the thief who stole his monthly pennies.' 'The sacrilegious villain!'

cried Ion; 'I hope he got a lesson. How was he punished? Do tell me: never mind Tychiades; he can be as incredulous as he likes.' 'At the feet of the statue a number of pence were laid, and other coins were attached to his thigh by means of wax; some of these were silver, and there were also silver plates, all being the thank-offerings of those whom he had cured of fever. Now we had a scamp of a Libyan groom, who took it into his head to filch all this coin under cover of night. He waited till the statue had descended from his pedestal, and then put his plan into effect. Pelichus detected the robbery as soon as he got back; and this is how he found the offender out and punished him. He caused the wretch to wander about in the court all night long, unable to find his way out, just as if he had been in a maze; till at daybreak he was caught with the stolen property in his possession. His guilt was clear, and he received a sound flogging there and then; and before long he died a villain's death. It seems from his own confession that he was scourged every night; and each succeeding morning the weals were to be seen on his body – *Now*, Tychiades, let me hear you laugh at Pelichus: I am a dotard, am I not? a relic from the time of Minos?'

'My dear Eucrates,' said I, 'if bronze is bronze, and if that statue was cast by Demetrius of Alopece, who dealt not in Gods but in men, then I cannot anticipate any danger from a statue of Pelichus; even the menaces of the original would not have alarmed me particularly.'

Here Antigonus, the doctor, put in a word. 'I myself,' he informed his host, 'have a Hippocrates in bronze, some eighteen inches high. Now the moment my candle is out, he goes clattering about all over the house, slamming the door, turning all my boxes upside-down, and mixing up all my drugs; especially when his annual sacrifice is overdue.' 'What are we coming to?' I cried; 'Hippocrates must have sacrifices, must he? He must be feasted with all pomp and circumstance, and punctually to the day, or his leechship is angry? Why, he ought to be only too pleased to be complimented with a cup of mead or a garland, like other dead men.'

'Now here,' Eucrates went on, 'is a thing that I saw happen five years ago, in the presence of witnesses. It was during the vintage. I had left the labourers busy in the vineyard at midday, and was walking off into the wood, occupied with my own thoughts. I had already got under the shade of the trees, when I heard dogs barking, and supposed that my boy Mnason was amusing himself in the chase as usual, and had penetrated into the copse with his friends. However, that was not it: presently there was an earthquake; I heard a voice like a thunderclap, and saw a terrible woman approaching, not much less than three hundred feet high. She carried a torch in her left hand, and a sword in her right; the sword might be thirty feet long. Her lower extremities were those of a dragon; but the upper half was like Medusa – as to the eyes, I mean; they were quite awful in their expression. Instead of hair, she had clusters of snakes writhing about her neck, and curling over her shoulders. See here: it makes my flesh creep, only to speak of it!' And he showed us all his arm, with the hair standing on end.

Ion and Dinomachus and Cleodemus and the rest of them drank down every word. The narrator led them by their venerable noses, and this least convincing of colossal bogies, this hundred-yarder, was the object of their mute adorations. And these (I was reflecting all the time) – these are the admired teachers from whom our youth are to learn wisdom! Two circumstances distinguish them from babies: they have white hair, and they have beards: but when it comes to swallowing a lie, they are babes and more than babes.

Dinomachus, for instance, wanted to know 'how big were the Goddess's dogs?' 'They were taller than Indian elephants,' he was assured, 'and as black, with coarse, matted coats. At the sight of her, I stood stock still, and turned the seal of my Arab's ring inwards; whereupon Hecate smote upon the ground with her dragon's foot, and caused a vast chasm to open, wide as the mouth of Hell. Into this she presently leaped, and was lost to sight. I began to pluck up courage, and looked over the edge; but first I took hold of a tree that grew near, for fear I should be giddy, and fall in. And then I saw the whole of Hades: there was Pyriphlegethon, the Lake of Acheron, Cerberus, the Shades. I even recognized some of them: I made out my father quite distinctly; he was still wearing the same clothes in which we buried him.' 'And what were the spirits doing?' asked Ion. 'Doing? Oh, they were just lying about on the asphodel, among their friends and kinsmen, all arranged according to their clans and tribes.' 'There now!' exclaimed Ion; 'after that I should like to hear the Epicureans say another word against the divine Plato and his account of the spiritual world. I suppose you did not happen to see Socrates or Plato among the Shades?' 'Yes, I did; I saw Socrates; not very plainly, though; I only went by the bald head and corpulent figure. Plato I did *not* make out; I will speak the plain truth; we are all friends here. I had just had a good look at everything, when the chasm began to close up; some of the servants who came to look for me (Pyrrhias here was among them) arrived while the gap was still visible – Pyrrhias, is that the fact?' 'Indeed it is,' says Pyrrhias; 'what is more, I heard a dog barking in the hole, and if I am not mistaken I caught a glimmer of torchlight.' I could not help a smile; it was handsome in Pyrrhias, this of the bark and the torchlight.

'Your experience,' observed Cleodemus, 'is by no means without precedent. In fact, I saw something of the same kind myself, not long ago. I had been ill, and Antigonus here was attending me. The fever had been on me for seven days, and was now aggravated by the excessive heat. All my attendants were outside, having closed the door and left me to myself; those were your orders, you know, Antigonus; I was to get some sleep if I could. Well, I woke up to find a handsome young man standing at my side, in a white cloak. He raised me up from the bed, and conducted me through a sort of chasm into Hades; I knew where I was at once, because I saw Tantalus and Tityus and Sisyphus. Not to go into details, I came to the Judgment Hall, and there were Aeacus and Charon and the Fates and the Furies. One person of a majestic appearance – Pluto, I suppose it was – sat reading out the names of those who were due to die, their term of life having lapsed. The young man took me and set me before him, but Pluto flew into a rage: "Away with him," he said to my conductor; "his thread is not yet out; go and fetch Demylus the smith; *he* has had his spindleful and more." I ran off home, nothing loath. My fever had now disappeared, and I told everybody that Demylus was as good as dead. He lived close by, and was said to have some illness, and it was not long before we heard the voices of mourners in his house.'

'This need not surprise us,' remarked Antigonus; 'I know of a man who rose from the dead twenty days after he had been buried; I attended him both before his death and after his resurrection.' 'I should have thought,' said I, 'that the body must have putrefied in all that time, or if not that, that he must have collapsed for want of nourishment. Was your patient a second Epimenides?'

At this point in the conversation, Eucrates' sons came in from the gymnasium, one of them quite a young man, the other a boy of fifteen or so. After saluting the company, they took their seats on the couch at their father's side, and a chair was brought for me. The appearance of the boys seemed to remind Eucrates of something: laying a hand upon each of them, he addressed me as follows: 'Tychiades, if what I am now about to tell you is anything but the truth, then may I never have joy of these lads. It is well known to everyone how fond I was of my sainted wife, their mother; and I showed it in my treatment of her, not only in her lifetime, but even after her death; for I ordered all the jewels and clothes that she had valued to be burnt upon her pyre. Now on the seventh day after her death, I was sitting here on this very couch, as it might be now, trying to find comfort for my affliction in Plato's book about the soul. I was quietly reading this, when Demaenete herself appeared, and sat down at my side exactly as Eucratides is doing now.' Here he pointed to the younger boy, who had turned quite pale during this narrative, and now shuddered in childish terror. 'The moment I saw her,' he continued, 'I threw my arms about her neck and wept aloud. She bade me cease; and complained that though I had consulted her wishes in everything else, I had neglected to burn one of her golden sandals, which she said had fallen under a chest. We had been unable to find this sandal, and had only burnt the fellow to it. While we were still conversing, a hateful little Maltese terrier that lay under the couch started barking, and my wife immediately vanished. The sandal, however, was found beneath the chest, and was eventually burnt. Do you still doubt, Tychiades, in the face of one convincing piece of evidence after another?' 'God forbid!' I cried; 'the doubter who should presume, thus to brazen it out in the face of Truth would deserve to have a golden sandal applied to him after the nursery fashion.'

Arignotus the Pythagorean now came in – the 'divine' Arignotus, as he is called; the philosopher of the long hair and the solemn countenance, you know, of whose wisdom we hear so much. I breathed again when I saw him. 'Ah!' thought I, 'the very man we want! here is the axe to hew their lies asunder. The sage will soon pull them up when he hears their cock-and-bull stories. Fortune has brought a *deus ex machina* upon the scene.' He sat down (Cleodemus rising to make room for him) and inquired after Eucrates' health. Eucrates replied that he was better. 'And what,' Arignotus next asked, 'is the subject of your learned conversation? I overheard your voices as I came in, and doubt not that your time will prove to have been profitably employed.' Eucrates pointed to me. 'We were only trying,' he said, 'to convince this man of adamant that there are such things as supernatural beings and ghosts, and that the spirits of the dead walk the earth and manifest themselves to whomsoever they will.' Moved by the august presence of Arignotus, I blushed, and hung my head. 'Ah, but, Eucrates,' said he, 'perhaps all that Tychiades means is, that a spirit only walks if its owner met with a violent end, if he was strangled, for instance, or beheaded or crucified, and not if he died a natural death. If that is what he means, there is great justice in his contention.' 'No, no,' says Dinomachus, 'he maintains that there is absolutely no such thing as an apparition.' 'What is this I hear?' asked Arignotus, scowling upon me; 'you deny the existence of the supernatural, when there is scarcely a man who has not seen some evidence of it?' 'Therein lies my exculpation,' I replied: 'I do not believe in the supernatural, because, unlike the rest of mankind, I do not see it: if I saw, I should doubtless believe, just as you all do.' 'Well,' said he, 'next time you are in Corinth, ask for the house of Eubatides, near the Craneum; and when you have found it, go up to Tibius the door-keeper, and tell him you would like to see the spot on which Arignotus the Pythagorean unearthed the demon, whose expulsion rendered the house habitable again.' 'What was that about, Arignotus?' asked Eucrates.

'The house,' replied the other, 'was haunted, and had been uninhabited for years: each intending occupant had been at once driven out of it in abject terror by a most grim and formidable apparition. Finally it had fallen into a ruinous state, the roof was giving way, and in short no one would have thought of entering it. Well, when I heard about this, I got my books together (I have a considerable number of Egyptian works on these subjects) and went off to the house about bedtime, undeterred by the remonstrances of my host, who considered that I was walking into the jaws of Death, and would almost have detained me by force when he learnt my destination. I took a lamp and entered alone, and, putting down my light in the principal room, I sat on the floor quietly reading. The spirit now made his appearance, thinking that he had to do with an ordinary person, and that he would frighten me as he had frightened so many others. He was pitch-black, with a tangled mass of hair. He drew near, and assailed me from all quarters, trying every means to get the better of me, and changing in a moment from dog to bull, from bull to lion. Armed with my most appalling adjuration, uttered in the Egyptian tongue, I drove him spellbound into the corner of a dark room, marked the spot at which he disappeared, and passed the rest of the night in peace. In the morning, to the amazement of all beholders (for everyone had given me up for lost, and expected to find me lying dead like former occupants), I issued from the house, and carried to Eubatides the welcome news that it was now cleared of its grim visitant, and fit to serve as a human habitation. He and a number of others, whom curiosity had prompted to join us, followed me to the spot at which I had seen the demon vanish. I instructed them to take spades and pickaxes and dig: they did so; and at about a fathom's depth we discovered a mouldering corpse, of which nothing but the bones remained entire. We took the skeleton up, and placed it in a grave; and from that day to this the house has never been troubled with apparitions.'

After such a story as this – coming as it did from Arignotus, who was generally looked up to as a man of inspired wisdom – my incredulous attitude towards the supernatural was loudly condemned on all hands. However, I was not frightened by his long hair, nor by his reputation. 'Dear, dear!' I exclaimed, 'so Arignotus, the sole mainstay of Truth, is as bad as the rest of them, as full of windy imaginings! Our treasure proves to be but ashes.' 'Now look here, Tychiades,' said Arignotus, 'you will not believe me, nor Dinomachus, nor Cleodemus here, nor yet Eucrates: we shall be glad to know who is your great authority on the other side, who is to outweigh us all?' 'No less a person,' I replied, 'than the sage of Abdera, the wondrous Democritus himself. *His* disbelief in apparitions is sufficiently clear. When he had shut himself up in that tomb outside the city gates, there to spend his days and nights in literary labours, certain young fellows, who had a mind to play their pranks on the philosopher and give him a fright, got themselves up in black palls and skull-masks, formed a ring round him, and treated him to a brisk dance. Was Democritus alarmed at the ghosts? Not he: "Come, enough of that nonsense," was all he had to say to them; and that without so much as looking up, or taking pen from paper. Evidently *he* had quite made up his mind about disembodied spirits.' 'Which simply proves,' retorted Eucrates, 'that Democritus was no wiser than yourself. Now I am going to tell you of another thing that happened to me personally; I did not get the story second-hand. Even you, Tychiades, will scarcely hold out against so convincing a narrative.

'When I was a young man, I passed some time in Egypt, my father having sent me to that country for my education. I took it into my head to sail up the Nile to Coptus, and thence pay a visit to the statue of Memnon, and hear the curious sound that proceeds from it at sunrise. In this respect, I was more fortunate than most people, who hear nothing but an indistinct voice: Memnon actually opened his lips, and delivered me an oracle in seven hexameters; it is foreign to my present purpose, or I would quote you the very lines. Well now, one of my fellow passengers on the way up was a scribe of Memphis, an extraordinarily able man, versed in all the lore of the Egyptians. He was said to have passed twenty-three years of his life underground in the tombs, studying occult sciences under the instruction of Isis herself.' 'You must mean the divine Pancrates, my teacher,' exclaimed Arignotus; 'tall, clean-shaven, snub-nosed, protruding lips, rather thin in the legs; dresses entirely in linen, has a thoughtful expression, and speaks Greek with a slight accent?' 'Yes, it was Pancrates himself. I knew nothing about him at first, but whenever we anchored, I used to see him doing the most marvellous things – for instance, he would actually ride on the crocodiles' backs, and swim about among the brutes, and they would fawn upon him and wag their tails; and then I realized that he was no common man. I made some advances, and by imperceptible degrees came to be on quite a friendly footing with him, and was admitted to a share in his mysterious arts. The end of it was, that he prevailed on me to leave all my servants behind at Memphis, and accompany him alone; assuring me that we should not want for attendance. This plan we accordingly followed from that time onwards. Whenever we came to an inn, he used to take up the bar of the door, or a broom, or perhaps a pestle, dress it up in clothes, and utter a certain incantation; whereupon the thing would begin to walk about, so that everyone took it for a man. It would go off and draw water, buy and cook provisions, and make itself generally useful. When we had no further occasion for its services, there was another incantation, after which the broom was a broom once more, or the pestle a pestle. I could never get him to teach me this incantation, though it was not for want of trying; open as he was about everything else, he guarded this one secret jealously. At last one day I hid in a dark corner, and overheard the magic syllables; they were three in number. The Egyptian gave the pestle its instructions, and then went off to the market. Well, next day he was again busy in the market: so I took the pestle, dressed it, pronounced the three syllables exactly as he had done, and ordered it to become a water-carrier. It brought me the pitcher full; and then I said, *Stop: be water-carrier no longer, but pestle as heretofore.* But the thing would take no notice of me: it went on drawing water the whole time, until at last the house was full of it. This was awkward: if Pancrates came back, he would be angry, I thought (and so indeed it turned out). I took an axe, and cut the pestle in two. The result was that both halves took pitchers and fetched water; I had two water-carriers instead of one. This was still going on, when Pancrates appeared. He saw how things stood, and turned the water-carriers back into wood; and then he withdrew himself from me, and went away, whither I knew not.'

'And you can actually make a man out of a pestle to this day?' asked Dinomachus. 'Yes, I can do *that*, but that is only half the process: I cannot turn it back again into its original form; if once it became a water-carrier, its activity would swamp the house.'

'Oh, stop!' I cried; 'if the thought that you are old men is not enough to deter you from talking this trash, at least remember who is present: if you do not want to fill these boys' heads with ghosts and hobgoblins, postpone your grotesque horrors for a more suitable occasion. Have some mercy on the lads: do not accustom them to listen to a tangle of superstitious stuff that will cling to them for the rest of their lives, and make them start at their own shadows.'

'Ah, talking of superstition, now,' says Eucrates, 'that reminds me: what do you make of oracles, for instance, and omens? of inspired utterances, of voices from the shrine, of the priestess's prophetic lines? You will deny all that too, of course? If I were to tell you of a certain magic ring in my possession, the seal of which is a portrait of the Pythian Apollo, and actually *speaks* to me, I suppose you would decline to believe it, you would think I was bragging? But I must tell you all of what I heard in the temple of Amphilochus at Mallus, when that hero appeared to me in person and gave me counsel, and of what I saw with my own eyes on that occasion; and again of all I saw at Pergamum and heard at Patara. It was on my way home from Egypt that the oracle of Mallus was mentioned to me as a particularly intelligible and veracious one: I was told that any question, duly written down on a tablet and handed to the priest, would receive a plain, definite answer. I thought it would be a good thing to take the oracle on my way home, and consult the God as to my future.'

I saw what was coming: this was but the prologue to a whole tragedy of the oracular. It was clear enough that I was not wanted, and as I did not feel called upon to pose as the sole champion of the cause of Truth among so many, I took my leave there and then, while Eucrates was still upon the high seas between Egypt and Mallus. 'I must go and find Leontichus,' I explained; 'I have to see him about something. Meanwhile, you gentlemen, to whom human affairs are not sufficient occupation, may solicit the insertion of divine fingers into your mythologic pie.' And with that I went out. Relieved of my presence, I doubt not that they fell to with a will on their banquet of mendacity.

That is what I got by going to Eucrates'; and, upon my word, Philocles, my overloaded stomach needs an emetic as much as if I had been drinking new wine. I would pay something for the drug that should work oblivion in me: I fear the effects of haunting reminiscence; monsters, demons, Hecates, seem to pass before my eyes.

Philocles – I am not much better off. They tell us it is not only the mad dog that inflicts hydrophobia: his human victim's bite is as deadly as his own, and communicates the evil as surely. You, it seems, have been bitten with many bites by the liar Eucrates, and have passed it on to me; no otherwise can I explain the demoniacal poison that runs in my veins.

Tychiades – What matter, friend? Truth and good sense: these are the drugs for our ailment; let us employ them, and that empty thing, a lie, need have no terrors for us.

Ghostly Episodes in the Life of Apollonius of Tyana
Philostratus

Philostratus's book entitled *The Life of Apollonius of Tyana* is a novelistic biography detailing the life and travels of the Greek Neopythagorean philosopher and teacher Apollonius (*c.* 15 AD–*c.* 100 AD). The following episodes feature various supernatural incidents said to have befallen Apollonius and his company of fellow travellers.

A Visitor from Beyond

Apollonius's home was Tyana, a Greek city amidst a population of Cappadocians. His father was of the same name, and the family descended from the first settlers. It excelled in wealth the surrounding families, though the district is a rich one. To his mother, just before he was born, there came an apparition of Proteus, who changes his form so much in Homer, in the guise of an Egyptian demon. She was in no way frightened, but asked him what sort of child she would bear. And he answered, "Myself." "And who are you?" she asked. "Proteus," answered he, "the god of Egypt." Well,

I need hardly explain to readers of the poets the quality of Proteus and his reputation as regards wisdom; how versatile he was, and for ever changing his form, and defying capture, and how he had a reputation of knowing both past and future. And we must bear Proteus in mind all the more, when my advancing story shows its hero to have been more of a prophet than Proteus, and to have triumphed over many difficulties and dangers in the moment when they beset him most closely.

An Encounter in the Mountains

Having passed the Caucasus, our travellers say they saw men four cubits in height, and they were already black, and that when they passed over the river Indus they saw others five cubits high. But on their way to this river our wayfarers found the following incidents worth of notice. For they were traveling by bright moonlight, when the figure of an *empusa* or hobgoblin appeared to them, that changed from one form into another, and sometimes vanished into nothing. And Apollonius realized what it was, and himself heaped abuse on the hobgoblin and instructed his party to do the same, saying that this was the right remedy for such a visitation. And the phantasm fled away shrieking even as ghosts do.

The Possessed Boy

[While Apollonius and his company were visiting India, a sage] brought forward a poor woman who interceded in behalf of her child, who was, she said, a boy of sixteen years of age, but had been for two years possessed by a devil. Now the character of the devil was that of a mocker and a liar. Here one of the sages asked, why she said this, and she replied: "This child of mine is extremely good-looking, and therefore the devil is amorous of him and will not allow him to retain his reason, nor will he permit him to go to school, or to learn archery, nor even to remain at home, but drives him out into desert places. And the boy does not even retain his own voice, but speaks in a deep hollow tone, as men do; and he looks at you with other eyes rather than with his own. As for myself I weep over all this and I tear my cheeks, and I rebuke my son so far as I well may; but he does not know me. And I made my mind to repair hither, indeed I planned to do so a year ago; only the demon discovered himself using my child as a mask, and what he told me was this, that he was the ghost of a man who fell long ago in battle, but that at death he was passionately attached to his wife.

Now he had been dead for only three days when his wife insulted their union by marrying another man, and the consequence was that he had come to detest the love of women, and had transferred himself wholly into this boy. But he promised, if I would only not denounce him to yourselves, to endow the child with many noble blessings. As for myself, I was influenced by these promises; but he has put me off and off for such a long time now, that he has got sole control of my household, yet has no honest or true intentions." Here the sage asked afresh, if the boy was at hand; and she said not, for, although she had done all she could to get him to come with her, the demon had threatened her with steep places and precipices and declared that he would kill her son, "in case," she added, "I haled him hither for trial." "Take courage," said the sage, "for he will not slay him when he has read this." And so saying, he drew a letter out of his bosom and gave it to the woman; and the letter, it appears, was addressed to the ghost and contained threats of an alarming kind.

A Mysterious Plague

When a plague began to rage in Ephesus, and no remedy sufficed to check it, [the people] sent a deputation to Apollonius, asking him to become physician of their infirmity; and he thought that he ought not to postpone his journey, but said, "Let us go." And forthwith he was in Ephesus, performing the same feat, I believe, as Pythagoras, who was in Thurii and Metapontum at one and the same moment. He therefore called together the Ephesians, and said, "Take courage, for I will today put a stop to the course of the disease." And with these words he led the population entire to the theatre, where the image of the Averting god had been set up. And there he saw what seemed an old mendicant artfully blinking his eyes as if blind, as he carried a wallet and a crust of bread in it; and he was clad in rags and was very squalid of countenance.

Apollonius therefore ranged the Ephesians around him and said, "Pick up as many stones as you can and hurl them at this enemy of the gods." Now the Ephesians wondered what he meant, and were shocked at the idea of murdering a stranger so manifestly miserable; for he was begging and praying them to take mercy upon him. Nevertheless, Apollonius insisted and egged on the Ephesians to launch themselves on him and not let him go. And as soon as some of them began to take shots and hit him with their stones, the beggar, who had seemed to blink and be blind, gave them all a sudden glance and his eyes were full of fire. Then the Ephesians recognized that he was a demon, and they stoned him so thoroughly that their stones were heaped into a great cairn around him. After a little pause, Apollonius bade them remove the stones and acquaint themselves with the wild animal they had slain. When therefore they had exposed the object which they thought they had thrown their missiles at, they found that he had disappeared, and instead of him there was a hound who resembled in form and look a Molossian dog, but was in size the equal of the largest lion; there he lay before their eyes, pounded to a pulp by their stones and vomiting foam as mad dogs do. Accordingly the statue of the Averting god, Heracles, has been set up over the spot where the ghost was slain.

The Devil Within

There chanced to be present in [Apollonius's] audience a young dandy who bore so evil a reputation for licentiousness that his conduct had long been the subject of coarse street-corner songs. His home was Corcyra, and he traced his pedigree to Alcinous the Phaeacian who entertained Odysseus. Apollonius then was talking about libations, and was urging them not to drink out of a particular cup, but to reserve it for the gods, without ever touching it or drinking out of it. But when he also urged them to have handles on the cup, and to pour the libation over the handle, because that is the part at which men are least likely to drink, the youth burst out into loud and coarse laughter, and quite drowned his voice. Then Apollonius looked up and said, "It is not yourself that perpetrates this insult, but the demon, who drives you without your knowing it." And in fact the youth was, without knowing it, possessed by a devil; for he would laugh at things that no one else laughed at, and then would fall to weeping for no reason at all, and he would talk and sing to himself.

Now most people thought that it was boisterous humour of youth which led him into excesses; but he was really the mouthpiece of a devil, though it only seemed a drunken frolic in which on that occasion he was indulging. Now, when Apollonius gazed on him, the ghost in him began to utter cries of fear and rage, such as one hears from people who are being branded or racked; and the ghost swore that he would leave the young man alone and never take possession of any man again. But Apollonius addressed him with anger, as a master might a shifty, rascally, and shameless slave and so on, and he ordered him to quit the young man and show by a visible sign that he had done so. "I will throw down yonder statue," said the devil, and pointed to one of the images which were there in the king's portico, for there it was that the scene took place. But when the statue began by moving gently, and then fell down, it would defy anyone to describe the hubbub which arose thereat and the way they clapped their hand with wonder. But the young man rubbed his eyes as if he had just woken up, and he looked towards the rays of the sun, and assumed a modest aspect, as all had their attention concentrated on him; for he no longer showed himself licentious, nor did he stare madly about, but he had returned to his own self, as thoroughly as if he had been treated with drugs; and he gave up his dainty dress and summery garments and the rest of his sybaritic way of life, and he fell in love with the austerity of philosophers, and donned their cloak, and, stripping off his old self, modelled his life and future upon that of Apollonius.

Ghoulish Guile

Now there was in Corinth at that time a man named Demetrius, who studied philosophy and had embraced in his system all the masculine vigour of the Cynics. Of him Favorinus in several of his works subsequently made the most generous mention, and his attitude towards Apollonius was exactly that which they say Antisthenes took up towards the system of Socrates: for he followed him and was anxious to be his disciple, and was devoted to his doctrines, and converted to the side of Apollonius the more esteemed of his own pupils. Among the latter was Menippus, a Lycian of twenty-five years of age, well endowed with good judgment, and of a physique so beautifully proportioned that in mien he resembled a fine and gentlemanly athlete.

Now this Menippus was supposed by most people to be loved by a foreign woman, who was good-looking and extremely dainty, and said that she was rich; although she was really, as it turned out, not one of these things, but was only so in semblance. For as he was walking all alone along the road towards Cenchraea, he met with an apparition, and it was a woman who clasped his hand and declared that she had been long in love with him, and that she was a Phoenician woman and lived in a suburb of Corinth, and she mentioned the name of the particular suburb, and said, "When you reach the place this evening, you will hear my voice as I sing to you, and you shall have wine such as you never before drank, and there will be no rival to disturb you; and we two beautiful beings will live together." The youth consented to this, for although he was in general a strenuous philosopher, he was nevertheless susceptible to the tender passion; and he visited her in the evening, and for the future constantly sought her company as his darling, for he did not yet realize that she was a mere apparition.

Then Apollonius looked over Menippus as a sculptor might do, and he sketched an outline of the youth and examined him, and having observed his foibles, he said, "You are a fine youth and are hunted by fine women, but in this case you are cherishing a serpent, and a serpent cherishes you." And when Menippus expressed his surprise, he added, "For this lady is of a kind you cannot marry. Why should you? Do you think that she loves you?" "Indeed I do," said the youth, "since she behaves to me as if she loves me." "And would you then marry her?" said Apollonius. "Why, yes, for it would be delightful to marry a woman who loves you." Thereupon Apollonius asked when the wedding was to be. "Perhaps tomorrow," said the other, "for it brooks no delay." Apollonius therefore waited for the occasion of the wedding breakfast, and then, presenting himself before the guests who had just arrived, he said, "Where is the dainty lady at whose instance ye are come?" "Here she is," replied Menippus, and at the same moment he rose slightly from his seat, blushing. "And to which of you belong the silver and gold and all the rest of the decorations of the banqueting hall?" "To the lady," replied the youth, "for this is all I have of my own," Menippus said, pointing to the philosopher's cloak which he wore.

And Apollonius said, "Have you heard of the gardens of Tantalus, how they exist and yet do not exist?" "Yes," they answered, "in the poems of Homer, for we certainly never went down to Hades." "As such," replied Apollonius, "you must regard this adornment, for it is not reality but the semblance of reality. And that you may realize the truth of what I say, this fine bride is one of the vampires, that is to say of those beings whom the many regard as lamias and hobgoblins. These beings fall in love, and they are devoted to the delights of Aphrodite, but especially to the flesh of human beings, and they decoy with such delights those whom they mean to devour in their feasts." And the lady said, "Cease your ill-omened talk and begone." And she pretended to be disgusted at what she heard, and in fact she was inclined to rail at philosophers and say that they always talked nonsense. When, however, the goblets of gold and the show of silver were proved as light as air and all fluttered away out of their sight, while the wine-bearers and the cooks and all the retinue of servants vanished before the rebukes of Apollonius, the phantom pretended to weep, and prayed him not to torture her nor to compel her to confess what she really was. But Apollonius insisted and would not let her off, and then she admitted that she was a vampire, and was fattening up Menippus with pleasures before devouring his body, for it was her habit to feed upon young and beautiful bodies, because their blood is pure and strong. I have related at length, because it was necessary to do so, this the best-known story of Apollonius; for many people are aware of it and know that the incident occurred in the centre of Hellas; but they have only heard in a general and vague manner that he once caught and overcame a lamia in Corinth, but they have never learned what she was about, nor that he did it to save Menippus, but I owe my own account to Damis and to the work which he wrote.

Taming the Satyr

After passing the cataracts [of the Nile River], [Apollonius and his company] halted in a village of the Ethiopians of no great size, and they were dining, towards the evening, mingling in their conversation the grave with the gay, when all on a sudden they heard the women of the village screaming and calling to one another to join in the pursuit and catch the thing; and they also summoned their husbands to help them in the matter. And the latter caught up sticks and stones and anything which came handy, and called upon one another to avenge the insult to their wives. And it appears that for ten months the ghost of a satyr had been haunting the village, who was mad after the women and was said to have killed two of them to whom he was supposed to be specially attached.

The companions, then, of Apollonius were frightened out of their wits till Apollonius said, "You need not be afraid, for it's only a satyr that is running amuck here." "Yes, by Zeus," said Nilus, "it's the one that we naked sages have found insulting us for a long time past and we could never stop his jumps and leaps." "But," said Apollonius, "I have a remedy against these hellhounds, which Midas is said once to have employed; for Midas himself had some of the blood of satyrs in his veins, as was clear from the shape of his ears; and a satyr once, trespassing on his kinship with Midas, made merry at the expense of his ears, not only singing about them, but piping about them. Well, Midas, I understand, had heard from his mother that when a satyr is overcome by wine he falls asleep, and at such times comes to his senses and will make friends with you; so he mixed wine which he had in his palace in a fountain and let the satyr get at it, and the latter drank it up and was overcome. And to show that the story is true, let us go to the head man of the village, and if the villagers have any wine, we will mix it with water for the satyr and he will share the fate of Midas's satyr."

They thought it a good plan, so he poured four Egyptian jars of wine into the trough out of which the village cattle drank, and then called the satyr by means of some secret rebuke or threat; and though as yet the latter was not visible, the wine sensibly diminished as if it was being drunk up. And when it was quite finished, Apollonius said, "Let us make peace with the satyr, for he is fast asleep." And with these words he led the villagers to the cave of the nymphs, which was not quite a furlong away from the village; and he showed them a satyr lying fast asleep in it, but he told them not to hit him or abuse him, "For," he said, "his nonsense is stopped for ever."

Such was this exploit of Apollonius, and, by heavens, we may call it not an incidental work in passing, but a masterwork of his passing by; and if you read the sage's epistle, in which he wrote to an insolent young man that he had sobered even a satyr demon in Ethiopia, you will perforce call to mind the above story. But we must not disbelieve that satyrs both exist and are susceptible to the passion of love; for I knew a youth of my own age in Lemnos whose mother was said to be visited by a satyr, as he well might to judge by this story; for he was represented as wearing in his back a fawn-skin that exactly fitted him, the front paws of which were drawn around his neck and fastened over his chest. But I must not go further into this subject; but, anyhow, credit is due as much to experience of facts as it is to myself.

Letters from Pliny
Pliny the Younger

The following two letters were written by the ancient Roman lawyer, author, and magistrate Pliny the Younger (*c.* 61 AD–*c.* 113 AD), who details several ghostly accounts from the time.

Letter to Sura

Our leisure furnishes me with the opportunity of learning from you, and you with that of instructing me. Accordingly, I particularly wish to know whether you think there exist such things as phantoms, possessing an appearance peculiar to themselves, and a certain supernatural power, or that mere empty delusions receive a shape from our fears. For my part, I am led to believe in their existence, especially by what I hear happened to Curtius Rufus. While still in humble circumstances and obscure, he was a hanger-on in the suite of the Governor of Africa. While pacing the colonnade one afternoon, there appeared to him a female form of superhuman size and beauty. She informed the terrified man that she was "Africa," and had come to foretell future events; for that he would go to Rome, would fill offices of state there, and would even return to that same province with the highest powers, and die in it. All which things were fulfilled. Moreover, as he touched at Carthage, and was disembarking from his ship, the same form is said to have presented itself to him on the shore. It is certain that, being seized with illness, and auguring the future from the past and misfortune from his previous prosperity, he himself abandoned all hope of life, though none of those about him despaired.

Is not the following story again still more appalling and not less marvellous? I will relate it as it was received by me:

There was at Athens a mansion, spacious and commodious, but of evil repute and dangerous to health. In the dead of night there was a noise as of iron, and, if you listened more closely, a clanking of chains was heard, first of all from a distance, and afterwards hard by. Presently a spectre used to appear, an ancient man sinking with emaciation and squalor, with a long beard and bristly hair, wearing shackles on his legs and fetters on his hands, and shaking them. Hence the inmates, by reason of their fears, passed miserable and horrible nights in sleeplessness. This want of sleep was followed by disease, and, their terrors increasing, by death. For in the daytime as well, though the apparition had departed, yet a reminiscence of it flitted before their eyes, and their dread outlived its cause. The mansion was accordingly deserted, and, condemned to solitude, was entirely abandoned to the dreadful ghost. However, it was advertised, on the chance of someone, ignorant of the fearful curse attached to it, being willing to buy or to rent it.

Athenodorus, the philosopher, came to Athens and read the advertisement. When he had been informed of the terms, which were so low as to appear suspicious, he made inquiries, and learned the whole of the particulars. Yet nonetheless on that account, nay, all the more readily, did he rent the house. As evening began to draw on, he ordered a sofa to be set for himself in the front part of the house, and called for his notebooks, writing implements, and a light. The whole of his servants he dismissed to the interior apartments, and for himself applied his soul, eyes, and hand to composition, that his mind might not, from want of occupation, picture to itself the phantoms of which he had heard, or any empty terrors. At the commencement there was the universal silence of night. Soon the shaking of irons and the clanking of chains was heard, yet he never raised his eyes nor slackened his pen, but hardened his soul and deadened his ears by its help. The noise grew and approached: now it seemed to be heard at the door, and next inside the door. He looked round, beheld and recognized the figure he had been told of. It was standing and signalling to him with its finger, as though inviting him. He, in reply, made a sign with his hand that it should wait a moment, and applied himself afresh to his tablets and pen. Upon this the figure kept rattling its chains over his head as he wrote. On looking round again, he saw it making the same signal as before, and without delay took up a light and followed it. It moved with a slow step, as though oppressed by its chains, and, after turning into the courtyard of the house, vanished suddenly and left his company. On being thus left to himself, he marked the spot with some grass and leaves which he plucked. Next day he applied to the magistrates, and urged them to have the spot in question dug up. There were found there some bones attached to and intermingled with fetters; the body to which they had belonged, rotted away by time and the soil, had abandoned them thus naked and corroded to the chains. They were collected and interred at the public expense, and the house was ever afterwards free from the spirit, which had obtained due sepulture.

The above story I believe on the strength of those who affirm it. What follows I am myself in a position to affirm to others. I have a freedman, who is not without some knowledge of letters. A younger brother of his was sleeping with him in the same bed. The latter dreamed he saw some one sitting on the couch, who approached with a pair of scissors to his head, and even cut the hair from the crown of it. When day dawned, he was found to be cropped round the crown, and his locks were discovered lying about. A very short time afterwards, a fresh occurrence of the same kind confirmed the truth of the former one. A lad of mine was sleeping, in company with several others, in the pages' apartment. There came through the windows (so he tells the story) two figures in white tunics, who cut his hair as he lay, and departed the way they came. In his case, too, daylight exhibited him shorn, and his locks scattered around. Nothing remarkable followed, except, perhaps, this, that I was not brought under accusation, as I should have been, if Domitian (in whose reign these events happened) had lived longer. For in his desk was found an information against me which had been presented by Carus; from which circumstance it may be conjectured – inasmuch as it is the custom of accused persons to let their hair grow – that the cutting off of my slaves' hair was a sign of the danger which threatened me being averted.

I beg, then, that you will apply your great learning to this subject. The matter is one which deserves long and deep consideration on your part; nor am I, for my part, undeserving of having the fruits of your wisdom imparted to me. You may even argue on both sides (as your way is), provided you argue more forcibly on one side than the other, so as not to dismiss me in suspense and anxiety, when the very cause of my consulting you has been to have my doubts put an end to.

Letter to Nonius Maximus

I am deeply afflicted with the news I have received of the death of Fannius; in the first place, because I loved one so eloquent and refined, in the next, because I was accustomed to be guided by his judgment – and indeed he possessed great natural acuteness, improved by practice, rendering him able to see a thing in an instant. There are some circumstances about his death which aggravate my concern. He left behind him a will which had been made a considerable time before his decease, by which it happens that his estate is fallen into the hands of those who had incurred his displeasure, whilst his greatest favourites are excluded. But what I particularly regret is that he has left unfinished a very noble work in which he was employed. Notwithstanding his full practice at the bar, he had begun a history of those persons who were put to death or banished by Nero, and completed three books of it. They are written with great elegance and precision; the style is pure, and preserves a proper medium between the plain narrative and the historical; and, as they were very favourably received by the public, he was the more desirous of being able to finish the rest. The hand of death is ever, in my opinion, too untimely and sudden when it falls upon such as are employed in some immortal work. The sons of sensuality, who have no outlook beyond the present hour, put an end every day to all motives for living, but those who look forward to posterity, and endeavour to transmit their names with honour to future generations by their works – to such, death is always immature, as it still snatches them from amidst some unfinished design.

Fannius, long before his death, had a presentiment of what has happened: he dreamed one night that as he was lying on his couch, in an undress, all ready for his work, and with his desk, as usual, in front of him, Nero entered and, placing himself by his side, took up the three first books of this history, which he read through and then departed. This dream greatly alarmed him, and he regarded it as an intimation, that he should not carry on his history any farther than Nero had read, and so the event has proved. I cannot reflect upon this accident without lamenting that he was prevented from accomplishing a work which had cost him so many toilsome vigils, as it suggests to me, at the same time, reflections on my own mortality, and the fate of my writings: and I am persuaded the same apprehensions alarm you for those in which you are at present employed. Let us then, my friend, while life permits, exert all our endeavours, that death, whenever it arrives, may find as little as possible to destroy. Farewell.

The Story of Damon
Plutarch

Peripoltas, the soothsayer, after he had brought back King Opheltas and the people under him to Boeotia, left a family which remained in high repute for many generations, and chiefly settled in Chaeronea, which was the first city which they conquered when they drove out the barbarians. As the men of this race were all brave and warlike, they were almost reduced to extinction in the wars with the Persians, and in later times with the Gauls during their invasion of Greece, so that there remained but one male of the family, a youth of the name of Damon, who was surnamed Peripoltas, and who far surpassed all the youth of his time in beauty and spirit, although he was uneducated and harsh-tempered. The commander of a detachment of Roman soldiers who were quartered during the winter in Chaeronea conceived a criminal passion for Damon, who was then a mere lad, and as he could not effect his purpose by fair means, it was evident that he would not hesitate to use force, as our city was then much decayed, and was despised, being so small and poor. Damon, alarmed and irritated at the man's behaviour, formed a conspiracy with a few young men of his own age, not many, for secrecy's sake, but consisting of sixteen in all. These men smeared their faces with soot, excited themselves by strong drink, and assaulted the Roman officer just at daybreak, while he was offering sacrifice in the marketplace. They killed him and several of his attendants, and then made their escape out of the city. During the confusion which followed, the senate of the city of Chaeronea assembled and condemned the conspirators to death – a decree which was intended to excuse the city to the Romans for what had happened. But that evening, when the chief magistrates, as is their custom, were dining together, Damon and his party broke into the senate-house, murdered them all, and again escaped out of the city. It chanced that at this time Lucius Lucullus was passing near Chaeronea with an armed force. He halted his troops, and, after investigating the circumstances, declared that the city was not to blame, but had been the injured party. As for Damon, who was living by brigandage and plunder of the country, and who threatened to attack the city itself, the citizens sent an embassy to him, and passed a decree guaranteeing his safety if he would return. When he returned they appointed him president of the gymnasium, and afterwards, while he was being anointed in the public baths, they murdered him there.

Our ancestors tell us that as ghosts used to appear in that place, and groans were heard there, the doors of the bath room were built up; and even at the present day those who live near the spot imagine that shadowy forms are to be seen, and confused cries heard. Those of his family who survive (for there are some descendants of Damon) live chiefly in Phokis, near the city of Steiris. They call themselves Asbolomeni, which in the Aeolian dialect means "sooty-faced," in memory of Damon having smeared his face with soot when he committed his crimes.

The Vision of Marcus Brutus
Plutarch

About the time that [Marcus Brutus and his army] were going to pass out of Asia into Europe, it is said that a wonderful sign was seen by Brutus. He was naturally given to much watching, and by practice and moderation in his diet had reduced his allowance of sleep to a very small amount of time. He never slept in the daytime, and in the night then only when all his business was finished, and when, everyone else being gone to rest, he had nobody to discourse with him. But at this time, the war being begun, having the whole state of it to consider and being solicitous of the event, after his first sleep, which he let himself take after his supper, he spent all the rest of the night in settling his most urgent affairs; which if he could dispatch early and so make a saving of any leisure, he employed himself in reading until the third watch, at which time the centurions and tribunes were used to come to him for orders.

Thus, one night before he passed out of Asia, he was very late all alone in his tent, with a dim light burning by him, all the rest of the camp being hushed and silent; and reasoning about something with himself and very thoughtful, he fancied someone came in, and, looking up towards the door, he saw a terrible and strange appearance of an unnatural and frightful body standing by him without speaking. Brutus boldly asked it, "What are you, of men or gods, and upon what business come to me?" The figure answered, "I am your evil genius, Brutus; you shall see me at Philippi." To which Brutus, not at all disturbed, replied, "Then I shall see you."

As soon as the apparition vanished, he called his servants to him, who all told him that they had neither heard any voice nor seen any vision. So then he continued watching till the morning, when he went to Cassius, and told him of what he had seen. He, who followed the principles of Epicurus's philosophy, and often used to dispute with Brutus concerning matters of this nature, spoke to him thus upon this occasion: "It is the opinion of our sect, Brutus, that not all that we feel or see is real and true; but that the sense is a most slippery and deceitful thing, and the mind yet more quick and subtle to put the sense in motion and affect it with every kind of change upon no real occasion of fact; just as an impression is made upon wax; and the soul of man, which has in itself both what imprints and what is imprinted on, may most easily, by its own operations, produce and assume every variety of shape and figure. This is evident from the sudden changes of our dreams; in which the imaginative principle, once started by anything matter, goes through a whole series of most diverse emotions and appearances. It is its nature to be ever in motion, and its motion is fantasy or conception. But besides all this, in your case, the body, being tired and distressed with continual toil, naturally works upon the mind, and keeps it in an excited and unusual condition. But that there should be any such thing as supernatural beings, or, if there were, that they should have human shape or voice or power that can reach to us, there is no reason for believing; though I confess I could wish that there were such beings, that we might not rely upon our arms only, and our horses and our navy, all which are so numerous and powerful, but might be confident of the assistance of gods also, in this our most sacred and honourable attempt." With such discourses as these Cassius soothed the mind of Brutus. But just as the troops were going on board, two eagles flew and lighted on the first two ensigns, and crossed over the water with them, and never ceased following the soldiers and being fed by them till they came to Philippi, and there, but one day before the fight, they both flew away.

Brutus had already reduced most of the places and people of these parts; but they now marched on as far as to the coast opposite Thasos, and, if there were any city or man of power that yet stood out, brought them all to subjection. At this point Norbanus was encamped in a place called the Straits, near Symbolum. Him they surrounded in such sort that they forced him to dislodge and quit the place; and Norbanus narrowly escaped losing his whole army, Caesar by reason of sickness being too far behind; only Antony came to his relief with such wonderful swiftness that Brutus and those with him did not believe when they heard he was come. Caesar came up ten days after, and encamped over against Brutus, and Antony over against Cassius.

The space between the two armies is called by the Romans the Campi Philippi. Never had two such large Roman armies come together to engage each other. That of Brutus was somewhat less in number than that of Caesar, but in the splendidness of the men's arms and richness of their equipage it wonderfully exceeded; for most of their arms were of gold and silver, which Brutus had lavishly bestowed among them. For though in other things he had accustomed his commanders to use all frugality and self-control, yet he thought that the riches which soldiers carried about them in their hands and on their bodies would add something of spirit to those that were desirous of glory, and would make those that were covetous and lovers of gain fight the more valiantly to preserve the arms which were their estate.

Caesar made a view and lustration of his army within his trenches, and distributed only a little corn and but five drachmas to each soldier for the sacrifice they were to make. But Brutus, either pitying this poverty, or disdaining this meanness of spirit in Caesar, first, as the custom was, made a general muster and lustration of the army in the open field, and then distributed a great number of beasts for sacrifice to every regiment, and fifty drachmas to every soldier; so that in the love of his soldiers and their readiness to fight for him Brutus had much the advantage.

But at the time of lustration it is reported that an unlucky omen happened to Cassius; for his lictor, presenting him with a garland that he was to wear at sacrifice, gave it him the wrong way up. Further, it is said that some time before, at a certain solemn procession, a golden image of Victory, which was carried before Cassius, fell down by a slip of him that carried it. Besides this there appeared many birds of prey daily about the camp, and swarms of bees were seen in a place within the trenches, which place the soothsayers ordered to be shut out from the camp, to remove the superstition which insensibly began to infect even Cassius himself and shake him in his Epicurean philosophy, and had wholly seized and subdued the soldiers; from whence it was that Cassius was reluctant to put all to the hazard of a present battle, but advised rather to draw out the war until further time, considering that they were stronger in money and provisions, but in numbers of men and arms inferior. But Brutus, on the contrary, was still, as formerly, desirous to come with all speed to the decision of a battle; that so he might either restore his country to her liberty, or else deliver from their misery all those numbers of people whom they harassed with the expenses and the service and exactions of the war. And finding also his light-horse in several skirmishes still to have had the better, he was the more encouraged and resolved; and some of the soldiers having deserted and gone to the enemy, and others beginning to accuse and suspect one another, many of Cassius's friends in the council changed their opinions to that of Brutus. But there was one of Brutus's party, named Atellius, who opposed his resolution, advising rather that they should tarry over the winter. And when Brutus asked him in how much better a condition he hoped to be a year after, his answer was, "If I gain nothing else, yet I shall live so much the longer." Cassius was much displeased at this answer; and among the rest, Atellius was had in much disesteem for it. And so it was presently resolved to give battle the next day.

Brutus that night at supper showed himself very cheerful and full of hope, and reasoned on subjects of philosophy with his friends, and afterwards went to his rest. But Messala says that Cassius supped privately with a few of his nearest acquaintance, and appeared thoughtful and silent, contrary to his temper and custom; that after supper he took him earnestly by the hand, and speaking to him, as his manner was when he wished to show affection, in Greek, said, "Bear witness for me, Messala, that I am brought into the same necessity as Pompey the Great was before me, of hazarding the liberty of my country upon one battle; yet ought we to be of courage, relying on our good fortune, which it were unfair to mistrust, though we take evil counsels." These, Messala says, were the last words that Cassius spoke before he bade him farewell; and that he was invited to sup with him the next night, being his birthday.

As soon as it was morning, the signal of battle, the scarlet coat, was set out in Brutus's and Cassius's camps, and they themselves met in the middle space between their two armies. There Cassius spoke thus to Brutus: "Be it as we hope, O Brutus, that this day we may overcome, and all the rest of our time may live a happy life together; but since the greatest of human concerns are the most uncertain, and since it may be difficult for us ever to see one another again, if the battle should go against us, tell me, what is your resolution concerning flight and death?" Brutus answered, "When I was young, Cassius, and unskilful in affairs, I was led, I know not how, into uttering a bold sentence in philosophy, and blamed Cato for killing himself, as thinking it an irreligious act, and not a valiant one among men, to try to evade the divine course of things, and not fearlessly to receive and undergo the evil that shall happen, but run away from it. But now in my own fortunes I am of another mind; for if Providence shall not dispose what we now undertake according to our wishes, I resolve to put no further hopes or warlike preparations to the proof, but will die contented with my fortune. For I already have given up my life to my country on the Ides of March; and have lived since then a second life for her sake, with liberty and honour."

Cassius at these words smiled, and, embracing Brutus said, "With these resolutions let us go on upon the enemy; for either we ourselves shall conquer, or have no cause to fear those that do." After this they discoursed among their friends about the ordering of the battle; and Brutus desired of Cassius that he might command the right wing, though it was thought that this was more fit for Cassius, in regard both of his age and his experience. Yet even in this Cassius complied with Brutus, and placed Messala with the valiantest of all his legions in the same wing, so Brutus immediately drew out his horse, excellently well equipped, and was not long in bringing up his foot after them.

Antony's soldiers were casting trenches from the marsh by which they were encamped, across the plain, to cut off Cassius's communications with the sea. Caesar was to be at hand with his troops to support them, but he was not able to be present himself, by reason of his sickness; and his soldiers, not much expecting that the enemy would come to a set battle, but only make some excursions with their darts and light arms to disturb the men at work in the trenches, and not taking notice of the boons drawn up against them ready to give battle, were amazed when they heard the confused and great outcry that came from the trenches. In the meanwhile Brutus had sent his tickets, in which was the word of battle, to the officers; and himself riding about to all the troops, encouraged the soldiers; but there were but few of them that understood the word before they engaged; the most of them, not staying to have it delivered to them, with one impulse and cry ran upon the enemy. This disorder caused an unevenness in the line, and the legions got severed and divided one from another; that of Messala first, and afterwards the other adjoining, went beyond the left wing of Caesar; and having just touched the extremity, without slaughtering any great number, passing round that wing, fell directly into Caesar's camp. Caesar himself, as his own memoirs tell us, had but just before been conveyed away, Marcus Artorius, one of his friends, having had a dream bidding Caesar be carried out of the camp. And it was believed that he was slain; for the soldiers had pierced his litter, which was left empty, in many places with their darts and pikes. There was a great slaughter in the camp that was taken, and two thousand Lacedaemonians that were newly come to the assistance of Caesar were all cut off together.

The rest of the army, which had not gone round but had engaged the front, easily overthrew them, finding them in great disorder, and slew upon the place three legions; and being carried on with the stream of victory, pursuing those that fled, fell into the camp with them, Brutus himself being there. But they that were conquered took the advantage in their extremity of what the conquerors did not consider. For they fell upon that part of the main body which had been left exposed and separated, where the right wing had broke off from them and hurried away in the pursuit; yet they could not break into the midst of their battle, but were received with strong resistance and obstinacy. Yet they put to flight the left wing, where Cassius commanded, being in great disorder, and ignorant of what had passed on the other wing; and, pursuing them to their camp, they pillaged and destroyed it, neither of their generals being present; for Antony, they say, to avoid the fury of the first onset, had retired into the marsh that was hard by; and Caesar was nowhere to be found after his being conveyed out of the tents; though some of the soldiers showed Brutus their swords bloody, and declared that they had killed him, describing his person and his age.

By this time also the centre of Brutus's battle had driven back their opponents with great slaughter; and Brutus was everywhere plainly conqueror, as on the other side Cassius was conquered. And this one mistake was the ruin of their affairs, that Brutus did not come to the relief of Cassius, thinking that he, as well as himself, was conqueror; and that Cassius did not expect the relief of Brutus, thinking that he too was overcome. For as a proof that the victory was on Brutus's side, Messala urges his taking three eagles and many ensigns of the enemy without losing any of his own.

But now, returning from the pursuit after having plundered Caesar's camp, Brutus wondered that he could not see Cassius's tent standing high, as it was wont, and appearing above the rest, nor other things appearing as they had been; for they had been immediately pulled down and pillaged by the enemy upon their first falling into the camp. But some that had a quicker and longer sight than the rest acquainted Brutus that they saw a great deal of shining armour and silver targets moving to and fro in Cassius's camp, and that they thought, by their number and the fashion of their armour, they could not be those that they left to guard the camp; but yet that there did not appear so great a number of dead bodies thereabouts as it was probable there would have been after the actual defeat of so many legions. This first made Brutus suspect Cassius's misfortune, and, leaving a guard in the enemy's camp, he called back those that were in the pursuit, and rallied them together to lead them to the relief of Cassius, whose fortune had been as follows.

First, he had been angry at the onset that Brutus's soldiers made, without the word of battle or command to charge. Then, after they had overcome, he was as much displeased to see them rush on to the plunder and spoil, and neglect to surround and encompass the rest of the enemy. Besides this, letting himself act by delay and expectation, rather than command boldly and with a clear purpose, he got hemmed in by the right wing of the enemy, and, his horse making with all haste their escape and flying towards the sea, the foot also began to give way, which he perceiving laboured as much as ever he could to hinder their flight and bring them back; and, snatching an ensign out of the hand of one that fled, he stuck it at his feet, though he could hardly keep even his own personal guard together. So that at last he was forced to fly with a few about him to a little hill that overlooked the plain. But he himself, being weak-sighted, discovered nothing, only the destruction of his camp, and that with difficulty. But they that were with him saw a great body of horse moving towards him, the same whom Brutus had sent. Cassius believed these were enemies, and in pursuit of him; however, he sent away Titinius, one of those that were with him, to learn what they were.

As soon as Brutus's horse saw him coming, and knew him to be a friend and a faithful servant of Cassius, those of them that were his more familiar acquaintance, shouting out for joy and alighting from their horses, shook hands and embraced him, and the rest rode round about him singing and shouting, through their excess of gladness at the sight of him. But this was the occasion of the greatest mischief that could be. For Cassius really thought that Titinius had been taken by the enemy, and cried out, "Through too much fondness of life, I have lived to endure the sight of my friend taken by the enemy before my face." After which words he retired into an empty tent, taking along with him only Pindarus, one of his freedmen, whom he had reserved for such an occasion ever since the disasters in the expedition against the Parthians, when Crassus was slain. From the Parthians he came away in safety; but now, pulling up his mantle over his head, he made his neck bare, and held it forth to Pindarus, commanding him to strike. The head was certainly found lying severed from the body. But no man ever saw Pindarus after, from which some suspected that he had killed his master without his command. Soon after they perceived who the horsemen were, and saw Titinius, crowned with garlands, making what haste he could towards Cassius. But as soon as he understood by the cries and lamentations of his afflicted friends the unfortunate error and death of his general, he drew his sword, and having very much accused and upbraided his own long stay, that had caused it, he slew himself.

Brutus, as soon as he was assured of the defeat of Cassius, made haste to him; but heard nothing of his death till he came near his camp. Then having lamented over his body, calling him "the last of the Romans," it being impossible that the city should ever produce another man of so great a spirit, he sent away the body to be buried at Thasos, lest celebrating his funeral within the camp might breed some disorder. He then gathered the soldiers together and comforted them; and, seeing them destitute of all things necessary, he promised to every man two thousand drachmas in recompense of what he had lost. They at these words took courage, and were astonished at the magnificence of the gift; and waited upon him at his parting with shouts and praises, magnifying him for the only general of all the four who was not overcome in the battle. And indeed the action itself testified that it was not without reason he believed he should conquer; for with a few legions he overthrew all that resisted him; and if all his soldiers had fought, and the most of them had not passed beyond the enemy in pursuit of the plunder, it is very likely that he had utterly defeated every part of them.

There fell of his side eight thousand men, reckoning the servants of the army, whom Brutus calls Briges; and on the other side, Messala says his opinion is that there were slain above twice that number. For which reason they were more out of heart than Brutus, until a servant of Cassius, named Demetrius, came in the evening to Antony, and brought to him the garment which he had taken from the dead body, and his sword; at the sight of which they were so encouraged, that, as soon as it was morning, they drew out their whole force into the field, and stood in battle array. But Brutus found both his camps wavering and in disorder; for his own, being filled with prisoners, required a guard more strict than ordinary over them; and that of Cassius was uneasy at the change of general, besides some envy and rancour, which those that were conquered bore to that part of the army which had been conquerors. Wherefore he thought it convenient to put his army in array, but to abstain from fighting. All the slaves that were taken prisoners, of whom there was a great number that were mixed up, not without suspicion, among the soldiers, he commanded to be slain; but of the freemen and citizens, some he dismissed, saying that among the enemy they were rather prisoners than with him, for with them they were captives and slaves, but with him freemen and citizens of Rome. But he was forced to hide and help them to escape privately, perceiving that his friends and officers were bent upon revenge against them.

Among the captives there was one Volumnius, a player, and Sacculio, a buffoon; of these Brutus took no manner of notice, but his friends brought them before him, and accused them that even then in that condition they did not refrain from their jests and scurrilous language. Brutus, having his mind taken up with other affairs, said nothing to their accusation; but the judgment of Messala Corvinus was, that they should be whipped publicly upon a stage, and so sent naked to the captains of the enemy, to show them what sort of fellow drinkers and companions they took with them on their campaigns. At this some that were present laughed; and Publius Casca, he that gave the first wound to Caesar, said, "We do ill to jest and make merry at the funeral of Cassius. But you, O Brutus," he added, "will show what esteem you have for the memory of that general, according as you punish or preserve alive those who will scoff and speak shamefully of him." To this Brutus, in great discomposure replied, "Why then, Casca, do you ask me about it, and not do yourselves what you think fitting?" This answer of Brutus was taken for his consent to the death of these wretched men; so they were carried away and slain.

After this he gave the soldiers the reward that he had promised them; and having slightly reproved them for having fallen upon the enemy in disorder without the word of battle or command, he promised them that if they behaved themselves bravely in the next engagement, he would give them up two cities to spoil and plunder, Thessalonica and Lacedaemon. This is the one indefensible thing of all that is found fault within the life of Brutus; though true it may be that Antony and Caesar were much more cruel in the rewards that they gave their soldiers after victory; for they drove out, one might almost say, all the old inhabitants of Italy, to put their soldiers in possession of other men's lands and cities. But indeed their only design and end in undertaking the war was to obtain dominion and empire, whereas Brutus, for the reputation of his virtue, could not be permitted either to overcome or save himself but with justice and honour, especially after the death of Cassius, who was generally accused of having been his adviser to some things that he had done with less clemency. But now, as in a ship, when the rudder is broken by a storm, the mariners fit and nail on some other piece of wood instead of it, striving against the danger not well, but as well as in that necessity they can, so Brutus, being at the head of so great an army, in a time of such uncertainty, having no commander equal to his need, was forced to make use of those that he had, and to do and to say many things according to their advice; which was, in effect, whatever might conduce to the bringing of Cassius's soldiers into better order. For they were very headstrong and intractable, bold and insolent in the camp for want of their general, but in the field cowardly and fearful, remembering that they had been beaten.

Neither were the affairs of Caesar and Antony in any better posture; for they were straitened for provision, and, the camp being in a low ground, they expected to pass a very hard winter. For being driven close upon the marshes, and a great quantity of rain, as is usual in autumn, having fallen after the battle, their tents were all filled with mire and water, which through the coldness of the weather immediately froze. And while they were in this condition, there was news brought to them of their loss at sea. For Brutus's fleet fell upon their ships, which were bringing a great supply of soldiers out of Italy, and so entirely defeated them, that but very few of the men escaped being slain, and they too were forced by famine to feed upon the sails and tackle of the ship. As soon as they heard this, they made what haste they could to come to the decision of a battle, before Brutus should have notice of his good success. For it had so happened that the fight both by sea and land was on the same day, but by some misfortune, rather than the fault of his commanders, Brutus knew not of his victory twenty days after. For had he been informed of this, he would not have been brought to a second battle, since he had sufficient provisions for his army for a long time, and was very advantageously posted, his camp being well sheltered from the cold weather, and almost inaccessible to the enemy, and his being absolute master of the sea, and having at land overcome on that side wherein he himself was engaged, would have made him full of hope and confidence. But it seems, the state of Rome not enduring any longer to be governed by many, but necessarily requiring a monarchy, the divine power, that it might remove out of the way the only man that was able to resist him that could control the empire, cut off his good fortune from coming to the ears of Brutus; though it came but a very little too late, for the very evening before the fight, Clodius, a deserter from the enemy, came and announced that Caesar had received advice of the loss of his fleet, and for that reason was in such haste to come to a battle. But his story met with no credit, nor was he so much as seen by Brutus, being simply set down as one that had had no good information, or invented lies to bring himself into favour.

The same night, they say, the vision appeared again to Brutus, in the same shape that it did before, but vanished without speaking. But Publius Volumnius, a philosopher, and one that had from the beginning borne arms with Brutus, makes no mention of this apparition, but says that the first eagle was covered with a swarm of bees, and that there was one of the captains whose arm of itself sweated oil of roses, and, though they often dried and wiped it, yet it would not cease; and that immediately before the battle, two eagles falling upon each other fought in the space between the two armies, that the whole field kept incredible silence and all were intent upon the spectacle, until at last that which was on Brutus's side yielded and fled. But the story of the Ethiopian is very famous, who, meeting the standard-bearer at the opening of the gate of the camp, was cut to pieces by the soldiers, that took it for an ill omen.

Brutus, having brought his army into the field and set them in array against the enemy, paused a long while before he would fight; for, as he was reviewing the troops, suspicions were excited, and information laid against some of them. Besides, he saw his horse not very eager to begin the action, and waiting to see what the foot would do. Then suddenly Camulatus, a very good soldier, and one whom for his valour he highly esteemed, riding hard by Brutus himself, went over to the enemy, the sight of which grieved Brutus exceedingly. So that partly out of anger, and partly out of fear of some greater treason and desertion, he immediately drew on his forces upon the enemy, the sun now declining, about three of the clock in the afternoon. Brutus on his side had the better, and pressed hard on the left wing, which gave way and retreated;

and the horse too fell in together with the foot, when they saw the
enemy in disorder. But the other wing, when the officers extended
the line to avoid its being encompassed, the numbers being inferior,
got drawn out too thin in the centre, and was so weak here that
they could not withstand the charge, but at the first onset fled. After
defeating these, the enemy at once took Brutus in the rear, who
all the while performed all that was possible for an expert general
and valiant soldier, doing everything in the peril, by counsel and by
hand, that might recover the victory. But that which had been his
superiority in the former fight was to his prejudice in this second.
For in the first fight, that part of the enemy which was beaten was
killed on the spot; but of Cassius's soldiers that fled, few had been
slain, and those that escaped, daunted with their defeat, infected
the other and larger part of the army with their want of spirit and
their disorder. Here Marcus, the son of Cato, was slain, fighting and
behaving himself with great bravery in the midst of the youth of the
highest rank and greatest valour. He would neither fly nor give the
least ground, but, still fighting and declaring who he was and naming
his father's name, he fell upon a heap of dead bodies of the enemy.
And of the rest, the bravest were slain in defending Brutus.

There was in the field one Lucilius, an excellent man and a friend
of Brutus, who, seeing some barbarian horse taking no notice of any
other in the pursuit, but galloping at full speed after Brutus, resolved
to stop them, though with the hazard of his life; and, letting himself
fall a little behind, he told them that he was Brutus. They believed
him the rather, because he prayed to be carried to Antony, as if he
feared Caesar, but durst trust him. They, overjoyed with their prey,
and thinking themselves wonderfully fortunate, carried him along
with them in the night, having first sent messengers to Antony of

their coming. He was much pleased, and came to meet them; and all the rest that heard that Brutus was taken and brought alive, flocked together to see him, some pitying his fortune, others accusing him of a meanness unbecoming his former glory, that out of too much love of life he would be a prey to barbarians.

When they came near together, Antony stood still, considering with himself in what manner he should receive Brutus. But Lucilius, being brought up to him, with great confidence said, "Be assured, Antony, that no enemy either has taken or ever shall take Marcus Brutus alive (forbid it, heaven, that fortune should ever so much prevail above virtue), but he shall be found, alive or dead, as becomes himself. As for me, I am come hither by a cheat that I put upon your soldiers, and am ready, upon this occasion, to suffer any severities you will inflict." All were amazed to hear Lucilius speak these words. But Antony, turning himself to those that brought him, said, "I perceive, my fellow soldiers, that you are concerned and take it ill that you have been thus deceived, and think yourselves abused and injured by it; but know that you have met with a booty better than that you sought. For you were in search of an enemy, but you have brought me here a friend. For indeed I am uncertain how I should have used Brutus, if you had brought him alive; but of this I am sure, that it is better to have such men as Lucilius our friends than our enemies." Having said this, he embraced Lucilius, and for the present commended him to the care of one of his friends, and ever after found him a steady and a faithful friend.

Brutus had now passed a little brook, running among trees and under steep rocks, and, it being night, would go no further, but sat down in a hollow place with a great rock projecting before it, with a few of his officers and friends about him. At first, looking up to heaven, that was then full of stars, he repeated two verses, one of which, Volumnius writes, was this:

Punish, great Jove, the author of these ills.

The other he says he has forgot. Soon after, naming severally all his friends that had been slain before his face in the battle, he groaned heavily, especially at the mentioning of Flavius and Labeo, the latter his lieutenant, and the other chief officer of his engineers. In the meantime, one of his companions, that was very thirsty and saw Brutus in the same condition, took his helmet and ran to the brook for water, when, a noise being heard from the other side of the river, Volumnius, taking Dardanus, Brutus's armour-bearer, with him, went out to see what it was. They returned in a short space, and inquired about the water. Brutus, smiling with much meaning, said to Volumnius, "It is all drunk; but you shall have some more fetched." But he that had brought the first water, being sent again, was in great danger of being taken by the enemy, and, having received a wound, with much difficulty escaped.

Now, Brutus guessing that not many of his men were slain in the fight, Statyllius undertook to dash through the enemy (for there was no other way), and to see what was become of their camp; and promised, if he found all things there safe, to hold up a torch for a signal, and then return. The torch was held up, for Statyllius got safe to the camp; but when after a long time he did not return, Brutus said, "If Statyllius be alive, he will come back." But it happened that in his return he fell into the enemy's hands, and was slain.

The night now being far spent, Brutus, as he was sitting, leaned his head towards his servant Clitus and spoke to him; he answered him not, but fell a weeping. After that, he drew aside his armour-bearer, Dardanus, and had some discourse with him in private. At last, speaking to Volumnius in Greek, he reminded him of their common studies and former discipline, and begged that he would take hold of his sword with him, and help him to thrust it through him. Volumnius put away his request, and several others did the like; and someone saying that there was no staying there but they needs must fly, Brutus, rising up, said, "Yes, indeed, we must fly, but not with our feet, but with our hands." Then giving each of them his right hand, with a countenance full of pleasure, he said that he found an infinite satisfaction in this, that none of his friends had been false to him; that as for fortune, he was angry with that only for his country's sake; as for himself, he thought himself much more happy than they who had overcome, not only as he had been a little time ago, but even now in his present condition; since he was leaving behind him such a reputation of his virtue as none of the conquerors with all their arms and riches should ever be able to acquire, no more than they could hinder posterity from believing and saying, that, being unjust and wicked men, they had destroyed the just and the good, and usurped a power to which they had no right.

After this, having exhorted and entreated all about him to provide for their own safety, he withdrew from them with two or three only of his peculiar friends; Strato was one of these, with whom he had contracted an acquaintance when they studied rhetoric together. Him he placed next to himself, and, taking hold of the hilt of his sword and directing it with both his hands, he fell upon it, and killed himself. But others say that not he himself, but Strato, at the earnest entreaty of Brutus, turning aside his head, held the sword, upon which he violently throwing himself, it pierced his breast, and he immediately died. This same Strato, Messala, a friend of Brutus, being, after reconciled to Caesar, brought to him once at his leisure, and with tears in his eyes said, "This, O Caesar, is the man that did the last friendly office to my beloved Brutus." Upon which Caesar received him kindly; and had good use of him in his labours and his battles at Actium, being one of the Greeks that proved their bravery in his service. It is reported of Messala himself, that, when Caesar once gave him this commendation, that though he was his fiercest enemy at Philippi in the cause of Brutus, yet he had shown himself his most entire friend in the fight of Actium, he answered, "You have always found me, Caesar, on the best and justest side."

Brutus's dead body was found by Antony, who commanded the richest purple mantle that he had to be thrown over it, and afterwards the mantle being stolen, he found the thief, and had him put to death. He sent the ashes of Brutus to his mother Servilia. As for Porcia his wife, Nicolaus the philosopher and Valerius Maximus write, that, being desirous to die, but being hindered by her friends, who continually watched her, she snatched some burning charcoal out of the fire, and, shutting it close in her mouth, stifled herself, and died. Though there is a letter current from Brutus to his friends, in which he laments the death of Porcia, and accuses them for neglecting her so that she desired to die rather than languish with her disease. So that it seems Nicolaus was mistaken in the time; for this epistle (if it indeed is authentic, and truly Brutus's) gives us to understand the malady and love of Porcia, and the way in which her death occurred.

The Haunted Pantry
Gaius Suetonius Tranquillus

Augustus was born in the consulship of Marcus Tullius Cicero and Caius Antonius, upon the ninth of the calends of October (the 23rd September), a little before sunrise, in the quarter of the Palatine Hill, and the street called The Ox-Heads, where now stands a chapel dedicated to him, and built a little after his death. For, as it is recorded in the proceedings of the senate, when Caius Laetorius, a young man of a patrician family, in pleading before the senators for a lighter sentence, upon his being convicted of adultery, alleged, besides his youth and quality, that he was the possessor, and as it were the guardian, of the ground which the Divine Augustus first touched upon his coming into the world; and entreated that he might find favour, for the sake of that deity, who was in a peculiar manner his; an act of the senate was passed, for the consecration of that part of his house in which Augustus was born.

His nursery is shewn to this day, in a villa belonging to the family, in the suburbs of Velitrae; being a very small place, and much like a pantry. An opinion prevails in the neighbourhood, that he was also born there. Into this place no person presumes to enter, unless upon necessity, and with great devotion, from a belief, for a long time prevalent, that such as rashly enter it are seized with great horror and consternation, which a short while since was confirmed by a remarkable incident. For when a new inhabitant of the house had, either by mere chance, or to try the truth of the report, taken up his lodging in that apartment, in the course of the night, a few hours afterwards, he was thrown out by some sudden violence, he knew not how, and was found in a state of stupefaction, with the coverlid of his bed, before the door of the chamber.

Nero's Mother
Gaius Suetonius Tranquillus

His mother being used to make strict inquiry into what he said or did, and to reprimand him with the freedom of a parent, Nero was so much offended that he endeavoured to expose her to public resentment, by frequently pretending a resolution to quit the government, and retire to Rhodes. Soon afterwards, he deprived her of all honour and power, took from her the guard of Roman and German soldiers, banished her from the palace and from his society, and persecuted her in every way he could contrive; employing persons to harass her when at Rome with lawsuits, and to disturb her in her retirement from town with the most scurrilous and abusive language, following her about by land and sea. But being terrified with her menaces and violent spirit, he resolved upon her destruction, and thrice attempted it by poison. Finding, however, that she had previously secured herself by antidotes, he contrived machinery, by which the floor over her bedchamber might be made to fall upon her while she was asleep in the night. This design miscarrying likewise, through the little caution used by those who were in the secret, his next stratagem was to construct a ship which could be easily shivered, in hopes of destroying her either by drowning, or by the deck above her cabin crushing her in its fall. Accordingly, under colour of a pretended reconciliation, he wrote her an extremely affectionate letter, inviting her to Baiae, to celebrate with him the festival of Minerva. He had given private orders to the captains of the galleys which were to attend her, to shatter to pieces the ship in which she had come, by falling foul of it, but in such manner that it might appear to be done accidentally. He prolonged the entertainment, for the more convenient opportunity of executing the plot in the night; and at her return for Bauli, instead of the old ship which had conveyed her to Baiae, he offered that which he had contrived for her destruction. He attended her to the vessel in a very cheerful mood, and, at parting with her, kissed her breasts; after which he sat up very late in the night, waiting with great anxiety to learn the issue of his project.

But receiving information that everything had fallen out contrary to his wish, and that she had saved herself by swimming – not knowing what course to take, upon her freedman, Lucius Agerinus bringing word, with great joy, that she was safe and well, he privately dropped a poniard by him. He then commanded the freedman to be seized and put in chains, under pretence of his having been employed by his mother to assassinate him; at the same time ordering her to be put to death, and giving out, that, to avoid punishment for her intended crime, she had laid violent hands upon herself. Other circumstances, still more horrible, are related on good authority; as that he went to view her corpse, and handling her limbs, pointed out some blemishes, and commended other points; and that, growing thirsty during the survey, he called for drink. Yet he was never afterwards able to bear the stings of his own conscience for this atrocious act, although encouraged by the congratulatory addresses of the army, the senate, and people. He frequently affirmed that he was haunted by his mother's ghost, and persecuted with the whips and burning torches of the Furies. Nay, he attempted by magical rites to bring up her ghost from below, and soften her rage against him. When he was in Greece, he durst not attend the celebration of the Eleusinian mysteries, at the initiation of which, impious and wicked persons are warned by the voice of the herald from approaching the rites.

Kî Fâ, or, The Law of Sacrifices
Confucian Canon

According to the law of sacrifices, (Shun), the sovereign of the line of Yü, at the Great Associate sacrifice, gave the place of honour to Hwang Tî, and at the border sacrifice made Khû the correlate of Heaven; he sacrificed (also) to Kwan-hsü as his ancestor (on the throne) and to Yâo as his honoured predecessor.

The sovereigns of Hsiâ, at the corresponding sacrifice, gave the place of honour also to Hwang Tî, and made Khwan the correlate at the border sacrifice; they sacrificed to Kwan-hsü as their ancestor, and to Yü as their honoured predecessor.

Under Yin, they gave the place of honour to Khû, and made Ming the correlate at the border sacrifice; they sacrificed to Hsieh as their ancestor, and to Thang as their honoured predecessor.

Under Kâu they gave the place of honour to Khû, and made Kî the correlate at the border sacrifice, they sacrificed to King Wân as their ancestor, and to king Wân as their honoured predecessor.

With a blazing pile of wood on the Grand Altar they sacrificed to Heaven; by burying (the victim) in the Grand Mound, they sacrificed to the Earth. (In both cases) they used a red victim.

By burying a sheep and a pig at the (Altar of) Great Brightness, they sacrificed to the seasons. (With similar) victims they sacrificed to (the spirits of cold and heat, at the pit and the altar, using prayers of deprecation and petition; to the sun, at the (altar called the) royal palace; to the moon, at the (pit called the) light of the night; to the stars at the honoured place of gloom; to (the spirits of) flood and drought at the honoured altar of rain; to the (spirits of the) four quarters at the place of the four pits and altars; mountains, forests, streams, valleys, hills, and mounds, which are able to produce clouds, and occasion winds and rain, were all regarded as (dominated by) spirits.

He by whom all under the sky was held sacrificed to all spirits. The princes of states sacrificed to those which were in their own territories; to those which were not in their territories, they did not sacrifice.

Generally speaking, all born between heaven and earth were said to have their allotted times; the death of all creatures is spoken of as their dissolution; but man when dead is said to be in the ghostly state. There was no change in regard to these points in the five dynasties. What, the seven dynasties made changes in, were the assessors at the Great Associate and the border sacrifices, and the parties sacrificed to in the ancestral temple – they made no other changes.

The sovereigns, coming to the possession of the kingdom, divided the land and established the feudal principalities; they assigned (great) cities (to their nobles), and smaller towns (to their chiefs); they made ancestral temples, and the arrangements for altering the order of the spirit-tablets; they raised altars, and they cleared the ground around them for the performance of their sacrifices. In all these arrangements they made provision for the sacrifices according to the nearer or more remote kinship, and for the assignment of lands of greater or lesser amount.

Thus the king made for himself seven ancestral temples, with a raised altar and the surrounding area for each. The temples were his father's, his grandfather's, his great-grandfather's, his great-great-grandfather's, and the temple of his (high) ancestor. At all of these a sacrifice was offered every month. The temples of the more remote ancestors formed the receptacles for the tablets as they were displaced; they were two, and at these only the seasonal sacrifices were offered. For the removed tablet of one more remote, an altar was raised and its corresponding area; and on occasions of prayer at this altar and area, a sacrifice was offered, but if there was no prayer, there was no sacrifice. In the case of one still more remote, (there was no sacrifice) – he was left in his ghostly state.

A feudal prince made for himself five ancestral temples, with an altar and a cleared area about it for each. The temples were his father's, his grandfather's, and his great-grandfather's, in all of which a sacrifice was offered every month. In the temples of the great-great-grandfather, and that of the (high) ancestor only, the seasonal sacrifices were offered. For one beyond the high ancestor a special altar was raised, and for one still more remote, an area was prepared. If there were prayer at these, a sacrifice was offered; but if there were no prayer, there was no sacrifice. In the case of one still more remote, (there was no service) – he was left in his ghostly state.

A Great Officer made for himself three ancestral temples and two altars. The temples were his father's, his grandfather's, and his great-grandfather's. In this only the seasonal sacrifices were offered.

To the great-great-grandfather and the (high) ancestor there were no temples. If there were occasion for prayer to them, altars were raised, and sacrifices offered on them. An ancestor still more remote was left in his ghostly state.

An officer of the highest grade had two ancestral temples and one altar – the temples of his father and grandfather, at which only the seasonal sacrifices were presented. There was no temple for his great-grandfather. If there was occasion to pray to him, an altar was raised, and a sacrifice offered to him. Ancestors more remote were left in their ghostly state.

An officer in charge merely of one department had one ancestral temple – that, namely, of his father. There was no temple for his grandfather, but he was sacrificed to (in the father's temple). Ancestors beyond the grandfather were left in their ghostly state.

The mass of ordinary officers and the common people had no ancestral temple. Their dead were left in their ghostly state (to have offerings presented to them in the back apartment, as occasion required).

The king, for all the people, erected an altar to (the spirit of) the ground, called the Grand Altar, and one for himself, called the Royal Altar.

A feudal prince, for all his people, erected one called the altar of the state, and one for himself called the altar of the prince.

Great Officers and all below them in association erected such an altar, called the Appointed Altar.

The king, for all the people, appointed (seven altars for) the seven sacrifices – one to the superintendent of the lot; one in the central court, for the admission of light and the rain from the roofs; one at the gates of the city wall; one in the roads leading from the city; one for the discontented ghosts of kings who had died without posterity; one for the guardian of the door; and one for the guardian of the furnace. He also had seven corresponding altars for himself.

A feudal prince, for his state, appointed (five altars for) the five sacrifices – one for the superintendent of the lot; one in the central court, for the admission of light and rain; one at the gates of the city wall; one in the roads leading from the city; one for the discontented ghosts of princes who had died without posterity. He also had five corresponding altars for himself.

A Great Officer appointed (three altars for) the three sacrifice – one for the discontented ghosts of his predecessors who had died without posterity, one at the gates of his city, and one on the roads leading from it.

An officer of the first grade appointed (two altars for) the two sacrifices – one at the gates, and one on the roads (outside the gates).

Other officers and the common people had one (altar and one) sacrifice. Some raised one altar for the guardian of the door; and others, one for the guardian of the furnace.

The king, carrying down (his favour), sacrificed to five classes of those who had died prematurely – namely, to the rightful eldest sons (of former kings); to rightful grandsons; to rightful great-grandsons; to rightful great-great-grandsons; and to the rightful sons of these last.

A feudal prince, carrying down (his favour), sacrificed to three classes; a Great Officer similarly to two; another officer of the first grade and the common people sacrificed only to the son who had died prematurely.

According to the institutes of the sage kings about sacrifices, sacrifice should be offered to him who had given (good) laws to the people to him who had laboured to the death in the discharge of his duties, to him who had strengthened the state by his laborious toil, to him who had boldly and successfully met great calamities, and to him who had warded off great evils.

Such were the following: Nang, the son of the lord of Lî-shan, who possessed the kingdom, and showed how to cultivate all the cereals; Khî (the progenitor) of Kâu, who continued his work after the decay of Hsiâ, and was sacrificed to under the name of Kî; Hâu-thû, a son of the line of Kung-kung, that swayed the nine provinces, who was able to reduce them all to order, and was sacrificed to as the spirit of the ground; the Tî Khû, who could define all the zodiacal stars, and exhibit their times to the people; Yâo, who rewarded (the worthy), made the penal laws impartial, and the end of whose course was distinguished by his righteousness; Shun, who, toiling amid all his affairs, died in the country (far from his capital); Yü, (the son of) Khwan, who was kept a prisoner till death for trying to dam up the waters of the flood, while Yü completed the work, and atoned for his father's failure; Hwang Tî, who gave everything its right name, thereby showing the people how to avail themselves of its qualities; Kwan-hsü, who completed this work of Hwang Tî; Hsieh, who was Minister of Instruction, and perfected the (condition and manners of the) people; Ming, who, through his attention to the duties of his office, died in the waters; Thang, who ruled the people with a benignant sway and cut off their oppressor; and King Wân, who by his peaceful rule, and King Wû, who by his martial achievements, delivered the people from their afflictions. All these rendered distinguished services to the people.

A Teaching from Confucius
Zisi

The Master said, "How abundantly do spiritual beings display the powers that belong to them! We look for them, but do not see them; we listen to, but do not hear them; yet they enter into all things, and there is nothing without them. They cause all the people in the kingdom to fast and purify themselves, and array themselves in their richest dresses, in order to attend at their sacrifices. Then, like overflowing water, they seem to be over the heads, and on the right and left of their worshippers.

"It is said in the Book of Poetry, 'The approaches of the spirits, you cannot sunrise; and can you treat them with indifference?' Such is the manifestness of what is minute! Such is the impossibility of repressing the outgoings of sincerity!"

The Master said, "How greatly filial was Shun! His virtue was that of a sage; his dignity was the throne; his riches were all within the four seas. He offered his sacrifices in his ancestral temple, and his descendants preserved the sacrifices to himself. Therefore, having such great virtue, it could not but be that he should obtain the throne, that he should obtain those riches, that he should obtain his fame, that he should attain to his long life.

"Thus it is that Heaven, in the production of things, is sure to be bountiful to them, according to their qualities. Hence the tree that is flourishing, it nourishes, while that which is ready to fall, it overthrows."

Japanese Legends of Fire Apparitions

Collected by F. Hadland Davis

Miraculous Lights

There are many varieties of fire apparitions in Japan. There is the ghost-fire, demon-light, fox-flame, flash-pillar, badger-blaze, dragon-torch, and lamp of Buddha. In addition, supernatural fire is said to emanate from certain birds, such as the blue heron, through the skin, mouth, and eyes. There are also fire-wheels, or messengers from Hades, and sea-fires, besides the flames that spring from the cemetery.

A Globe of Fire

From the beginning of March to the end of June there may be seen in the province of Settsu a globe of fire resting on the top of a tree, and within this globe there is a human face. In ancient days there once lived in the Nikaido district of Settsu Province a priest named Nikōbō, famous for his power to exorcise evil spirits and evil influences of every kind. When the local governor's wife fell sick, Nikōbō was requested to attend and see what he could do to restore her to health again. Nikōbō willingly complied, and spent many days by the bedside of the suffering lady. He diligently practised his art of exorcism, and in due time the governor's wife recovered. But the gentle and kind-hearted Nikōbō was not thanked for what he had done; on the contrary, the governor became jealous of him, accused him of a foul crime, and caused him to be put to death. The soul of Nikōbō flashed forth in its anger and took the form of a miraculous globe of fire, which hovered over the murderer's house. The strange light, with the justly angry face peering from it, had its effect, for the governor was stricken with a fever that finally killed him. Every year, at the time already indicated, Nikōbō's ghost pays a visit to the scene of its suffering and revenge.

The Ghostly Wrestlers

In Omi province, at the base of the Katada hills, there is a lake. During the cloudy nights of early autumn, a ball of fire emerges from the margin of the lake, expanding and contracting as it floats toward the hills. When it rises to the height of a man it reveals two shining faces, to develop slowly into the torsos of two naked wrestlers, locked together and struggling furiously. The ball of fire, with its fierce combatants, floats slowly away to a recess in the Katada hills. It is harmless so long as no one interferes with it, but it resents any effort to retard its progress. According to a legend concerning this phenomenon, we are informed that a certain wrestler, who had never suffered a defeat, waited at midnight for the coming of this ball of fire. When it reached him he attempted to drag it down by force, but the luminous globe proceeded on its way, and hurled the foolish wrestler to a considerable distance.

Yama, the First Man, and King of the Dead

Donald A. Mackenzie

The following is a discussion of traditional cultural practices in India concerning the dead, and views on the afterlife.

In early Vedic times the dead might be either buried or cremated. These two customs were obviously based upon divergent beliefs regarding the future state of existence. A Varuna hymn makes reference to the "house of clay", which suggests that among some of the Aryan tribes the belief originally obtained that the spirits of the dead hovered round the place of sepulture. Indeed, the dread of ghosts is still prevalent in India; they are supposed to haunt the living until the body is burned.

Those who practised the cremation ceremony in early times appear to have conceived of an organized Hades, to which souls were transferred through the medium of fire, which drove away all spirits and demons who threatened mankind. Homer makes the haunting ghost of Patroklos exclaim, "Never again will I return from Hades when I have received my meed of fire." The Vedic worshippers of Agni burned their dead for the same reason as did the ancient Greeks. "When the remains of the deceased have been placed on the funeral pile, and the process of cremation has commenced, Agni, the god of fire, is prayed not to scorch or consume the departed, not to tear asunder his skin or his limbs, but, after the flames have done their work, to convey to the fathers the mortal who has been presented to him as an offering. Leaving behind on earth all that is evil and imperfect, and proceeding by the paths which the fathers trod, invested with a lustre like that of the gods, it soars to the realms of eternal light in a car, or on wings, and recovers there its ancient body in a complete and glorified form; meets with the forefathers who are living in festivity with Yama; obtains from him, when recognized by him as one of his own, a delectable abode, and enters upon a more perfect life, which is crowned with the fulfilment of all desires, is passed in the presence of the gods, and employed in the fulfilment of their pleasure."

Agni is the god who is invoked by the other deities: "Make straight the pathways that lead to the gods; be kind to us, and carry the sacrifice for us."

In this connection, however, Professor Macdonell says, "Some passages of the *Rigveda* distinguish the path of the fathers or dead ancestors from the path of the gods, doubtless because cremation appeared as a different process from sacrifice."

It would appear that prior to the practice of cremation, was a belief in Paradise ultimately obtained: the dead walked on foot towards it. Yama, King of the Dead, was the first man. Like the Aryan pioneers who discovered the Punjab, he explored the hidden regions and discovered the road which became known as "the path of the fathers".

> *To Yama, mighty king, be gifts and homage paid.*
> *He was the first of men that died, the first to brave*
> *Death's rapid rushing stream, the first to point the road*
> *To heaven, and welcome others to that bright abode.*

Professor Macdonell gives a new rendering of a Vedic hymn in which Yama is referred to as follows:

> *Him who along the mighty heights departed,*
> *Him who searched and spied the path for many,*
> *Son of Vivasvat, gatherer of the people,*
> *Yama the king, with sacrifices worship.*

Yama and his sister Yami, the first human pair, are identical with the Persian Yima and Yimeh of Avestan literature; they are the primeval "twins", the children of Vivasvat, or Vivasvant, in the *Rigveda* and of Vivahvant in the *Avesta*. *Yama* signifies twin, and Dr. Rendel Harris, in his researches on the Greek Dioscuri cult, shows that among early peoples the belief obtained widely that one of each pair of twins was believed to be a child of the sky. "This conjecture is borne out by the name of Yama's father (Vivasvant), which may well be a cult-epithet of the bright sky, 'shining abroad' (from the root *vas*, 'to shine')." In the *Avesta* "Yima, the bright" is referred to: he is the Jamshid of Fitzgerald's Omar.

Yima, the Iranian ruler of Paradise, is also identical with Mitra (Mithra), whose cult "obtained from 200–400 AD a worldwide diffusion in the Roman Empire, and came nearer to monotheism than the cult of any other god in paganism."

Professor Moulton wonders if the Yama myth "owed anything to Babylon?" It is possible that the worshippers of Agni represented early Iranian beliefs, and that the worshippers of Mitra, Varuna, and the twins (Yama and Yima and the twin Aswins) were influenced by Babylonian mythology as a result of contact, and that these opposing sects were rivals in India in early Vedic times.

In one of the hymns Yami is the wooer of her brother Yama. She declares that they were at the beginning intended by the gods to be husband and wife, but Yama replies:

> *"Who has sure knowledge of that earliest day? Who has seen it with his eyes and can tell of it? Lofty is the law of Mitra and Varuna; how canst thou dare to speak as a temptress?"*

In the Vedic "land of the fathers", the shining Paradise, the two kings Varuna and Yama sit below a tree. Yama, a form of Mitra, plays on a flute and drinks Soma with the Celestials, because Soma gives immortality. He gathers his people to him as a shepherd gathers his flock; indeed he is called the "Noble Shepherd". He gives to the faithful the draught of Soma; apparently unbelievers were destroyed or committed to a hell called Put. Yama's messengers were the pigeon and the owl; he had also two brindled watchdogs, each with four eyes. The dead who had faithfully fulfilled religious ordinances were addressed:

> *Fear not to pass the guards –*
> *The four-eyed brindled dogs – that watch for the departed.*
> *Return unto thy home, O soul! Thy sin and shame*

Leave thou behind on earth; assume a shining form –
Thine ancient shape – refined and from all taint set free.

Yama judged men as Dharma-rajah, "King of righteousness"; he was Pitripati, "lord of the fathers"; Samavurti, "the impartial judge"; Kritana, "the finisher"; Antaka, "he who ends life"; Samana, "the leveller", etc.

In post-Vedic times he presided over a complicated system of Hells; he was Dandadhara, "the wielder of the rod or mace". He had a noose with which to bind souls; he carried out the decrees of the gods, taking possession of souls at their appointed time.

In one of the *Brahmanas,* death, or the soul which Death claims as his own, is "the man in the eye". The reflection of a face in the pupil of the eye was regarded with great awe by the early folk; it was the spirit looking forth. We read, "Now that man in yonder orb (of the sun) and that man in the right eye truly are no other than Death; his feet have stuck fast in the heart, and having pulled them out, he comes forth; and when he comes forth then that man dies; whence they say of him who has passed away, *'he has been cut off'* (life or life-string has been severed)".

Yama might consent to prolong the life of one whose days had run out, on condition that another individual gave up part of his own life in compensation; he might even agree to restore a soul which he had bound to carry away, in response to the appeal of a mortal who had attained to great piety. The Vedic character of Yama survives sometimes in Epic narrative even after cremation had become general.

The Brahman and His Bride
Vyasa

Once upon a time Menaka, the beautiful Apsara (celestial fairy), who is without shame or pity, left beside a hermitage her newborn babe, the daughter of the King of Gandharvas (celestial elves). A pious Rishi, named Sthula-kesha, found the child and reared her. She was called Pramadarva, and grew to be the most beautiful and most pious of all young women. Ruru, the great grandson of Bhrigu, looked upon her with eyes of love, and at the request of his sire, Pramati, the virgin was betrothed to the young Brahman.

It chanced that Pramadarva was playing with her companions a few days before the morning fixed for the nuptials. As her time had come, she trod upon a serpent, and the death-compelling reptile bit her, whereupon she fell down in a swoon and expired. She became more beautiful in death than she had been in life.

Brahmans assembled round the body of Pramadarva and sorrowed greatly. Ruru stole away alone and went to a solitary place in the forest where he wept aloud. "Alas!" he cried, "the fair one, whom I love more dearly than ever, lieth dead upon the bare ground. If I have performed penances and attained to great ascetic merit, let the power which I have achieved restore my beloved to life again."

Suddenly there appeared before Ruru an emissary from the Celestial regions, who spake and said, "Thy prayer is of no avail, O Ruru. That one whose days have been numbered can never get back her own life again. Thou shouldst not therefore abandon thine heart to grief. But the gods have decreed a means whereby thou canst receive back thy beloved."

Said Ruru, "Tell me how I can comply with the will of the Celestials, O messenger, so that I may be delivered from my grief."

The messenger said, "If thou wilt resign half of thine own life to this maiden, Pramadarva, she will rise up again."

Said Ruru, "I will resign half of my own life so that my beloved may be restored unto me."

Then the king of the Gandharvas and the Celestial emissary stood before Dharma-rajah (Yama) and said, "If it be thy will, O Mighty One, let Pramadarva rise up endowed with a part of Ruru's life."

Said the Judge of the Dead, "So be it."

When Dharma-rajah had spoken thus, the serpent-bitten maiden rose from the ground, and Ruru, whose life was curtailed for her sake, obtained the sweetest wife upon earth. The happy pair spent their days deeply devoted to each other, awaiting the call of Yama at the appointed time.

Inca Demons and Spirits
Lewis Spence

Spirits roam throughout the mythology of the Incas, as highlighted here in a discussion of some traditions, beliefs, and practices observed by ancient Peruvians.

Totemism

Garcilasso el Inca de la Vega, an early Spanish writer on matters Peruvian, states that tradition ran that in pre-Inca times, every district, family, and village possessed its own god, each different from the others. These gods were usually such objects as trees, mountains, flowers, herbs, caves, large stones, pieces of jasper, and animals. The jaguar, puma, and bear were worshipped for their strength and fierceness, the monkey and fox for their cunning, the condor for its size and because several tribes believed themselves to be descended from it. The screech-owl was worshipped for its beauty, and the common owl for its power of seeing in the dark. Serpents, particularly the larger and more dangerous varieties, were especially regarded with reverence.

Although Payne classes all these gods together as totems, it is plain that those of the first class – the flowers, herbs, caves, and pieces of jasper – are merely fetishes. A fetish is an object in which the savage believes to be resident a spirit which, by its magic, will assist him in his undertakings. A totem is an object or an animal, usually the latter, with which the people of a tribe believe themselves to be connected by ties of blood and from which they are descended. It later becomes the type or symbol of the tribe.

Paccariscas

Lakes, springs, rocks, mountains, precipices, and caves were all regarded by the various Peruvian tribes as *paccariscas* – places whence their ancestors had originally issued to the upper world. The *paccarisca* was usually saluted with the cry, "Thou art my birthplace, thou art my life-spring. Guard me from evil, O *Paccarisca!*" In the holy spot a spirit was supposed to dwell which served the tribe as a kind of oracle. Naturally the *paccarisca* was looked upon with extreme reverence. It became, indeed, a sort of life-centre for the tribe, from which they were very unwilling to be separated.

Worship of Stones

The worship of stones appears to have been almost as universal in ancient Peru as it was in ancient Palestine. Man in his primitive state believes stones to be the framework of the earth, its bony structure. He considers himself to have emerged from some cave – in fact, from the entrails of the earth. Nearly all South American creation myths regard man as thus emanating from the bowels of the great terrestrial mother. Rocks which were thus chosen as *paccariscas* are found, among many other places, at Callca, in the valley of the Yucay, and at Titicaca there is a great mass of red sandstone on the top of a high ridge with almost inaccessible slopes and dark, gloomy recesses where the sun was thought to have hidden himself at the time of the great deluge which covered all the earth. The rock of Titicaca was, in fact, the great *paccarisca* of the sun itself.

We are thus not surprised to find that many standing stones were worshipped in Peru in aboriginal times. Thus Arriaga states that rocks of great size which bore some resemblance to the human figure were imagined to have been at one time gigantic men or spirits who, because they disobeyed the creative power, were turned into stone. According to another account they were said to have suffered this punishment for refusing to listen to the words of Thonapa, the son of the creator, who, like Quetzalcoatl or Manco Ccapac, had taken upon himself the guise of a wandering Indian, so that he might have an opportunity of bringing the arts of civilization to the aborigines. At Tiahuanaco a certain group of stones was said to represent all that remained of the villagers of that place, who, instead of paying fitting attention to the wise counsel which Thonapa the Civilizer bestowed upon them, continued to dance and drink in scorn of the teachings he had brought to them.

Again, some stones were said to have become men, as in the old Greek creation legend of Deucalion and Pyrrha. In the legend of Ccapac Inca Pachacutic, when Cuzco was attacked in force by the Chancas, an Indian erected stones to which he attached shields and weapons so that they should appear to represent so many warriors in hiding. Pachacutic, in great need of assistance, cried to them with such vehemence to come to his help that they became men, and rendered him splendid service.

Huacas

Whatever was sacred, of sacred origin, or of the nature of a relic, the Peruvians designated a *huaca*, from the root *huacan*, to howl, native worship invariably taking the form of a kind of howl, or weird, dirge-like wailing. All objects of reverence were known as *huacas*, although those of a higher class were also alluded to as *viracochas*. The Peruvians had, naturally, many forms of *huaca*, the most popular of which were those of the fetish class which could be carried about by the individual. These were usually stones or pebbles, many of which were carved and painted, and some made to represent human beings. The llama and the ear of maize were perhaps the most usual forms of these sacred objects. Some of them had an agricultural significance. In order that irrigation might proceed favourably, a *huaca* was placed at intervals in proximity to the acequias, or irrigation canals, which was supposed to prevent them leaking or otherwise failing to supply a sufficiency of moisture to the parched maize fields. *Huacas* of this sort were known as *ccompas*, and were regarded as deities of great importance, as the food supply of the community was thought to be wholly dependent upon their assistance. Other *huacas* of a similar kind were called *chichics* and *huancas*, and these presided over the fortunes of the maize, and ensured that a sufficient supply of rain should be forthcoming. Great numbers of these agricultural fetishes were destroyed by the zealous commissary Hernandez de Avendaño.

A Journey to Xibalba

Lewis Spence

Mystery veils the commencement of the Second Book of the *Popol Vuh,* the sacred narrative text of the K'iche' Maya people. The theme is the birth and family of Hun-Ahpu and Xbalanque, and the scribe intimates that only half is to be told concerning the history of their father. Xpiyacoc and Xmucane, the father and mother deities, had two sons, Hunhun-Ahpu and Vukub-Hunahpu, the first being, so far as can be gathered, a bi-sexual personage. He had by a wife, Xbakiyalo, two sons, Hunbatz and Hunchouen, men full of wisdom and artistic genius. All of them were addicted to the recreation of dicing and playing at ball, and a spectator of their pastimes was Voc, the messenger of Hurakan. Xbakiyalo having died, Hunhun-Ahpu and Vukub-Hunahpu, leaving the former's sons behind, played a game of ball which in its progress took them into the vicinity of the realm of Xibalba (the Underworld). This reached the ears of the monarchs of that place, Hun-Came and Vukub-Came, who, after consulting their counsellors, challenged the strangers to a game of ball, with the object of defeating and disgracing them.

For this purpose they dispatched four messengers in the shape of owls. The brothers accepted the challenge, after a touching farewell with their mother Xmucane, and their sons and nephews, and followed the feathered heralds down the steep incline to Xibalba from the playground at Ninxor Carchah. After an ominous crossing over a river of blood, they came to the residence of the kings of Xibalba, where they underwent the mortification of mistaking two wooden figures for the monarchs. Invited to sit on the seat of honour, they discovered it to be a red-hot stone, and the contortions which resulted from their successful trick caused unbounded merriment among the Xibalbans. Then they were thrust into the House of Gloom, where they were sacrificed and buried. The head of Hunhun-Ahpu was, however, suspended from a tree, which speedily became covered with gourds, from which it was almost impossible to distinguish the bloody trophy. All in Xibalba were forbidden the fruit of that tree.

But one person in Xibalba had resolved to disobey the mandate. This was the virgin princess Xquiq (Blood), the daughter of Cuchumaquiq, who went unattended to the spot. Standing under the branches gazing at the fruit, the maiden stretched out her hand, and the head of Hunhun-Ahpu spat into the palm. The spittle caused her to conceive, and she returned home, being assured by the head of the hero-god that no harm should result to her. This thing was done by order of Hurakan, the Heart of Heaven. In six months' time her father became aware of her condition, and despite her protestations the royal messengers of Xibalba, the owls, received orders to kill her and return with her heart in a vase. She, however, escaped by bribing the owls with splendid promises for the future to spare her and substitute for her heart the coagulated sap of the bloodwort.

In her extremity Xquiq went for protection to the home of Xmucane, who now looked after the young Hunbatz and Hunchouen.

Xmucane would not at first believe her tale. But Xquiq appealed to the gods, and performed a miracle by gathering a basket of maize where no maize grew, and thus gained her confidence.

Shortly afterwards Xquiq became the mother of twin boys, the heroes of the First Book, Hun-Ahpu, and Xbalanque. These did not find favour in the eyes of Xmucane, their grandmother. Their infantile cries aroused the wrath of this venerable person, and she vented it upon them by turning them out of doors. They speedily took to an outdoor life, however, and became mighty hunters, and expert in the use of their blowpipes, with which they shot birds and other small game. The ill-treatment which they received from Hunbatz and Hunchouen caused them at last to retaliate, and those who had made their lives miserable were punished by being transformed by the divine children into apes. The venerable Xmucane, filled with grief at the metamorphosis and flight of her ill-starred grandsons, who had made her home joyous with their singing and flute-playing, was told that she would be permitted to behold their faces once more if she could do so without losing her gravity, but their antics and grimaces caused her such merriment that on three separate occasions she was unable to restrain her laughter and the men-monkeys appeared no more. Hun-Ahpu and Xbalanque now became expert musicians, and one of their favourite airs was that of "Hun-Ahpu qoy," the "monkey of Hun-Ahpu."

The divine twins were now old enough to undertake labour in the field, and their first task was the clearing of a milpa or maize plantation. They were possessed of magic tools, which had the merit of working themselves in the absence of the young hunters at the chase, and those they found a capital substitute for their own directing presence upon the first day. Returning at night from hunting, they smeared their faces and hands with dirt so that Xmucane might be deceived into imagining that they had been hard at work in the maize field. But during the night the wild beasts met and replaced all the roots and shrubs which the brothers – or rather their magic tools – had removed. The twins resolved to watch for them on the ensuing night, but despite all their efforts the animals succeeded in making good their escape, save one, the rat, which was caught in a handkerchief. The rabbit and deer lost their tails in getting away. The rat, in gratitude that they had spared its life, told them of the glorious deeds of their great fathers and uncles, their games at ball, and of the existence of a set of implements necessary to play the game which they had left in the house. They discovered these, and went to play in the ball-ground of their fathers.

It was not long, however, until Hun-Came and Vukub-Came, the princes of Xibalba, heard them at play, and decided to lure them to the Underworld as they had lured their fathers. Messengers were despatched to the house of Xmucane, who, filled with alarm, despatched a louse to carry the message to her grandsons. The louse, wishing to ensure greater speed to reach the brothers, consented to be swallowed by a toad, the toad by a serpent, and the serpent by the great bird Voc. The other animals duly liberated one another; but despite his utmost efforts, the toad could not get rid of the louse, who had played him a trick by lodging in his gums, and had not been swallowed at all. The message, however, was duly delivered, and the players returned home to take leave of their grandmother and mother. Before their departure they each planted a cane in the middle of the house, which was to acquaint those they left behind with their welfare, since it would wither if any fatal circumstance befell them.

Pursuing the route their fathers had followed, they passed the river of blood and the river Papuhya. But they sent an animal called Xan as *avant courier* with orders to prick all the Xibalbans with a hair from Hun-Ahpu's leg, thus discovering those of the dwellers in the Underworld who were made of wood – those whom their fathers had unwittingly bowed to as men – and also learning the names of the others by their inquiries and explanations when pricked. Thus they did not salute the mannikins on their arrival at the Xibalban court, nor did they sit upon the red-hot stone. They even passed scatheless through the first ordeal of the House of Gloom. The Xibalbans were furious, and their wrath was by no means allayed when they found themselves beaten at the game of ball to which they had challenged the brothers. Then Hun-Came and Vukub-Came ordered the twins to bring them four bouquets of flowers, asking the guards of the royal gardens to watch most carefully, and committed Hun-Ahpu and Xbalanque to the "House of Lances" – the second ordeal – where the lancers were directed to kill them. The brothers, however, had at their beck and call a swarm of ants, which entered the royal gardens on the first errand, and they succeeded in bribing the lancers. The Xibalbans, white with fury, ordered that the owls, the guardians of the gardens, should have their lips split, and otherwise showed their anger at their third defeat.

Then came the third ordeal in the "House of Cold". Here the heroes escaped death by freezing by being warmed with burning pinecones. In the fourth and fifth ordeals they were equally lucky, for they passed a night each in the "House of Tigers" and the "House of Fire" without injury. But at the sixth ordeal misfortune overtook them in the "House of Bats", Hun-Ahpu's head being cut off by Camazotz, "Ruler of Bats," who suddenly appeared from above.

The beheading of Hun-Ahpu does not, however, appear to have terminated fatally, but owing to the unintelligible nature of the text at this juncture, it is impossible to ascertain in what manner he was cured of such a lethal wound. This episode is followed by an assemblage of all the animals, and another contest at ball-playing, after which the brothers emerged uninjured from all the ordeals of the Xibalbans.

But in order to further astound their "hosts", Hun-Ahpu and Xbalanque confided to two sorcerers named Xulu and Pacaw that the Xibalbans had failed because the animals were not on their side, and directing them what to do with their bones, they stretched themselves upon a funeral pile and died together. Their bones were beaten to powder and thrown into the river, where they sank, and were transformed into young men. On the fifth day they reappeared like men-fish, and on the sixth in the form of ragged old men, dancing, burning and restoring houses, killing and restoring each other to life, with other wonders. The princes of Xibalba, hearing of their skill, requested them to exhibit their magical powers, which they did by burning the royal palace and restoring it, killing and resuscitating the king's dog, and cutting a man in pieces, and bringing him to life again. The monarchs of Xibalba, anxious to experience the novel sensation of a temporary death, requested to be slain and resuscitated. They were speedily killed, but the brothers refrained from resuscitating their arch-enemies.

Announcing their real names, the brothers proceeded to punish the princes of Xibalba. The game of ball was forbidden them, they were to perform menial tasks, and only the beasts of the forest were they to hold in vassalage. They appear after this to achieve a species of doubtful distinction as plutonic deities or demons. They are described as warlike, ugly as owls, inspiring evil and discord. Their faces were painted black and white to show their faithless nature.

Xmucane, waiting at home for the brothers, was alternately filled with joy and grief as the canes grew green and withered, according to the varying fortunes of her grandsons. These young men were busied at Xibalba with paying fitting funeral honours to their father and uncle, who now mounted to heaven and became the sun and moon, whilst the four hundred youths slain by Zipacna became the stars. Thus concludes the Second Book.

The Christianization of Norse Mythology: From Gods to Ghosts

George Webbe Dasent

It is far easier to change a form of religion than to extirpate a faith. The first indeed is no easy matter, as those students of history well know, who are acquainted with the tenacity with which a large proportion of the English nation clung to the Church of Rome, long after the State had declared for the Reformation. But to change the faith of a whole nation in block and bulk on the instant, was a thing contrary to the ordinary working of Providence, and unknown even in the days of miracles, though the days of miracles had long ceased when Rome advanced against the North. There it was more politic to raise a cross in the grove where the Sacred Tree had once stood, and to point to the sacred emblem which had supplanted the old object of national adoration, when the populace came at certain seasons with songs and dances to perform their heathen rites. Near the cross soon rose a church; and both were girt by a cemetery, the soil of which was doubly sacred as a heathen fane and a Christian sanctuary, and where alone the bodies of the faithful could repose in peace. But the songs and dances, and processions in the churchyard round the cross, continued long after Christianity had become dominant. So also the worship of wells and spring was christianized when it was found impossible to prevent it. Great churches arose over or near them, as at Walsingham, where an abbey, the holiest place in England, after the shrine of St. Thomas at Canterbury, threw its majestic shade over the heathen wishing well, and the worshippers of Odin and the Nornir were gradually converted into votaries of the Virgin Mary. Such practices form a subject of constant remonstrance and reproof in the treatises and penitential epistles of medieval divines, and in some few places and churches, even in England, such rites are still yearly celebrated.

So, too, again with the ancient gods. They were cast down from honour, but not from power. They lost their genial kindly influence as the protectors of men and the origin of all things good; but their existence was tolerated; they became powerful for ill, and degenerated into malignant demons. Thus the worshippers of Odin had supposed that at certain times and rare intervals the good powers shewed themselves in bodily shape to mortal eye, passing through the land in divine progress, bringing blessings in their train, and receiving in return the offerings and homage of their grateful votaries. But these were naturally only exceptional instances; on ordinary occasions the pious heathen recognized his gods sweeping through the air in cloud and storm, riding on the wings of the wind, and speaking in awful accents, as the tempest howled and roared, and the sea shook his white mane and crest. Nor did he fail to see them in the dust and din of battle, when Odin appeared with his terrible helm, succouring his own, striking fear into their foes, and turning the day in many a doubtful fight; or in the hurry and uproar of the chase, where the mighty huntsman on his swift steed, seen in glimpses among the trees, took up the hunt where weary mortals laid it down, outstripped them all, and brought the noble quarry to the ground.

Looking up to the stars and heaven, they saw the footsteps of the gods marked out in the bright path of the Milky Way; and in the Bear they hailed the war chariot of the warrior's god. The great goddesses too, Frigga and Freyja, were thoroughly old-fashioned domestic divinities. They help women in their greatest need, they spin themselves, they teach the maids to spin, and punish them if the wool remains upon their spindle. They are kind, and good, and bright, for *Holda*, *Bertha*, are the epithets given to them.

And so, too, this mythology which, in its aspect to the stranger and the external world, was so ruthless and terrible, when looked at from within and at home, was genial, and kindly, and hearty, and affords another proof that men, in all ages and climes, are not so bad as they seem; that after all, peace and not war is the proper state for man, and that a nation may make war on others and exist; but that unless it has peace within, and industry at home, it must perish from the face of the earth. But when Christianity came, the whole character of this goodly array of divinities was soured and spoilt. Instead of the stately procession of the God, which the intensely sensuous eye of man in that early time connected with all the phenomena of nature, the people were led to believe in a ghastly grisly band of ghosts, who followed an infernal warrior or huntsman in hideous tumult through the midnight air. No doubt, as Grimm rightly remarks, the heathen had fondly fancied that the spirits of those who had gone to Odin followed him in his triumphant progress either visibly or invisibly; that they rode with him in the whirlwind, just as they followed him to battle, and feasted with him in Valhalla; but now the Christian belief, when it had degraded the mighty god into a demon huntsman, who pursued his nightly round in chase of human souls, saw in the train of the infernal master of the hunt only the spectres of suicides, drunkards, and ruffians; and, with all the uncharitableness of a dogmatic faith, the spirits of children who died unbaptized, whose hard fate had thrown them into such evil company.

This was the way in which that widespread superstition arose, which sees in the phantoms of the clouds the shapes of the Wild Huntsman and his accursed crew, and bears, in spring and autumn nights, when seafowl take the wing to fly either south or north, the strange accents and uncouth yells with which the chase is pressed on in the upper air. Thus, in Sweden it is still Odin who passes by; in Denmark it is King Waldemar's Hunt; in Norway it is *Aaskereida*, that is *Asgard's Car*. [...]

Odin and the Aesir then were dispossessed and degraded by our Saviour and his Apostles, just as they had of old thrown out the Frost Giants, and the two are mingled together, in mediaeval Norse tradition, as Trolls and Giants, hostile alike to Christianity and man. Christianity had taken possession indeed, but it was beyond her power to kill. To this half-result the swift corruption of the Church of Rome lent no small aid. Her doctrines, as taught by Augustine and Boniface, by Anschar and Sigfrid, were comparatively mild and pure; but she had scarce swallowed the heathendom of the North, much in the same way as the Wolf was to swallow Odin at the "Twilight of the Gods," than she fell into a deadly lethargy of faith, which put it out of her power to digest her meal.

The Drowning of Thorkell, AD 1026

Unknown Icelandic Author

On Maundy Thursday, early in the morning, Thorkell got ready for his journey. Thorstein set himself much against it: "For the weather looks to me uncertain," said he.

Thorkell said the weather would do all right. "And you must not hinder me now, kinsman, for I wish to be home before Easter."

So now Thorkell ran out the ferryboat, and loaded it. But Thorstein carried the lading ashore from out of the boat as fast as Thorkell and his followers put it on board.

Then Thorkell said, "Give over now, kinsman, and do not hinder our journey this time; you must not have your own way in this."

Thorstein said, "He of us two will now follow the counsel that will answer the worst, for this journey will cause the happening of great matters."

Thorkell now bade them farewell till their next meeting, and Thorstein went home, and was exceedingly downcast. He went to the guesthouse, and bade them lay a pillow under his head, the which was done. The servant-maid saw how the tears ran down upon the pillow from his eyes. And shortly afterwards a roaring blast struck the house, and Thorstein said, "There, we now can hear roaring the slayer of kinsman Thorkell."

Now to tell of the journey of Thorkell and his company: they sail this day out, down Broadfirth, and were ten on board. The wind began to blow very high, and rose to full gale before it blew over. They pushed on their way briskly, for the men were most plucky. Thorkell had with him the sword Skofnung, which was laid in the locker. Thorkell and his party sailed till they came to Bjorn's isle, and people could watch them journey from both shores. But when they had come thus far, suddenly a squall caught the sail and overwhelmed the boat. There Thorkell was drowned and all the men who were with him. The timber drifted ashore wide about the islands, the corner-staves (pillars) drove ashore in the island called Staff Isle. Skofnung stuck fast to the timbers of the boat, and was found in Skofnungs Isle. That same evening that Thorkell and his followers were drowned, it happened at Holyfell that Gudrun went to the church, when other people had gone to bed, and when she stepped into the lichgate she saw a ghost standing before her.

He bowed over her and said, "Great tidings, Gudrun."

She said, "Hold then your peace about them, wretch."

Gudrun went on to the church, as she had meant to do, and when she got up to the church she thought she saw that Thorkell and his companions were come home and stood before the door of the church, and she saw that water was running off their clothes. Gudrun did not speak to them, but went into the church, and stayed there as long as it seemed good to her. After that she went to the guestroom, for she thought Thorkell and his followers must have gone there; but she came into the chamber, there was no one there. Then Gudrun was struck with wonder at the whole affair.

On Good Friday Gudrun sent her men to find out matters concerning the journeying of Thorkell and his company, some up to Shawstrand and some out to the islands. By then the flotsam had already come to land wide about the islands and on both shores of the firth. The Saturday before Easter, the tidings got known and great news they were thought to be, for Thorkell had been a great chieftain. Thorkell was eight-and-forty years old when he was drowned, and that was four winters before Olaf the Holy fell. Gudrun took much to heart the death of Thorkell, yet bore her bereavement bravely. Only very little of the church timber could ever be gathered in. Gellir was now fourteen years old, and with his mother he took over the business of the household and the chieftainship. It was soon seen that he was made to be a leader of men. Gudrun now became a very religious woman. She was the first woman in Iceland who knew the Psalter by heart. She would spend a long time in the church at nights saying her prayers, and Herdis, Bolli's daughter, always went with her at night. Gudrun loved Herdis very much. It is told that one night the maiden Herdis dreamed that a woman came to her who was dressed in a woven cloak, and coifed in a head cloth, but she did not think the woman winning to look at.

She spoke, "Tell your grandmother that I am displeased with her, for she creeps about over me every night, and lets fall down upon me drops so hot that I am burning all over from them. My reason for letting you know this is that I like you somewhat better, though there is something uncanny hovering about you too. However, I could get on with you if I did not feel there was so much more amiss with Gudrun."

Then Herdis awoke and told Gudrun her dream. Gudrun thought the apparition was of good omen. Next morning Gudrun had planks taken up from the church floor where she was wont to kneel on the hassock, and she had the earth dug up, and they found blue and evil-looking bones, a round brooch, and a wizard's wand, and men thought they knew then that a tomb of some sorceress must have been there; so the bones were taken to a place far away where people were least likely to be passing.

Biographies
& Sources

Lacy Collison-Morley

Greek and Roman Stories of Haunting; Greek and Roman Tales of Necromancy; Greek and Roman Visions of the Dead in Sleep; Greek and Roman Apparitions of the Dead; Greek and Roman Warning Apparitions

(Originally published in *Greek and Roman Ghost Stories*, 1912)

Lacy Collison-Morley (1875–1958) was born in Croydon, in the United Kingdom. Her best-known work is her book entitled *Greek and Roman Ghost Stories* (1912). Her other publications include *Modern Italian Literature* (1911), *Shakespeare in Italy* (1916), and *Naples Through the Centuries* (1925).

George Webbe Dasent

The Christianization of Norse Mythology: From Gods to Ghosts

(Originally published in *Popular Tales from the Norse*, 1904)

British author George Webbe Dasent (1817–1896) was born in St. Vincent, British West Indies. After studying Classical literature at university and then serving in a diplomatic role in Sweden, Dasent discovered his great passion for Scandinavian mythology and literature. Going on to become an assistant editor at *The Times* and then a professor of English literature and modern history at King's College London, Dasent also worked as a translator of Scandinavian folk tales. Among his best-known works are *Viking Folk Tales and Tales from the Fjeld*.

F. Hadland Davis

Japanese Legends of Fire Apparitions

(Originally published in *Myths and Legends of Japan*, 1912)
Frederick Hadland Davis was a writer and historian – author
of *The Land of the Yellow Spring and Other Japanese Stories*
(1910) and *The Persian Mystics* (1908 and 1920). His books
describe these cultures to the Western world and tell stories
of ghosts, creation, mystical creatures and more. He is best
known for his book *Myths and Legends of Japan* (1912).

Camilla Grudova

Introduction

Camilla Grudova is author of the critically acclaimed *The
Doll's Alphabet*, and *Children of Paradise*, longlisted for the
Women's Prize for fiction. In 2023 she was named one of
Granta's Best Young British Novelists. She is the winner of a
Shirley Jackson award for Best Novelette. Her new collection
of stories, *The Coiled Serpent*, is out in November 2023.

Homer

The Visit to the Dead

(Originally published in *The Odyssey*, translated by Samuel
Butler, 1900)
Little is known for certain about the life of Homer, the Greek
poet credited as the author of the great epics *The Iliad* and
The Odyssey, although he is believed to have been born
sometime between the twelfth and eighth centuries BC. *The
Odyssey* describes the trials of the hero Odysseus on his
journey home to Ithaca following the Trojan War. The work

has had a huge influence on Western literature, inspiring extensive translations, poems, plays and novels.

Lucian

The Liar

(Originally published in *The Works of Lucian of Samosata, Vol. 3*, translated by H.W. Fowler and F.G. Fowler, 1781)

Lucian of Samosata (*c.* 120–*c.* 200) was a satirist and pamphleteer, known for his sarcasm and humour. His works were written in Ancient Greek, however his native language was likely Syriac, as he originated from the city of Samosata, in the Roman province of Syria. Little can be confirmed about his life – what we do know derives from his writings – however he was likely apprenticed to become a sculptor but, unsuccessful, ran away to pursue his education, later becoming a teacher and writer.

Philostratus

Ghostly Episodes in The Life of Apollonius of Tyana

(Originally published in *The Life of Apollonius of Tyana*, translated by F.C. Conybeare, 1912)

Philostratus (*c.* 170–*c.* 250) was a Greek sophist and writer who lived during the Roman imperial period, under the reign of Emperor Philip I. Philostratus was likely born on the island of Lemnos, and he studied and lectured in Athens before moving to Rome. With the Roman empress Julia Domna as his patron, Philostratus composed at least five known works, the best known of which are *Lives of the Sophists* and *The Life of Apollonius of Tyana*, which he wrote between 217 and 238 AD.

Pliny the Younger

Letters from Pliny

(Originally published variously in *Library of the World's Best Mystery and Detective Stories*, edited by Julain Hawthorne, 1907; Letters of Pliny, translated by William Melmoth)

Pliny the Younger (*c.* 61–*c.* 113) was an ancient Roman author, lawyer, and magistrate. Born in *Novum Comum* (today Como, in northern Italy), he was raised and educated by his uncle, Pliny the Elder. After his uncle's death while attempting to rescue victims of the eruption of Mount Vesuvius, Pliny the Younger inherited his uncle's estate. He rose in the ranks of various civil and military offices, served as an imperial governor, and worked in the Roman legal system. His 247 surviving letters, some of which were sent to emperors and other significant figures of the time, preserve various aspects of ancient Roman culture and workings of its government.

Plutarch

The Story of Damon; The Vision of Marcus Brutus

(Originally published variously in *Plutarch's Lives, Vol. 2*, translated by Aubrey Stewart and George Long, 1899; *Plutarch: Lives of the Noble Grecians and Romans*, translated by A.H. Clough)

Plutarch (*c.* 46–*c.* 119) was a Greek philosopher, author, essayist, historian, and priest of the Temple of Apollo in Delphi. After studying philosophy and mathematics in Athens, Plutarch worked as a magistrate in Chaeronea. As a priest at the Temple of Apollo, Plutarch likely took part in the temple's renowned religious rites known as the Eleusinian Mysteries.

Much of his writing preserves biographical information on the lives of various Roman emperors and significant figures in Greek and Roman society. His best-known works include *Parallel Lives* and *Moralia*.

Lewis Spence

Inca Demons and Spirits; A Journey to Xibalba
(Originally published in *The Myths of Mexico and Peru*, 1913; *The Popol Vuh*, 1908)

James Lewis Thomas Chalmers Spence (1874–1955) was a scholar of Scottish, Mexican and Central American folklore, as well as that of Brittany, Spain and the Rhine. He was also a poet, journalist, author, editor and nationalist who founded the party that would become the Scottish National Party. He was a Fellow of the Royal Anthropological Institute of Great Britain and Ireland, and Vice President of the Scottish Anthropological and Folklore Society.

Gaius Suetonius Tranquillus

The Haunted Pantry; Nero's Mother
(Originally published in *The Lives of the Twelve Caesars*, translated by Alexander Thomson, revised and corrected by T. Forester, 1796)

Gaius Suetonius Tranquillus (*c.* 69–*c.* 122), also known simply as Suetonius, was a Roman author and historian. He wrote during the Roman Empire's Imperial era. A close friend of Pliny the Younger, Suetonius likely served on Pliny's staff during Pliny's imperial governorship. Suetonius's best-known work, entitled *De vita Caesarum*, is a collection of biographies of twelve Roman emperors, from Julius Caesar to Domitian. His writing also helped preserve information on Roman culture, politics, daily life, and significant public figures of the time.

Vyasa

The Brahman and His Bride

(Originally published in *Indian Myth and Legend*, edited by Donald A. Mackenzie, 1913)

Vyasa was a venerated Indian sage, and he is credited as the author of the *Mahabharata*, a Sanskrit epic of ancient India. He is also credited with compiling the mantras of the *Vedas* and authoring the eighteen *Puranas* and *Brahma Sutras*. He is believed by many Hindus to be a partial reincarnation of the god Vishnu. Some theorize that Vyasa was not an individual but in fact a series of sages, each given the title of Vyasa upon composing a new *Purana*.

Alfred Wiedemann

The Ancient Egyptian Doctrine of the Immortality of the Soul

(Originally published in *The Ancient Egyptian Doctrine of the Immortality of the Soul*, 1895)

Alfred Wiedemann (1856–1936) was a German Egyptologist. After studying Egyptology and Classical history at the Universities of Leipzig, Berlin, Paris, and Tübingen and earning his PhD in 1878, Wiedemann worked as an associate professor at the University of Bonn. He eventually became a full professor of Egyptology there. His published works focus on various aspects of ancient Egyptian life, cultural practices, and myths.

Ziharpto

The Adventure of Setne Khamwas with the Mummies

(Originally published in *Popular Stories of Ancient Egypt*, translated by C.H.W. Johns, 1915)

Ziharpto was an ancient Egyptian scribe and, according to the original source material, was the creator of the version of 'The Adventure of Setne Khamwas with the Mummies' used in this collection. The life of Ziharpto is obscure, though reference to his name can be found on certain Ptolemaic monuments, and he has been written about by J. Krall in *Der Name des Schreibers der Chamois-Sage* (1886).

Zisi

A Teaching from Confucius

(Originally published in *The Doctrine of the Mean*, translated by James Legge, 1893)

Zisi (c. 481–402 BC) was a Chinese author and philosopher. Born Kong Ji, he lived during the Zhou Dynasty and was the only grandson of the philosopher and politician Confucius. Zisi is credited with preserving and passing on the teachings of Confucius, and authoring *The Doctrine of the Mean*. The text serves as a central doctrine of Confucianism, significantly influencing Chinese and Eastern philosophy and culture.

A Selection of Fantastic Reads

A range of Gothic novels, horror, crime,
mystery, fantasy, adventure, dystopia, utopia,
science fiction, myth, folklore and more:
available and forthcoming from Flame Tree 451

Categories: Bio = Biographical, BL = Black Literature, C = Crime,
F = Fantasy, FL = Feminist Literature, G = Gothic, H = Horror, L = Literary,
M = Mystery, MF = Myth & Folklore, P = Political, SF = Science Fiction,
TH = Thriller. Organized by year of first publication.

1764	*The Castle of Otranto*, Horace Walpole	G
1786	*The History of the Caliph Vathek*, William Beckford	G
1768	*Barford Abbey*, Susannah Minifie Gunning	G
1783	*The Recess Or, a Tale of Other Times*, Sophia Lee	G
1791	*Tancred: A Tale of Ancient Times*, Joseph Fox	G
1872	*In a Glass Darkly*, Sheridan Le Fanu	C, M
1794	*Caleb Williams*, William Godwin	C, M
1794	*The Banished Man*, Charlotte Smith	G
1794	*The Mysteries of Udolpho*, Ann Radcliffe	G
1795	*The Abbey of Clugny*, Mary Meeke	G
1796	*The Monk*, Matthew Lewis	G
1798	*Wieland*, Charles Brockden Brown	G
1799	*St. Leon*, William Godwin	H, M
1799	*Ormond, or The Secret Witness*, Charles Brockden Brown	H, M
1801	*The Magus,* Francis Barrett	H, M
1807	*The Demon of Sicily*, Edward Montague	G
1811	*Undine*, Friedrich de la Motte Fouqué	G
1814	*Sintram and His Companions*, Friedrich de la Motte Fouqué	G
1818	*Northanger Abbey*, Jane Austen	G
1818	*Frankenstein*, Mary Shelley	H, G
1820	*Melmoth the Wanderer*, Charles Maturin	G
1826	*The Last Man*, Mary Shelley	SF

1828	*Pelham*, Edward Bulwer-Lytton	C, M
1831	*Short Stories & Poetry*, Edgar Allan Poe (to 1949)	C, M
1838	*The Amber Witch*, Wilhelm Meinhold	H, M
1842	*Zanoni*, Edward Bulwer-Lytton	H, M
1845	*Varney the Vampyre*, Thomas Preskett Prest	H, M
1846	*Wagner, the Wehr-wolf*, George W.M. Reynolds	H, M
1847	*Wuthering Heights*, Emily Brontë	G
1850	*The Scarlet Letter*, Nathaniel Hawthorne	H, M
1851	*The House of the Seven Gables*, Nathaniel Hawthorne	H, M
1852	*Bleak House*, Charles Dickens	C, M
1853	*Twelve Years a Slave*, Solomon Northup	Bio, BL
1859	*The Woman in White*, Wilkie Collins	C, M
1859	*Blake, or the Huts of America*, Martin R. Delany	BL
1860	*The Marble Faun*, Nathaniel Hawthorne	H, M
1861	*East Lynne*, Ellen Wood	C, M
1861	*Elsie Venner*, Oliver Wendell Holmes	H, M
1862	*A Strange Story*, Edward Bulwer-Lytton	H, M
1862	*Lady Audley's Secret*, Mary Elizabeth Braddon	C, M
1864	*Journey to the Centre of the Earth*, Jules Verne	SF
1868	*The Huge Hunter*, Edward Sylvester Ellis	SF
1868	*The Moonstone*, Wilkie Collins	C, M
1870	*Twenty Thousand Leagues Under the Sea*, Jules Verne	SF
1872	*Erewhon*, Samuel Butler	SF
1874	*The Temptation of St. Anthony*, Gustave Flaubert	H, M
1874	*The Expressman and the Detective*, Allan Pinkerton	C, M

1876	*The Man-Wolf and Other Tales*, Erckmann-Chatrian	H, M
1878	*The Haunted Hotel*, Wilkie Collins	C, M
1878	*The Leavenworth Case*, Anna Katharine Green	C, M
1886	*The Mystery of a Hansom Cab*, Fergus Hume	C, M
1886	*Robur the Conqueror*, Jules Verne	SF
1886	*The Strange Case of Dr Jekyll & Mr Hyde*, R.L. Stevenson	SF
1887	*She*, H. Rider Haggard	F
1887	*A Study in Scarlet*, Arthur Conan Doyle	C, M
1890	*The Sign of Four*, Arthur Conan Doyle	C, M
1891	*The Picture of Dorian Gray*, Oscar Wilde	G
1892	*The Big Bow Mystery*, Israel Zangwill	C, M
1894	*Martin Hewitt, Investigator*, Arthur Morrison	C, M
1895	*The Time Machine*, H.G. Wells	SF
1895	*The Three Imposters*, Arthur Machen	H, M
1897	*The Beetle*, Richard Marsh	G
1897	*The Invisible Man*, H.G. Wells	SF
1897	*Dracula*, Bram Stoker	H
1898	*The War of the Worlds*, H.G. Wells	SF
1898	*The Turn of the Screw*, Henry James	H, M
1899	*Imperium in Imperio*, Sutton E. Griggs	BL, SF
1899	*The Awakening*, Kate Chopin	FL
1899	*The Conjure Woman*, Charles W. Chesnutt	H
1902	*The Hound of the Baskervilles*, Arthur Conan Doyle	C, M
1902	*Of One Blood: Or, The Hidden Self*, Pauline Hopkins	FL, BL
1903	*The Jewel of Seven Stars*, Bram Stoker	H, M

1904	*Master of the World*, Jules Verne	SF
1905	*A Thief in the Night*, E.W. Hornung	C, M
1906	*The Empty House & Other Ghost Stories*, Algernon Blackwood	G
1906	*The House of Souls*, Arthur Machen	H, M
1907	*Lord of the World*, R.H. Benson	SF
1907	*The Red Thumb Mark*, R. Austin Freeman	C, M
1907	*The Boats of the 'Glen Carrig'*, William Hope Hodgson	H, M
1907	*The Exploits of Arsène Lupin*, Maurice Leblanc	C, M
1907	*The Mystery of the Yellow Room*, Gaston Leroux	C, M
1908	*The Mystery of the Four Fingers*, Fred M. White	SF
1908	*The Ghost Kings*, H. Rider Haggard	F
1908	*The Circular Staircase*, Mary Roberts Rinehart	C, M
1908	*The House on the Borderland*, William Hope Hodgson	H, M
1909	*The Ghost Pirates*, William Hope Hodgson	H, M
1909	*Jimbo: A Fantasy*, Algernon Blackwood	G
1909	*The Necromancers*, R.H. Benson	SF
1909	*Black Magic*, Marjorie Bowen	H, M
1910	*The Return*, Walter de la Mare	H, M
1911	*The Lair of the White Worm*, Bram Stoker	H
1911	*The Innocence of Father Brown*, G.K. Chesterton	C, M
1911	*The Centaur*, Algernon Blackwood	G
1912	*Tarzan of the Apes*, Edgar Rice Burroughs	F
1912	*The Lost World*, Arthur Conan Doyle	SF
1913	*The Return of Tarzan*, Edgar Rice Burroughs	F
1913	*Trent's Last Case*, E.C. Bentley	C, M

1913	*The Poison Belt*, Arthur Conan Doyle	SF
1915	*The Valley of Fear*, Arthur Conan Doyle	C, M
1915	*Herland*, Charlotte Perkins Gilman	SF, FL
1915	*The Thirty-Nine Steps*, John Buchan	TH
1917	*John Carter: A Princess of Mars*, Edgar Rice Burroughs	F
1917	*The Terror*, Arthur Machen	H, M
1917	*The Job*, Sinclair Lewis	L
1917	*The Sturdy Oak*, Ed. Elizabeth Jordan	FL
1918	*When I Was a Witch & Other Stories,* Charlotte Perkins Gilman	FL
1918	*Brood of the Witch-Queen*, Sax Rohmer	H, M
1918	*The Land That Time Forgot*, Edgar Rice Burroughs	F
1918	*The Citadel of Fear*, Gertrude Barrows Bennett (as Francis Stevens)	FL, TH
1919	*John Carter: A Warlord of Mars*, Edgar Rice Burroughs	F
1919	*The Door of the Unreal*, Gerald Biss	H
1919	*The Moon Pool*, Abraham Merritt	SF
1919	*The Three Eyes*, Maurice Leblanc	SF
1920	*A Voyage to Arcturus*, David Lindsay	SF
1920	*The Metal Monster*, Abraham Merritt	SF
1920	*Darkwater*, W.E.B. Du Bois	BL
1922	*The Undying Monster*, Jessie Douglas Kerruish	H
1925	*The Avenger*, Edgar Wallace	C
1925	*The Red Hawk*, Edgar Rice Burroughs	SF
1926	*The Moon Maid*, Edgar Rice Burroughs	SF
1927	*Witch Wood*, John Buchan	H, M
1927	*The Colour Out of Space*, H.P. Lovecraft	SF

1927	*The Dark Chamber*, Leonard Lanson Cline	H, M
1928	*When the World Screamed*, Arthur Conan Doyle	F
1928	*The Skylark of Space*, E.E. Smith	SF
1930	*Last and First Men*, Olaf Stapledon	SF
1930	*Belshazzar*, H. Rider Haggard	F
1934	*The Murder Monster*, Brant House (Emile C. Tepperman)	H
1934	*The People of the Black Circle*, Robert E. Howard	F
1935	*Odd John*, Olaf Stapledon	SF
1935	*The Hour of the Dragon*, Robert E. Howard	F
1935	*Short Stories Selection 1*, Robert E. Howard	F
1935	*Short Stories Selection 2*, Robert E. Howard	F
1936	*The War-Makers*, Nick Carter	C, M
1937	*Star Maker*, Olaf Stapledon	SF
1936	*Red Nails*, Robert E. Howard	F
1936	*The Shadow Out of Time*, H.P. Lovecraft	SF
1936	*At the Mountains of Madness*, H.P. Lovecraft	SF
1938	*Power*, C.K.M. Scanlon writing in *G-Men*	C, M
1939	*Almuric*, Robert E. Howard	SF
1940	*The Ghost Strikes Back*, George Chance	SF
1937	*The Road to Wigan Pier*, George Orwell	P, Bio
1938	*Homage to Catalonia*, George Orwell	P, Bio
1945	*Animal Farm*, George Orwell	P, F
1949	*Nineteen Eighty-Four*, George Orwell	P, F
1953	*The Black Star Passes*, John W. Campbell	SF
1959	*The Galaxy Primes*, E.E. Smith	SF

New Collections of Ancient Myths, Folklore and Early Literature

2014	*Celtic Myths*, J.K. Jackson (ed.)	MF
2014	*Greek & Roman Myths*, J.K. Jackson (ed.)	MF
2014	*Native American Myths*, J.K. Jackson (ed.)	MF
2014	*Norse Myths*, J.K. Jackson (ed.)	MF
2018	*Chinese Myths*, J.K. Jackson (ed.)	MF
2018	*Egyptian Myths*, J.K. Jackson (ed.)	MF
2018	*Indian Myths*, J.K. Jackson (ed.)	MF
2018	*Myths of Babylon*, J.K. Jackson (ed.)	MF
2019	*African Myths*, J.K. Jackson (ed.)	MF
2019	*Aztec Myths*, J.K. Jackson (ed.)	MF
2019	*Japanese Myths*, J.K. Jackson (ed.)	MF
2020	*Arthurian Myths*, J.K. Jackson (ed.)	MF
2020	*Irish Fairy Tales*, J.K. Jackson (ed.)	MF
2020	*Polynesian Myths*, J.K. Jackson (ed.)	MF
2020	*Scottish Myths*, J.K. Jackson (ed.)	MF
2021	*Viking Folktales*, J.K. Jackson (ed.)	MF
2021	*West African Folktales*, J.K. Jackson (ed.)	MF
2022	*East African Folktales*, J.K. Jackson (ed.)	MF
2022	*Persian Myths*, J.K. Jackson (ed.)	MF
2022	*The Tale of Beowulf*, Dr Victoria Symons (Intro.)	MF
2022	*The Four Branches of the Mabinogi*, Shân Morgain (Intro.)	MF
2023	*Slavic Myths*, Ema Lakinska (Intro.)	MF
2023	*Turkish Folktales*, Nathan Young (Intro.)	MF
2023	*Gawain and the Green Knight*, Alan Lupack (Intro.)	MF

2023   *Hungarian Folktales*, Boglárka Klitsie-Szabad (Intro.)   MF

2023   *Korean Folktales*, Dr Perry Miller (Intro.)   MF

2023   *Southern African Folktales*, Prof. Enongene Mirabeau Sone (Intro.)   MF

New Collections of Ancient, Folkloric and Classic Ghost Stories

2022   *American Ghost Stories*, Brett Riley (Intro.)   H, G

2022   *Irish Ghost Stories*, Maura McHugh (Intro.)   H, G

2022   *Scottish Ghost Stories*, Helen McClory (Intro.)   H, G

2022   *Victorian Ghost Stories*, Reggie Oliver (Intro.)   H, G

2023   *Ancient Ghost Stories*, Camilla Grudova (Intro.)   H, G

2023   *Haunted House Stories*, Hester Fox (Intro.)   H, G

2023   *Indian Ghost Stories*, Dr Mithuraaj Dusiya (Intro.)   H, G

2023   *Japanese Ghost Stories*, Hiroko Yoda (Intro.)   H, G

A TASTE FOR THE FANTASTIC

FLAME TREE offers several series with stories from the distant past to the far future, covering the entire range of imaginative literature and great works that shaped our world.

From the fireside tradition of oral storytelling, early written versions of mythology (such as Norse, African, Egyptian and Aztec) emerge in the majestic works of literature of the Middle Ages (Dante, Chaucer, Boccaccio), the Early Modern period (Shakespeare, Milton, Cervantes) and the classic speculative tales by way of Shelley, Stoker, Lovecraft and H.G. Wells.

You'll find too, early Feminist adventure fiction, and the foundations of Black proto-science fiction literature from the 1900s.

Our short story collections also gather new tales by modern writers to bring together the sensibilities of humankind from the past, the present and the future.

Find us in all good bookshops, and at *flametreepublishing.com*